"In case you decide to send me away, or you need extra defense," Freya said, "I want you to have this."

In one smooth motion, Freya dropped to her knee. She lifted the fabric of her tunic—so high, Astrid thought she would remove it entirely, but that was absurd, no matter how Astrid's eyes locked onto the strip of exposed skin—and extracted her bone-handled dagger from her side. Freya proffered it to Astrid, rolling the light blade on the tips of her gloved fingers.

"For your protection," Freya said.

HUMAN TERRITORY
Northgate
ELVEN ISLANDS
OLWEN
Vakker
Ceridwen
LYNBY
Westgate
TORDEN
ANWEN
BRANWEN
Ravn
Ulfur's Base
ORC COUNTRY
Sydlig Forest
AEGIR OCEAN
DWYRAIN OCEAN
SYDLIG
TORDEN
AND SURROUNDING ENVIRONS

ALSO BY LILA GWYNN

OLYMPIA THE BOUNTY HUNTER

Kissed the Mark

Falling for the Fugitive

Undead at Large

THE SAPPHIC ORCS OF TORDEN

The Orc and Her Bride

The Orc and Her Spy

The Orc and Her Captive

STANDALONE

The Yuletide Fairy's Curse

SHORT FICTION

"The Scavenger of the Skies" (Indie Bites, Vol. 7)

"A Curse Is on Her If She Stay" (Indie Bites, Vol. 9)

"Here Be Salt and Dragons" (Indie Bites, Vol. 10)

"Blooming in Brimstone" (She Was Monstress, Vol. 1)

"The Wedding Heist of Ellen o' the Dale" (Indie Bites, Vol. 18)

THE ORC —AND— HER SPY

BOOK TWO OF THE SAPPHIC ORCS OF TORDEN

LILA GWYNN

Eldest of Three

Cover & map design by Sarah Waites at The Illustrated Page Design
https://theillustratedpage.net/design/

Published by Eldest of Three
https://lilagwynn.com

ISBN-13 (eBook): 979-8-9940024-0-7
ISBN-13 (Paperback): 979-8-9940024-1-4

For information about content warnings, spice level, and happily ever afters, please visit: https://lilagwynn.com/books/sapphic-orcs-of-torden

For stubborn women who carve their own paths

THE CAST SO FAR

Though this book is a sequel, it may be read as a standalone.

ASTRID KARRSDAUGHTER

The orc queen of Torden; Ruga's older sister

FREYA WEDD

Astrid's human spymaster posing as her handmaiden; a refugee from the human wars

RUGA KARRSDAUGHTER

Queen Consort of Branwen; Astrid's younger sister; Elketh's wife; Hedda's ex-girlfriend

ELKETH CERIDWEN

The elvish queen of Branwen; Ruga's wife

HEDDA LIVSDAUGHTER

Orc captain of the queen's félag; Ruga's ex-girlfriend; had an outburst at the midsummer festival

VERA BRIGID

Vakker Castle's elf librarian

BRENN

A human priestess and seer; close friends with Freya; a refugee from the human wars

ULFUR ROWANSDAUGHTER

Orc warlord of Lynby, who killed Torden's previous ruler and caused the country to divide in two

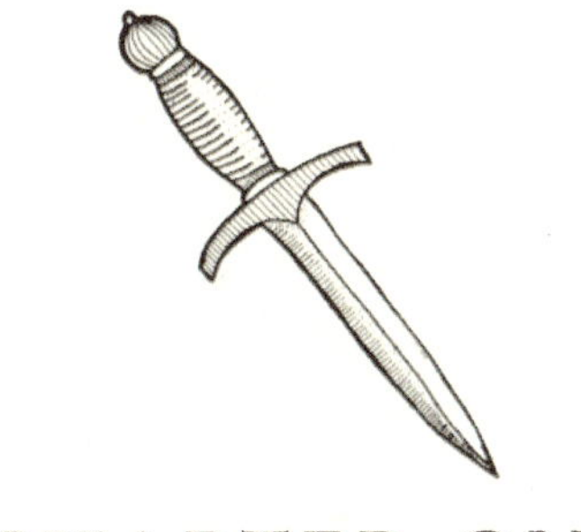

CHAPTER ONE

Rain-battered Freya reached the priestess's house to find the door already open for her. Of course—Brenn's precognition had prepared her for Freya's arrival. Prophetic visions from the goddess lent Brenn that advantage.

The inside of Brenn's house was so bright, Freya had to squint to see. It was crowded in the way only people who lived in deliberate clutter and kept everything in one specific place could understand. Keys dangled on strings from the ceiling, catching the light of a ring of candles. Bits of iron, gold, and marble glittered at Freya, causing her to put up her hand to shield her eyes. In theory, this mystical stuff helped Brenn work, but Freya would never comprehend how, exactly. There were large, open windows on every wall, letting in the gloomy light of the afternoon and giving off a glow from within that could be seen from a mile away.

Over the fire, a kettle began to whistle.

"Freya!" Brenn rose from her pile of blankets in front of the hearth.

She stood a foot taller than Freya, but they were otherwise similar in appearance—both human, originating from the same region up north in the human territories, with dark hair and sun-toned skin.

Despite that they were both thirty-five years of age, Brenn's devotion to the goddess had paused her body in time. On the other hand, the furrow between Freya's brows was permanent, though none of her wrinkles could be said to come from smiling too often.

Notably, a live raven and a falcon perched on Brenn's shoulders.

The falcon chirped as she took her spot comfortably on Freya's extended forearm. Freya cooed at the bird, stroking her feathers. In her jesses was the scrolled note Freya had sent, unopened.

Brenn kissed Freya's cheek, smiled, and then said, "Aren't you supposed to be at the assembly?"

"Are you spying on me? I'm not sure the goddess would appreciate your powers used for such nefarious purposes," said Freya.

"Yet somehow she never revokes my magic," Brenn said. "Tea?"

Freya removed her boots and shook out her drenched cloak. Brenn had set out two cups of tea on a clutter-strewn table between two mismatched armchairs. She clutched her iron staff in white-knuckled hands. From her armrest, Brenn's raven cocked its head at Freya.

"So," Brenn said.

Freya took her seat. Rain pattered the roof in a gentle, steady flow, and the cup of tea warmed her hands through her leather gloves. "You didn't bother reading my message?"

Brenn raised an eyebrow. "You never come for anything else."

"How about to see my dear old friend?" Freya asked, showing her teeth.

Brenn laughed. "All right, let's get this over with."

From her pocket, Freya extracted a frayed red thread and passed it over.

Brenn twisted it between her fingers. "The alliance was a brilliant idea, Freya. Any attempts to invade Torden are dissuaded. The goddess would have warned me otherwise."

Freya moodily put her chin in her hand. "It *was* a brilliant idea. But I can't shake the feeling something bad is coming."

"You always think something bad is coming," Brenn pointed out.

"Only because it always does." Freya sipped her tea, thinking. "Why, am I bothering you?"

"Never," Brenn said. She wrapped the thread around the tip of her staff. "I wish you'd come more often for tea and less for prophecy. I love to see you, of course, but nothing ever changes. And you worry and worry no matter the outcome."

The beginning of their oldest argument: though Brenn received prophetic visions and hunches from the goddess, she only knew what the goddess wished to impart to her. Which was vague, and sometimes nonsense, and hardly ever helpful for Freya's purposes.

Freya considered giving in. She considered arguing, too, but Brenn did not deserve that. In the end, she decided on one simple word, gently spoken: "Please."

The fire reflected in Brenn's eyes. The raven took flight and began to peck at some fabric on the wall.

"It never helps," Brenn insisted.

This was true, too: Freya was never assured by good news and only took heed of the bad. Good news meant something bad could still happen, but bad news meant something bad *would* happen.

But the raven knew Brenn almost as well as Freya did. Brenn was going to help anyway.

Freya squeezed her eyes shut. A rhythmic chanting started to her right, deeper than her old friend's voice; a flash of light brightened the backs of her eyelids; the floor itself trembled, keys and metals smacking into each other in a ruckus. Tea sloshed over the sides of Freya's cup and over her gloves, and her falcon took off. Just as suddenly as the shaking started, it stopped. Freya waited with her heart in her throat.

Brenn slumped in her armchair. The skin under her eyes was sallow.

Freya wanted to grab her by the collar of her priestess robes and shake answers out of her. "Did you see something?" she asked.

"I did," Brenn said. "Why don't we finish our tea first?"

"If it's something bad, I need to know now."

Brenn stared into the hearth.

"Tell me."

"I saw two things. One of them may need your immediate attention," Brenn said in warning.

"Yes?" Freya croaked.

"You shouldn't have skipped out on the assembly. There's important news."

"That's specific and helpful." Freya looked up at the ceiling. "Thanks a lot."

"The other thing is more abstract." Brenn took a deep breath and rushed through her next words. "It's about Queen Astrid. The goddess showed me that she will experience a loss. But this doesn't mean—"

Freya jumped to her feet. Scalding hot tea splashed over her trousers. "A loss of *what*?"

Loss of her queendom? Loss of her life?

"Like I said, I do not know. It could be a financial loss," Brenn reasoned. "Or a friend dying of natural causes."

Like Freya, Astrid had few friends. Freya laughed dryly. Her throat caught on the laugh and transformed it into a cough. "Why hasn't the goddess shown this to you before? Has the loss been coming all along?"

Brenn held two fingers to her temple. "I love you, Freya, truly. But that's not how wyrd works, and you know it. We are not worthy of the goddess's full knowledge, and we will only ever see glimpses of our fate."

The raven and the falcon circled overhead, cawing at each other in a reflection of their owners.

Freya was already at the door, donning her wet boots. "I'll be back if I need more. Keep your window open for Huginn."

"Freya, it's going to be okay. It's not—"

"If you remember more details, please get in touch with me right away." Her voice had gone stiff, formal. "I'll see you later."

Brenn followed Freya into the rain, pleading. "Freya. There are things you don't understand about the goddess and her magic. It's okay not to know, but please don't act rashly."

The things Freya did not know were ahead of her, not behind. She mounted her horse, one word echoing through her mind over and over again, all-consuming.

Loss.

CHAPTER TWO

Queen Astrid Karrsdaughter, orc ruler of Torden, would've rather been anywhere but here.

She listened with waning patience to the steward's rundown of issues brought up at the assembly. Often, the complaints Torden's citizens raised with Varin filled Astrid with unease—either because she had not thought of addressing something herself, or because they seemed so insignificant as to hardly be worth the administrative effort. The steward was a tolerant orc. More tolerant than Astrid was capable of.

As the steward droned on, Astrid glanced behind her. Her spymaster was missing. Astrid had known this instinctively; she felt the absence of Freya even when she did not see her, like a draft against her side. Astrid had not seen Freya slip out of the meeting, but that was no surprise.

The steward's spectacles repeatedly fell to the end of his nose and had to be pushed back up. Astrid watched the rhythmic nature of this action, the inevitability—the slow descent downward, the quick, precise push upward, and the sniffle that followed, his tusks wavering as if preparing for a sneeze. Maybe she needed to order him a new pair of spectacles. She fiddled with her dark red cloak and absently noticed some of the thread was coming loose on the left side.

Astrid glanced back once more.

"Your Majesty?" the steward said.

With a flush, Astrid realized it was not the first time he'd called for her attention. "Yes?"

Varin coughed. "We received a letter of some importance today." Which was a nice way of him saying, *You will actually want to listen to this part.*

"From whom?" Astrid asked.

Varin's eyes darted to the left and right. The room was full of Astrid's félag—the guards she trusted the most, her inner circle. None of them would spread confidential information that could put Astrid at risk.

Astrid nodded to Varin.

"It's from King Skarde of Sydlig, Your Majesty," said Varin.

Astrid leaned forward in her chair, suddenly alert. The king to the south, communicating with her by a letter sent to her steward? "What does it say, Varin?" And why was she not told of this important letter earlier? Was Freya aware?

"King Skarde is sending an ambassador to Vakker Castle," Varin said, "and a consul to every major city in Torden."

A ringing sounded in Astrid's ears. "Did Skarde share his rationale?"

"The letter states he was made aware of our international relations with the Elven Islands. He desires to have a more active role in Torden's future."

Astrid slumped in her throne.

This year, she had married off her sister, Ruga, to the elf princess Elketh Ceridwen of Branwen in exchange for the support of their renowned military. But King Skarde...

The last time Astrid had seen Skarde, she'd traveled on horse for a month through the notoriously difficult Sydlig Forest to meet with him to discuss whether he would offer Torden military support. In response, he had constantly changed the subject, laughed in her face. The orc king had a serious set to his brow that made his laughter unnatural in contrast.

Astrid had reached out to Skarde on other occasions—she'd written him pleasant letters to congratulate him on his marriage to his fourth wife, and to commend the fantastic harvest Sydlig had a few years back—but only received responses from his steward. Generic "*thank you, we hope you have been well,*" messages that did not inquire about whether Astrid and Torden were actually doing well.

For a king, Skarde struck Astrid as apolitical when it came to anything other than himself. And if her assessment of this were true, then it also had to be true Skarde thought something happening in Torden would negatively impact him or his country.

Which begged the question: Did Skarde know something Astrid didn't about the future of Torden?

"I'll write the earls to warn them about Sydlig's incoming consuls," said Astrid. *That* would go over well.

Varin's eyelids drooped and he stifled a yawn.

Astrid felt a pang of remorse. Her sister Ruga had done a lot of the administrative work around here, things no one else thought to do, and everyone was working overtime to fill in the gaps ever since Ruga left.

Astrid began to look back again and stopped herself. Only then did she notice the room was unnaturally quiet. She looked from the guards, who stared at her, to the steward, whose forehead was coated in a sheen of sweat.

"Queen Astrid," said Hedda at her side. "I believe you would like us to get back to business?" And then, in a lower voice: "I'm on kitchen mop duty today."

"Stars," Astrid murmured. "Meeting adjourned."

As she walked back to her rooms surrounded by guards, she heard Freya fall into step behind her, and finally relaxed her shoulders.

When Astrid's wrist cramped from writing to the earls, constructing a half-truth about why they needn't worry, she forced herself to take a break. The words on the paper blurred in her vision. She had an urge to scream. The félag would come running into her rooms, but she could do it just once. Get it out of her system.

"Shall I take these to the courier when you're finished, My Queen?" Freya asked.

Sometimes it seemed as though Freya could disappear and reappear like a breeze, tumbling in and then back out of Astrid's presence. Astrid had a strong preference for *in.*

"Yes, that would be wonderful, Freya. Thank you."

Though there were two chairs in Astrid's sparsely furnished antechamber, Freya always opted for standing.

Astrid stared into the low embers of the fire. Freya took her duties seriously, but Astrid truly missed the ease with which she had been able to talk to her sister.

Astrid had been at this politics game for a long time, and it was easier when others shared her burden. Ruga had always helped, uncomplaining, up until the end. Tears welled in Astrid's eyes. She blinked them away before Freya could see.

"Is something the matter?" Freya asked.

Of course Freya would notice her mood anyway. "I'm wondering how much of an imposition the ambassador and the consuls will be. It bothers me that the king reached out to my steward rather than me. I don't suppose you caught word of this first? Have you had a chance to look into the identities of the consuls?"

"No, not yet."

"Where were you, then?" Astrid turned to face Freya. "During the meeting?"

Freya stood with her mouth slightly ajar. In moments like this, Astrid was reminded of how vulnerable Freya could be—she was a weapon, yes, but she was just a woman, too, a human who barely reached five feet in height. Astrid had always been impressed that Freya could make herself seem much taller through sheer force of presence or much smaller at will.

Freya ran fingers through her short, ink-black hair before she spoke, and Astrid found her eyes tracking Freya's gloved hands.

"You were well protected by the félag. I didn't realize you would notice me missing, Your Majesty."

I always notice you, Astrid thought to say, but she held her tongue. Freya had not answered her, which meant Astrid would not be getting an answer any time soon. "What do you think of Skarde sending the consuls?"

"I worry King Skarde may know something we don't."

Astrid swallowed. "About Ulfur's plans?"

Ulfur, who had rallied against Torden's last ruler to divide the country in two. Astrid and Freya had been working under the assumption that Ulfur was too busy with her own headstrong warlords in Lynby to turn her attention to Torden—especially knowing Torden had a much more organized military and the Elven Islands on their side—but nothing was ever a given now. Things that once made sense didn't follow the old rules anymore.

"Yes, if Ulfur is plotting something, and Sydlig caught whiff of it," Freya said. Her hands were behind her back, her posture unusually rigid. Freya had worked for Astrid for over a decade, and Astrid liked to think she understood her body language by now. Freya hoarded information the way the greedy hoarded gold. Not knowing would tear her up inside.

"May I make a suggestion?" Freya asked.

"Of course."

"I think it would be wise to demote Hedda for your safety."

Astrid blinked. Hedda was the captain of Astrid's félag—she'd had restricted duties after an outburst several months back wherein she'd publicly denounced the queen, embarrassing Astrid's entire legion of guards and making her control over her people appear weak. Granted, Hedda was quick to anger, but she'd served the ruler before Astrid, too, and cared deeply about protecting Torden.

The incident had taken Astrid aback and planted a seed of doubt in her heart about Hedda's loyalty. She suspected the outburst was more about Astrid's involvement in ending the romantic relationship Hedda had shared with Ruga prior to Ruga's engagement, but there was a worse possibility. It could also mean Hedda secretly hated Astrid, and had for a long time.

How Astrid disliked questioning her own people.

"We've put Hedda through enough," Astrid said. "She's apologized for her actions. The castle floors sparkle with her punishment."

"She harbors resentment toward Your Majesty," Freya said. Her voice was toneless; she spoke not out of passion but logic, something Astrid always found impossible to argue with. "For separating her from Ruga, and for how we've approached her punishment."

Astrid considered. "I'm reluctant to demote her completely. Perhaps we can discuss the change with her? Give her the chance to argue her case."

"We need someone stronger. Less emotionally charged," Freya said.

"Who do you have in mind?"

"Hrothgar. They're strong, loyal, and have never had an outburst like Hedda. They don't drink, either."

The quick response shouldn't have surprised Astrid, but for Freya to have a solution ready, she'd been considering it for some time. Freya was always two steps ahead of everyone else, it seemed.

"I wish you'd discuss these matters with me as soon as you think of them," Astrid said, keeping her tone light, keeping the frustration out.

"I don't like to present you with information until I'm really sure, My Queen."

Stars, but Freya was stubborn. Maybe one day, the two of them could come up with solutions together, if Freya didn't tire of working for Torden.

That was an unpleasant thought. Eager to distract herself, Astrid began the laborious process of folding the letters. "Bring me my seal?"

The door to Astrid's bedroom opened and closed, the only indication Freya had left. She returned a moment later. Without looking up, Astrid held out her palm to accept her seal and wax.

Cool skin grazed her hand instead. Startled, Astrid stared and stared at the bare hand in hers, crossed with pale scars. She followed the length of the arm up to Freya's face—frozen as if in a trance, her wide, dark pupils reflecting the flickering flames of the fire. Astrid sat similarly frozen, wondering what would happen next, what she was supposed to do, if anything.

Wondering what this meant.

Her fingers twitched, almost giving in to the temptation to close her hand over Freya's smaller one, just as Freya snatched her hand back. Both Freya's hands were ungloved, the other tightly gripping the wax and seal.

As far as Astrid knew, Freya only removed the gloves in front of her.

Astrid held her breath. A second passed, then two.

"Sorry," Freya said. She shook her head as if shedding her trance. "I... I'm sorry."

"What—?" Astrid started. *What's on your mind?* she thought she may have been about to ask. *What compelled you to touch me?*

With a clatter, Freya dropped the wax and seal onto Astrid's side table, then disappeared into the shadows. Astrid gawked at the space she'd occupied. Freya's silhouette lingered in her vision like a ghost.

Astrid brought the wax over to the fire to warm. Probably nothing, she reasoned. Freya was worried about the consuls, just like Astrid was, and she'd been distracted enough to pass her the wrong hand. The goddess knew Astrid did that every once in a while, too.

But Freya was usually so calculated and mindful.

Astrid watched, transfixed, as the wax melted, puddling in its metal warming cup. The phantom sensation of Freya's hand lingered on Astrid's own.

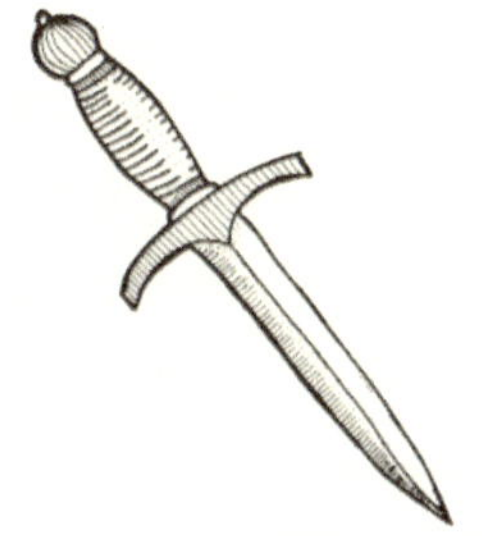

CHAPTER THREE

A rosy-cheeked human from the castle's laundry staff arched her back into the wall and let out a moan Freya had to stifle with her hand.

Freya's other hand was two fingers and two knuckles deep in Mara, pumping at a rhythm that made Mara tremble until she finally grabbed Freya's shoulder and rode out the rest against Freya's hand.

Freya stepped back, panting. Mara giggled. The room—an empty chamber reserved for visitors on the fourth floor of the castle—was heavy with the smells of sweat and sex.

Freya went to the basin to wipe down her hands, then shook them out and put them back in her gloves.

"Always lovely meeting up with you, Freya," Mara said between gulps of air. She found her stockings and began the process of rolling them back up her sticky legs. "This will be the last time, I think."

"Oh?" Freya said.

"I found someone," Mara said, and her already-flushed cheeks reddened.

"How wonderful. I'm happy for you," said Freya.

She meant it. Mara was a single mother of three—busy doing laundry during the week, cutting cards on the weekend, and raising her kids for the rest. No time for romance, just like Freya. This what had made their arrangement easy to fall into.

"He works at the docks," Mara said without prompting. "Steady income. Keeps buying me flowers." She rolled her eyes at the last part, but she was grinning.

"Sounds like a good man," Freya said.

"Oh, he is. And second-generation, too. He's never even seen war." This last part was said with a sparkle in her eye that made Freya's gut twist.

The underlying assumption was that all humans in Vakker Castle were refugees from the human wars up north, and the polite thing to do was not to ask what someone else had been through. To survive up in the human territories, one had to swear allegiance to one warband or another. Whatever Mara's experience, she fell into the camp that liked to pretend the wars had never happened.

Freya didn't have that luxury. The things she'd done for those warlords would haunt her for the rest of her life.

This was why Freya chose not to talk much during their rendezvouses. Some of these things were better left unknown.

Mara tugged down her skirts, still grinning. "I'd love for you to find someone too, Freya."

Freya nearly choked. "I'm busy, but thank you. I hope he makes you happy."

"Too busy tending to the queen to find your own happiness?" Mara said, teasing.

"Something like that."

"Well, don't let her work you too hard."

Freya left the room before she could say something bitter and defensive that Mara didn't deserve.

She'd specifically sought out Mara to take her mind *off* of the embarrassing interaction where she had put her bare hand in Astrid's.

What in the goddess's name had Freya been thinking? She'd been distracted by Brenn's prediction. The history fair was coming up, and she'd spent long nights doing thorough background checks on all of the visitors. She'd not been sleeping well. Deep within herself, Freya admitted she craved touch of some sort. Mara had allowed her to let off some of the frustration and embarrassment, but Freya had not satisfied the source of the craving.

Now, Freya couldn't use Mara as a release. Finding someone new might be wise before Freya did something foolish.

And foolish it had been. Freya's brain replayed the scene of her reaching for Astrid like a woman possessed. The feeling of skin on skin. She couldn't mess up again. It embarrassed her all over again to wonder what Astrid must have thought of her. The last thing Freya wanted was for Astrid to suspect Freya of being too weak or distracted to serve well. The trust Freya had garnered was hard-earned. She could spoil it with the wrong move in a second.

She shook out her hands in the hallway. Forced herself to feel the leather gloves rubbing against her skin.

The ambassador would need at least a month to reach Vakker Castle. The consuls coming with him would reach some of the southernmost cities of Torden first, and Freya had more background checks to do, people to interrogate, provisions to make.

She had to get started right away.

The month before the ambassador came passed quickly. Every day, Freya made use of her contacts and presented Astrid's félag with the history of each orc coming to Torden. She paid special attention to the ambassador himself, but it was impossible to know how big a group he would bring with him until she laid eyes on everyone. Servants, guards, attendants, stewards—those people were hard to track down, not to mention that any of those positions could come and go. Freya would have much more work to do once the ambassador's retinue reached Vakker Castle.

The night the ambassador was set to arrive, Freya lurked in Astrid's room as the queen dressed. She had put so much effort into preparing, and yet part of her still felt as clueless as the day she'd begun her investigation.

The ambassador's name was Elgir, and according to a message he'd sent ahead, he was due to arrive with his entourage about an hour before dinner, giving Astrid enough time to conduct a brief tour of the castle as the ambassador's staff dealt with his belongings.

As for Freya, she analyzed every action of Astrid's—the way her hands trembled slightly when she brushed her hair, the way she stopped what she was doing every few minutes to take a deep breath.

Freya did not ask if the queen was all right. She stood at the open door to the balcony, listening to the evening sounds of lovers crunching crisp leaves underfoot and the quiet jokes of the guards on the other side of the door to the antechamber. Everyone was anticipating the meal, which would be more lavish than usual for their guests.

Everyone but Freya and Astrid.

A shuffling of fabric sliding over skin came from the center of the room, followed by a frustrated grunt.

"Freya, could you lend a hand?"

Freya pushed the balcony door closed and went to Astrid and her untied dress.

It was a bit of a joke whenever Freya had to do things queen's attendants were actually intended to do. Though Freya presented to the castle as Astrid's particularly dutiful attendant, her true responsibilities seldom overlapped with that of a typical lady's maid. Freya gathered intelligence and served as Astrid's discreet eyes around the castle; she was not accustomed to helping a queen in and out of her clothes. Like most of Torden's nobility, Astrid was self-sufficient, and Freya had absolutely no training in the role she purported to serve.

Freya grimaced at the many ribbons to lace. The dress itself was a stunning shade of green. Out of season, Freya thought, but then it would make Astrid look eternal like the trees that did not turn with autumn. Calculated to give off the impression she was unchanging, strong.

Astrid had gotten the bottom three ribbons tied haphazardly.

"I'm not good at this, Your Majesty," Freya warned.

"Just had this damn dress ordered," Astrid muttered under her breath. "I don't know what Dag was thinking. They know I can't get into this kind of garment without assistance."

In truth, Ruga might have been called in for tasks like this in the past. She was more feminine than either Astrid or Freya, and good with fabrics.

Freya tried to think of how Ruga's hands worked when faced with these kinds of ribbons. Ruga was competent at doing up dresses. Children could do this. How hard could it be?

"I'll try my best," said Freya.

As Freya untangled the knots, one formed at the base of her throat. The room felt unbearably stuffy, though the fire was not set, and the door had just been open. Freya faced a smooth strip of skin on Astrid's back—the curve of Astrid's spine, muscles that shifted under cool-toned brown skin as she fidgeted.

"Stars," Freya muttered to herself.

"Is it so difficult? Perhaps I should wear another dress."

Damn Mara for finding her true love.

Instead of filling her time with locating spare rooms for a tryst, Freya had spent the last month distracting herself with what she was best at—gathering intel, preparing for any possible outcome.

Freya had spent less and less time around Astrid, always making sure to leave her with trusted members of her guard. To Freya's relief, moving Hrothgar to captain of the félag had been a good decision. Freya hadn't needed to worry about Hedda's bursts of anger weakening the queen's defense.

There had been no plausible threats as of yet. Still, Freya was almost positive the incoming ambassador was the cause of Astrid's future "loss." She would have to keep diligent watch from the second he stepped through the castle gates.

But first, this complicated dress. Freya removed her gloves and wiped sweaty palms on her trousers. "I've got it," she said, her voice unusually husky.

She powered through the laces by pretending she was tying up a prisoner, tie after tie and knot after knot. The resulting effect was... Well. Efficient, if not beautiful. She realized when she was done that some of the ribbon was intended to be tied into bows.

Astrid turned in the mirror. Her loose braid of thick, brunette hair swung as she moved. Though Astrid had a muscular build—

not inherently soft, or Freya had never thought of her as such—there was a grace, a smoothness, an elegance to her step.

Stop noticing her movements, you fool.

"Oh, it's not so bad," Astrid said. "Thank you."

"Of course, Your Majesty. He's supposed to be here soon; shall we go?"

"No putting it off, I suppose," said Astrid, shooting such a soft, trusting smile at Freya that she was left flustered.

Freya opened the door for Astrid. The queen's dress swished against Freya's boots as she filtered past.

CHAPTER FOUR

The ambassador was late.

Astrid waited with her retinue at the castle gates as her hands grew numb with the cold. Her guards had no qualms about hiding their impatience—they shuffled so frequently, Astrid's determination not to shiver bothered her like an itch.

She glanced to her side at Freya, who faced directly forward with her arms crossed, eyes straight ahead like she could see something Astrid couldn't. Freya had sent her falcon to the ambassador's entourage, so they knew precisely when the ambassador was set to arrive. To cover their bases, Freya had also consulted Brenn to be sure of the time.

And yet he was not here.

They'd been waiting for nearly two hours. The general chatter that accompanied a large group of people had ended twenty minutes ago when everyone realized they would be out here for a long time. Every now and then, someone's stomach grumbled loudly.

Astrid's eye twitched.

"I am old," the steward said, breaking the silence, "and I am going to the dining hall to eat."

"Yes, of course," Astrid said, ashamed she had not thought to let him go. "Anyone outside of the félag may go to dinner." She bit back an apology on the ambassador's behalf.

"Thank the goddess," the elf librarian, Vera, muttered. Astrid had hoped to use Vera as a kind of cultural liaison, as she was worldly and educated about Sydlig's history. Torden and Sydlig had much in common, certainly, but Astrid had found oversights in her knowledge of Sydlig in the past, and she was terrified of stumbling upon one now, facing this ambassador.

Her upbringing had taken her around orc country and occasionally into the Elven Islands, traveling with her merchant family, but she had never paid much attention to politics until it was apparent she was a serious contender for queen.

It wasn't like she had expected to rule a country.

She continued to wait with the félag. Freya remained at her side in spite of being dismissed. She'd acted odd earlier, Astrid thought. True, Astrid did not often make Freya complete the maid duties Freya had technically signed up for, but Freya had seemed uncomfortable when faced with the back of Astrid's dress. Was it unprofessional to request that Freya lace up her clothing? The urge to ask her was strong, but the embarrassment Astrid would feel at the answer was stronger.

She remained quiet.

They waited some more. The hour stretched on, leaving Astrid with little sense of the passage of time and a cold ache in her bones. The sun set magnificently, orange and pinks and purples reflected on bits of jewelry—armbands, the rings of the félag, gleaming sword and axe pommels. Her own simple crown left a crenelated half-circle of light around her, and only when she noticed it did someone whisper under their breath, "Thank fuck." She was fairly certain it was Hrothgar, who as far as she knew was not prone to swearing.

In the distance, the ambassador's retinue was visible in silhouette. There weren't as many of them as Astrid had feared—a smallish group, maybe a dozen or so horses. The horses were overburdened with baggage, but it could have been much worse.

Astrid finally allowed herself to shift, to subtly shake out her limbs, as they got closer. The sun finished setting and left them in the dark, and the cold turned brittle.

"Nine," Freya whispered. Nine people. A collection of attendants, if Astrid had to guess. Maybe some soldiers or guards who had helped them get here safely, not that traveling through Torden was unsafe. She hoped some of them would head right back after dinner.

When the group was close enough to hear, Astrid stepped forward. An orc at the head of the group swung down from his horse. He had broad shoulders and a softness around his stomach, and his skin was smooth and unblemished, unaccustomed to labor.

"Welcome to Vakker Castle," Astrid said with a tiny dip of her head.

The orc bowed grandly. "Ambassador Guthmar at your service, Your Majesty."

Something was off, but Astrid couldn't discern what, exactly. "We were anticipating you earlier."

Two of the orcs on the horses flanking Guthmar's dismounted and bowed to Astrid. They did not have the look of attendants. The woman to Guthmar's left wore finer fabrics than even Astrid dared to wear lest she ruin them, though the orc did have the hard look in her eyes of someone who hadn't lived her entire life in the lap of luxury. Her hair was a striking magenta, tied into the same kind of loose braid Astrid preferred. The orc man to Guthmar's right was shorter than him and stocky, his horns looking a tad too big for his head, and his hair was short-cropped. The two orcs were similarly dressed in the royal purple and stag motifs of Sydlig's court.

"My husband, Tassi," Guthmar said, gesturing to his right, "and my wife, Alvor."

Astrid forced a smile. She had not invited this ambassador here, and she certainly had not invited his spouses. "Welcome. We have prepared a meal for you, if you are hungry from your travels."

Guthmar laughed throatily. His entire retinue joined in, like hunger was an inside joke they'd developed on their journey. "Much appreciated, Your Majesty. Please, lead the way."

Astrid caught Freya's eye as she turned to the great hall.

"Your Majesty," Freya whispered loud enough for the félag to hear. "The ambassador we were expecting is named Elgir."

The ambassador brought his spouses and his two bodyguards with him into the dining hall, forcing everyone who usually dined with Astrid to move over to make room. The benches were overcrowded and hot. The food was good, though the hall was half-full of people who'd already eaten, waiting for the queen to finish her own meal.

They'd spared no expense to greet the ambassador. The skald stood in one corner, enthusiastically reciting a love story with the musical accompaniment of a lyre.

"How were your travels?" Astrid asked lightly. She was tempted to pry into why Elgir had been replaced with Guthmar, but was unsure whether it was rude to ask outright. She had no idea if Freya had dug into Guthmar's background.

Next to Astrid, Hrothgar dipped a spoon into their stew. Her captain ate next to her, both as a sign of their respected status and as extra protection in case something were to happen in the great hall, which Astrid did not find likely. She did find, however, that Hedda had been a better conversationalist than Hrothgar.

"We traveled well," Guthmar said. He swirled his goblet of mead. Astrid had not counted how many times it had been refilled, but she thought the staff had stopped by at least thrice. "I always forget how lovely Torden's towns are. Hospitable, too."

Astrid nearly flinched, thinking of humble inns housing this grand orc and his people.

The husband and wife were quiet, observing, which made Astrid distrust them instantly. She wished she'd had time to consult Freya. Neither Freya nor Astrid had predicted the spouses would be here, and Astrid didn't know their histories.

As time went on, Astrid's sense of alarm dimmed. She found it easy enough to engage in conversation. If she didn't please the ambassador, she at least avoided offending him. The more they conversed, the more she relaxed—he was prone to talking, sharing more than he needed to, and she could sit there and give the occasional nod.

The ambassador hardly seemed a threat. Astrid noted he did not wear a sword. Of his entourage, only his bodyguards carried weapons. After a while, the ambassador's attendants came for dinner. Astrid had witnessed them bearing Guthmar's generous travel bags, and she was not surprised at their fatigue from carrying the luggage up the stairs. The attendants joined the housekeeping staff at their table, and the kitchen scrambled to bring them fresh food. Some were human and some were orcs. They did not look ready for battle, either, though Astrid was not sure how the ambassador kept four attendants busy.

When he'd heaped more food onto his plate, Guthmar settled back, cradling the goblet close to him. "You're probably wondering what I'm doing here, aren't you?"

Astrid's eye twitched. "It was clear enough in His Majesty's letter to my steward."

"Well, what I'm doing here rather than Elgir, I mean." He lowered his voice. "Elgir is His Majesty's brother, and not of good temperament. They got into a fight shortly before he was meant to leave." He tsked, like fighting with one's sibling was childish, and Astrid felt a pang of guilt at her past conflict with her own sister. Becoming royalty did divide people so.

"I am King Skarde's cousin," Guthmar said. "And I was meant to be the consul of… Stars, what was it? Alvor?"

"Ravn," his wife supplied.

"Right. Ravn. But I got promoted, so you're stuck with me." He laughed then, full-bellied, and launched into some story clearly designed to brag about his closeness with the king.

Good, then. Freya would at least have done some research into his background, as she had for all of the consuls.

Astrid's attention wandered as Guthmar's story became more convoluted and harder to follow. As if by instinct, she sought out Freya, who stood against the wall closer to the staff table, practically invisible. She was some distance from the on-duty guards, but when two orcs from the kitchen came in with a heavy platter, she rushed forward to help them carry it to the attendants. After they'd delivered the food, the orcs patted her on the back in a familiar way that put a knot in Astrid's stomach.

But that was silly, Astrid reasoned. Freya had cultivated relationships with the castle staff because it helped her stay informed of things Astrid had no way of figuring out for herself. That was what spymasters were for.

Astrid couldn't remember how she'd gotten by before Freya had come around. She'd had no spymaster before, hadn't even considered the possibility of hiring one. It was the kind of position only shady, corrupt rulers would need, she'd thought, before Freya had proved her usefulness.

And Astrid was a queen, anyway, not someone who could be familiar with people the way Freya could. Patting someone on the shoulder could be seen as construing favoritism. Fodder for a rumor mill. People would think they had the chance to get close to her, that she could succumb to undue influence.

Keeping her distance was something Astrid had done her entire reign. She just wished it didn't necessitate total isolation.

Was Astrid imagining the additional distance grown between herself and Freya? Freya was always busy in advance of big events at Vakker Castle, and they had the consuls to think about now, and the history fair to think about soon, so it was not abnormal for her to be absent. And she never left Astrid completely on her own. Certainly never unprotected. Staff at the castle came and went with time, but Freya was a constant, just as constant as the félag Astrid had built up over her fifty-some years of rule.

Unbidden, Astrid remembered the soft touch of Freya's fingers on the sensitive skin of her palm, the way an awkwardness had permeated her room when Freya laced up her dress.

As if sensing Astrid's thoughts, Freya's gaze flicked to hers and held her there. For one beat—two beats—Astrid couldn't breathe. Freya lifted her hand slightly, pushing back the fabric of her tunic so Astrid could see the gleam of Freya's dagger sheathed at her hip. A message Astrid understood implicitly: *You have my protection.*

Freya let the fabric of her tunic fall back over her hip, and Astrid saw the strip of skin that vanished under it burned into her sight the way flames remain when staring too long at a fire. She continued to stare. Freya's brow furrowed, and she gave a nod of assurance, a half-bow. Devotion emanated from her, and suddenly the attention was too much.

Astrid slammed down her mead.

"Is everything all right, Your Majesty?" the ambassador asked.

Astrid had not listened to anything he'd said for the last ten minutes, and he had not noticed.

"Yes, of course," Astrid said, hiding behind her smile. "It's just that the mead is a bit strong tonight."

CHAPTER FIVE

How could this have happened? Freya had planned so meticulously, sought out every detail, extracted and organized and memorized. She had anticipated the need to keep close watch over the ambassador, but not that King Skarde might send someone else.

She could not fathom a benign reason for the old ambassador's replacement.

On her way to the dining hall, she tapped Mara on the shoulder and asked her to introduce the topic of the replacement to Guthmar's attendants during the meal.

In the dining hall, three long tables seated the entire castle: one for the staff, one for the garrison, and one where Astrid, the félag, and Guthmar and his spouses sat.

Freya waited against the wall near the staff table, listening in on the attendants' conversation. They were unhappy to be here; traveling for a month was rough, and Guthmar was an orc who stopped at every town to see the sights. They told stories of him holding them up at rustic inns, interesting houses with oddly shaped windows, beds of flowers with unusual colors, bustling markets with trinkets he'd peruse for hours. Easily distracted, they said. Not scared of inconveniencing others by taking up their time. But nobody mentioned anything about him being cruel.

In fact, the impression was that Guthmar was foolish. He'd been sent in lieu of the king's brother, Elgir, who from all rumors was a hostile, unpredictable person. Was the replacement a good indication, then? Had King Skarde intended to intimidate Torden with Elgir, then changed his mind and sent the less frightening Guthmar instead? Or was it meant as an insult? As in, *here is this silly man, and this is how much of a threat we think you are?*

Freya couldn't make head nor tail of it.

Was it possible the change was a mere coincidence? Brenn would say nothing was a coincidence and everything was in the hands of the goddess. Their wyrd had been set in stone long before they were born. Freya, of course, did not believe in anything this simple.

The worst part of the switch was that Astrid relied on Freya to handle these matters, and Freya had failed. How disappointed the queen must've been. Freya was seldom wrong about anything, seldom caught by surprise. And here they were, completely unaware of a significant change the goddess apparently had not seen fit to share with Brenn.

Freya itched to sneak away and speak to Brenn about this development, but from now on, she wouldn't be able to leave the queen's side. The castle staff were discussing the upcoming history fair with the new attendants—something Freya had already prepared for. Only those invited would be allowed through the castle gates, but *more* strangers in the castle while they were already dealing with this ambassador crisis...

Sometimes Freya wished she could split herself in two.

Freya would write to Brenn. She needed her nearby: her guidance and her steady presence were invaluable. From now until Sydlig saw fit to recall their ambassador, Freya would have to use every resource available to her.

"And who's this?" one of the ambassador's human attendants asked. Ingirun, Freya thought her name was.

Everyone at the staff table turned to Freya. She waved.

"That's the queen's shadow," a kitchen girl said behind her hand.

"The what? Is that an official position here?"

"She's Queen Astrid's attendant," the kitchen girl clarified. "You won't see the queen without Freya."

Subconsciously, Freya's hand went to her dagger. She felt the hard, comforting ridge of the pommel through the fabric of her tunic. She liked her nickname and what it implied. Astrid was never alone under her watch, never vulnerable. Freya was Astrid's sword, the whisper in her ear, the shadow at her feet.

"A bit overbearing for a lady's maid," Ingirun commented.

"Yes," the kitchen girl agreed.

Freya was not offended by this assessment.

"She's handsome," one of the orc attendants said, and Freya snapped to attention, puffing out her chest. She did a quick sweep of the table and caught the orc attendant ogling her. She was picking up on their names quickly—this was Hjotra.

Freya winked.

It couldn't hurt, especially with Mara unavailable, to get close to Guthmar's attendants. They could be good sources of inside information, and Freya could let out some of the tension that wound her up every day. Freya had been with an orc before, early on when she had come to Vakker—a woman from the kitchens who had since moved away. At the time, the orc's penetrative tongue had been a shock, but Freya'd gotten used to it.

The idea of forging a new connection exhausted Freya, however. Questions about the scars on her hands. Boundaries to set, emotions to evade. The dynamic with Mara had been simple. With these new attendants, Freya didn't know what to expect.

When Guthmar's people left the hall, Freya followed them silently. They went to their respective assigned rooms without wandering. Good. She'd check in on them later and make sure they were still there, but for now, her confidence in the attendants being exactly who they said they were had grown.

Freya waited in the queen's bedroom as Astrid removed her crown, brushed out her braid, and slid off her armbands. Freya was called over to undo the laces she'd done earlier. This time, she removed her gloves right away and got it over with. Untying the prisoner, she told herself. Not undressing her queen.

"What are you thinking, Freya?" Astrid asked.

Freya hadn't spoken since they'd come back, so lost in thought had she been.

"I don't like the ambassador switch." Freya ran a hand through her hair and her fingers came back oily. She was suddenly embarrassed to be so close to the queen. When was the last time she'd washed her hair?

"What do we know of Guthmar?" Astrid asked. "Other than the things he told me at the table."

Freya had noticed the ambassador's penchant for talking someone's ear off. "I haven't gleaned as much as I'd like. He's the king's cousin—I'm sure he shared that with you. His attendants don't think highly of him, though not for the reason you'd expect. He made many sojourns on the way up here. Not just in the towns, though he always wanted to try every variety of mead. Apparently, he also stopped for flowers he didn't recognize. To smell them."

"Well. That's not exactly malicious, is it?"

"No. If anyone in his entourage was set on harming you, I doubt it would be him."

"Harming me?" Astrid's hand went to her throat. "I was more worried about... Court sabotage, maybe. Or Sydlig having information we don't. How much influence he expects to have over me. The imposition of it all."

Stars. Freya really was deprived of sleep. She hadn't told Astrid about Brenn's prediction, and she didn't plan on doing so. She could help Astrid avoid catastrophe on her own.

"The political side. Of course," said Freya.

"Have you any indication Guthmar's entourage would cause me physical harm?"

"They would all be dead if I thought they would hurt you," Freya said.

Her words hung in the air between them, and after an extended silence, Astrid laughed. "Was that a joke, Freya?"

"Too dry, I suppose." Freya's cheeks warmed. She wasn't sure if it was a joke, but her sense of humor tended toward the dark side.

"I would have understood sooner if I wasn't so exhausted," said Astrid. "Listening to Guthmar all night... However long he plans to stay, it will feel like an eternity."

"That, we do agree on, My Queen."

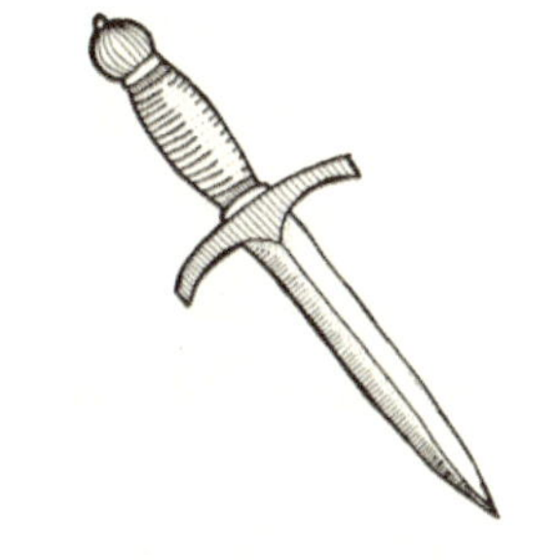

CHAPTER SIX

Astrid woke when the sky was still dark and promptly tripped over something at the foot of her bed.

She blinked away the last of sleep as she took in the sight of a crumpled human on the ground: Freya, swaddled in an eiderdown blanket. For a beat, she imagined something was wrong, that Freya was injured, and her pulse raced.

And then Freya moved.

"Whatever are you doing in here?" Astrid asked. Freya's rooms were connected to Astrid's, but she'd never known Freya to sleep in her bedroom.

To her credit, Freya did little other than grunt, massaging her side where Astrid had kicked her. "I couldn't sleep."

Freya was curled at the foot of Astrid's bed with a blanket and pillow; the arrangement was premeditated. Her eyes were red with fatigue.

"You don't have to guard me overnight. It's not like I'll be stabbed in my sleep," Astrid joked.

She bent down to put a hand on Freya's shoulder, and Freya jolted. There was no humor in her expression.

Did Freya think Astrid *could* be killed in her own bed?

She remembered what Freya had said last night about the possibility of harm coming to Astrid. Her dark joke about the action she would take. Astrid had no doubt Freya was fully capable of following through. Unfortunately for all of them, Guthmar did not deserve to die, and his death would be the start of an international incident. The last thing Astrid needed was enemies to the west *and* south.

"There are two guards outside the door," Astrid reminded Freya, "and the rest of my félag down the hall. Not to mention you in the next room over. I'm well protected."

"I know, Your Majesty." Freya's voice was scratchy. She smoothed down her hair, which had taken to sticking up every which way. Despite herself, Astrid relished in seeing Freya mussed and undone.

"I'm being extra cautious because of the ambassador switch," said Freya.

Astrid didn't know what to say. They'd already discussed the ambassador last night. How if he was a threat, he was a diplomatic one, not an...assassin.

The idea of an assassin in her apartments made her shudder. She searched for words of assurance—why did *Astrid* need to assure Freya that she herself wasn't in bodily danger?—when someone knocked at the door.

"Hrothgar?" Astrid called.

"Yes, Your Majesty. Ambassador Guthmar is here, and he would like a tour of the castle."

"He should have come on time yesterday if he wanted a tour," Freya muttered.

Astrid waved her protest away. "I'll get ready as fast as I can, Hrothgar. You can let him into my antechamber."

Silence from the other side of the door. Freya shook her head in disagreement.

"He has brought his spouses and his bodyguards, Your Majesty," Hrothgar said.

Five orcs crowding up Astrid's antechamber. Just envisioning this made Astrid want to crawl back into bed. "Leave them in the hall, then," she said. "I'll be quick."

"Yes, Your Majesty." Hrothgar's steps echoed away. There was booming laughter down the hall, unmistakably the ambassador's, and both Astrid and Freya flinched.

"You should get ready, too, Freya," Astrid said as she splashed her face in the basin.

"I'm going to follow you closely today," Freya warned.

Astrid glanced up through her wet eyelashes. Always, Freya insisted on guarding Astrid as her duty. She rejected gifts and other displays of thanks, but Astrid felt gratitude well up in her chest anyway. "Why?"

"I don't trust the newcomers, and I still have much to learn about them," Freya said. She was standing now, and though she'd been sleeping a moment ago and was wearing only a light tunic, she looked ready for the day.

"You'll let me know what you learn?" Astrid asked.

Freya didn't look up to meet her gaze. The column of her throat bobbed as she swallowed. "Of course, My Queen."

The ambassador was surrounded by a small crowd when Astrid left her rooms ten minutes or so later. He was regaling the onlookers with a tale—or he would have been, if any of his words made it through his boisterous laughter. His wife and husband wore indulgent smiles, but the bodyguards he'd brought with him were stoic as could be, and Astrid's félag wore the stony faces of those forced to pander to a small, petulant child.

It was going to be a long day.

"Is there anything in particular you want to see?" Astrid asked as they headed down the stairs. The light padding of Freya's feet followed her, comforting and familiar.

"Oh, I'd like to see everything," he said, and Astrid's stomach nearly fell out of her ass. She recalled what Freya had said about his attendants: *He wanted to stop for every little thing.*

He actually, literally, meant he wanted to see *everything.*

Astrid brought him to the meadery first. It smelled of honey and yeast and reminded her of summer. She thought about Guthmar's loose tongue last night, brought on by the mead. "Perhaps we should try some," she suggested, and the meadery staff rushed to find something worthy to give an ambassador. Soon, everyone had a drinking horn in hand. Astrid pretended to politely sip at hers as the conversation went on.

The bodyguards were on alert at all times for Guthmar's safety. This was, in part, because he was known to be clumsy when he drank. They would reach out at times, anticipating his stumble into things made of glass. Astrid mouthed *thank you* to them when they stopped Guthmar from falling into a set of armor in the meadery, worn by a legendary hero of yore who was known to have beaten an army single-handedly after having drunk an entire barrel of mead on his own. Vera would have shrieked if the armor was so much as dented. It would not do well to ruin something valuable right before the history fair.

In the scullery, Guthmar wanted a demonstration of how the kitchen staff washed the dishes. Guthmar's wife shouldered past him right away. "You don't have to do anything special for him," Alvor assured the two men assigned to cleaning duty. "He would just like to see how you work normally."

Astrid was oddly touched by the gesture. The two men displayed immediate relief. They showed Guthmar how they scrubbed every nook and cranny of the fancier goblets. "Fascinating," Guthmar said with genuine awe. It was also possible he was drunk.

"He's full of wonder about the world," Astrid whispered to Freya. Freya hummed noncommittally in response.

Guthmar did, indeed, want to stop literally everywhere. He stopped at windows to admire the architecture; he stopped at a sconce to appreciate the metalsmithing that went into it; he stopped people in the halls to ask their names and what they did here. Once, he even sent an older orc on the kitchen staff away blushing after complimenting his hairstyle.

As the day went on, it was hard to be annoyed with Guthmar. Astrid hardly had time to do as much stopping as he did, but how could she begrudge someone who took time to appreciate all of life's little pleasures? She began to envy him, after a time. She understood what his spouses saw in him.

"He notices everything," Freya whispered from behind Astrid.

"Yes," Astrid said, a bit fondly.

"He's *cataloging*."

Astrid saw Guthmar's actions through new eyes. Thank the goddess for Freya. It was a good cover to look through the accounting books—not that he'd find anything amiss—among other things that could be fed back to King Skarde.

But how much of this was true, and how much was Freya's overcaution?

"Library," Freya murmured as Astrid turned the corner toward the aviary.

Astrid paused, shuffled her feet, and pivoted to the other direction. "Do you like to read, Ambassador?" she said. "Our library is the finest in Torden."

At this, the ambassador wrinkled his nose. He truly was inebriated. "I don't care much for books. The effort required to read is...vast. Why stay inside and read when we can be out experiencing the world?"

Astrid pursed her lips. Novelty—this was someone who craved novelty. "We have an elf librarian."

"*My*, but that is fascinating. Lead the way."

Vera—said elf librarian—was not pleased to see them. She lifted her spectacles up her nose and brushed long red hair over one shoulder, giving the entourage an impressive glower.

"Your Majesty," she greeted in a tone that could only be described as ironic. "And the ambassador from Sydlig, I take it."

The ambassador held out a somewhat sweaty palm to greet her. Vera frowned at it and did not reciprocate the gesture.

"Lovely to meet you. How did you end up in orc country?" he asked.

Vera peered over the ambassador's shoulder and straight at Freya. Astrid had never truly understood the relationship between Vera and Freya. They'd come to the castle together a decade ago, but they were not friends. What Astrid could tell was that Vera knew Freya was responsible for their presence today.

"Would you like a tour?" Vera asked unkindly.

"Oh, no. I don't care for literature," he said, and Astrid smothered a smile at the horror-struck look on Vera's face.

"I do, dear," Tassi said. "Perhaps we can have a look around?"

Tassi nudged Guthmar away from Vera. The three spouses and their two bodyguards found a corner with a chair and began to rifle through the books as Guthmar sat there, trying to peer around the corner at the librarian.

"What do you think, Vera?" Freya asked, leaning against the librarian's counter.

"He's ridiculous," Vera said. "Whyever would the king send him? If he won't so much as read a book, how can he be expected to read and understand legal contracts? Or write and receive correspondence?"

"Why, indeed?" said Astrid.

Freya ran a finger over the book Vera was reading. "I was wondering if you knew anything about Sydlig marriage customs."

Vera snorted. "Of course I know about Sydlig marriage customs."

"The three of them—Ambassador Guthmar and then Alvor and Tassi, who do not have titles. They've been introduced as his spouses, but not each other's. Are they...all together, do you know?"

"It's much like here," Vera said. "Their relationship would work however it does on an individual basis. The ambassador is part of the royal family. They don't necessarily have greater or fewer spouses than anyone else in Sydlig."

This was the good thing about having Freya around. Astrid had been paying attention to Alvor and Tassi's interactions with the castle staff, but she had not been paying attention to their relationship dynamic.

"Freya?" Astrid prodded.

"There's a distance," said Freya, "between Alvor and Tassi. I get the impression they don't like each other much."

Astrid watched them openly. Tassi managed to distract Guthmar from gazing at Vera with a book about mead-making. While Tassi and Alvor didn't stand close, they didn't avoid each other either. Both spouses touched Guthmar with ease—affection, even. Resting their hands on his shoulder, leaning over him to turn the page. Astrid wasn't sure how to read into them.

To be fair, she was out of practice with romance these days.

"We'll keep an eye on them," Freya said. "Thanks, Vera."

"Get him out of my library, or you'll regret it," Vera said.

"Understood," said Freya.

It occurred to Astrid that Vera was the only person who could threaten Freya without any consequences.

"Ambassador Guthmar," Astrid called, "is there anywhere else you would like to see?" Hopefully outside, she thought to add, but she didn't want him to feel unwelcome.

Guthmar's finger hovered over a picture from a book. His smile screamed true delight, saliva clinging to his tusks. Completely and totally uninhibited. "Birds," the ambassador said, as though he had never heard of the concept. "How magnificent are these!"

He held up the book for Astrid to see. The page was indeed graced with a breathtaking image of a bird. If Vera had been feeling more indulgent, she might have told them who had illustrated it and what sort of bird it was.

"We have an aviary just down the hall," Astrid said.

Guthmar jumped up from the chair, slamming his book shut. He passed it off to Tassi, who politely replaced it on the shelf. "Let us go at once," he said.

Astrid led the way to the aviary. It was open, two stories tall, with its own tower and huge windows. Even though she couldn't be outside, she felt like she could breathe in here, with the cold wind coming in from the outdoors.

The aviarist greeted them when they arrived, but they'd taken him by surprise. He dabbed sweat from the base of his horns. Astrid tried to leave him alone as much as she could; he was an orc who loved birds more than he loved other people.

Upon their entrance to the aviary, Freya's peregrine falcon made a little squawk and descended from its perch. She lifted her arm for it to land. Her hands were gloved in leather, but her hawking gauntlet was thicker and went farther up her arms, and she was not wearing it. The falcon's talons sank into her arm, and she did not so much as flinch.

"How fascinating," Guthmar said. He cautiously approached the bird, lifting up a hand as if he meant to touch.

Freya shook her head once.

"He does not like to be pet," the ambassador guessed, his voice laced with sorrow.

"No," Freya said. "She does not."

"Female peregrine falcons are much larger than males," the aviarist supplied in a small voice.

The ambassador recovered quickly. "What is her name?"

"Huginn," said Freya.

"Huginn," Guthmar repeated, feeling the name in his mouth. "An odd name for a bird."

"Tassi is an odd name for a man," Freya countered.

The air was sucked out of the room. Astrid's diplomatic side kicked in, ready to smooth things over, when a great guffaw bubbled out of Alvor's throat first, followed by Tassi. Guthmar joined in. The aviarist pretended to be busy with a merlin on the other side of the room.

Guthmar spoke first after the bout of laughter. Belatedly, Astrid realized she should have participated, and Freya might have laughed, too, and now it was too late and it looked as though nobody on her court had a sense of humor. Embarrassment flushed her skin.

"It is so intriguing that your maid has an interest in falconry," he said. "When does she have the time?"

"Oh, you know," Astrid said, fumbling for an explanation, "much like you, Freya takes pleasure in learning new things."

"Indeed, Your Majesty," said Freya. "May I speak with Your Majesty to the side? I think I may be coming down ill."

Huginn lifted from Freya's arm and circled above Guthmar, stunning him into silence with her broad wingspan. Astrid turned to Freya, shielding her from the others with her body.

"He knows I'm more than a maid," Freya said. It was a wonder her voice did not echo around that large place when everything else did. "I need to conduct a more thorough background check on him and his retinue. Do you mind if I go?"

Astrid stole a peek at the ambassador. Hrothgar was distracting him, forcing the aviarist to interact with Guthmar and tell them bird facts that invoked delighted responses.

Hedda would have done the same, Astrid couldn't help but think. And she might have done it without bothering the aviarist.

"Of course you can go," Astrid said. "I'm safe here."

The protest was clear on Freya's face. She was made of sharp angles: her straight nose, her severe brows, the triangle of her widow's peak and the beginning of her hair, short on the sides and longer on top. Something was different about her hair up close—and close they were, Astrid realized with a start, so close she could smell the citrus soap Freya preferred, fresh as summer.

"Did you do something with your hair?" Astrid asked.

Freya's brow scrunched. "No?"

"Oh," said Astrid. "Forgive me."

"There is nothing to forgive, Your Majesty."

Neither of them spoke. The voices of the others echoed across the room, and Astrid knew she should be paying attention to them, but all she could register was Freya.

"I'll take my leave, then," Freya said at last, breaking eye contact. She bowed to Astrid and exited the room.

The aviary was too spacious now, and Astrid felt exposed. The wind blew around the fabric of her trousers and her cloak.

"Where to next?" Guthmar asked, and Astrid's sore feet whined.

CHAPTER SEVEN

Freya wished she could be in two places at once more than ever. She would have to make this quick. Ask her contacts for information on the bodyguards, the spouses, Ambassador Guthmar's relationship to King Skarde—whether it matched up with Guthmar's claims or not, whether anything was amiss. Attendants knew everything. She would start there first, then reach out to her people at the other major cities, see if they knew anything she didn't.

So much to do. So little time. She was half-tempted to ride down to Sydlig herself for answers.

Freya did not make it to the attendants' rooms. Instead, halfway into the castle's foyer, she stopped in her tracks at the sound of a familiar voice: Brenn.

Brenn was not dressed in her priestess robes; she wore a flowy dress the color of midnight. Half in disguise, and half not, because she had her priestess's staff.

Brenn spoke to one of the guards at the entrance to the main hallway. The guard leaned too close into Brenn's space, and Freya rushed forward to intervene.

"Stars, Freya," Brenn murmured, holding the staff close to her chest like a shield. "You might have told the guards I was coming."

"This is the priestess Brenn," Freya said. "She has been invited."

"My sincerest apologies to the queen," the guard said, bowing. They never assumed Freya would invite people of her own volition, only on the queen's orders.

And, well. Brenn didn't come to the castle often.

Freya dragged Brenn into an alcove with a mullioned window.

Brenn set her staff against the stone wall and smoothed down her dress to sit along the windowsill. "I got your letter," she said, "obviously."

"Sorry I was not there to greet you. We have had a busy morning."

"The ambassador?" Brenn asked.

"Yes," said Freya. "He's demanding, though not in the way you'd expect."

"I'm planning to stay per your wishes. But know the sacrifice I am making."

Freya leaned her head against the wall. "I know. Thank you."

Brenn watched the sight through the window. It looked out onto the courtyard, where a couple sat at a fountain that no longer ran. They whispered to each other, completely unaware of their onlookers. So carefree.

A dull ache throbbed in Freya's chest.

Brenn broke the silence. "If something bad is going to happen, I can't prevent it. Neither can you."

"Of course. Anything we can do is better than nothing." Not true, but what else could be done?

"And...I'm worried about you."

Freya dropped next to Brenn on the small lip of the sill. "About me?"

"I remember how it was back when we first escaped the human wars. How protective you were. Looking out for me before yourself."

Discomfort itched at Freya's skin. She did not like the attention on her, nor did she know how to react to the gratitude in Brenn's voice.

"I don't need looking after anymore." Brenn traced the pattern on the window with one finger.

"No, you've carried on well," Freya said.

"I'm not talking about me. I'm talking about *you*."

Freya waited for one furious beat. Her instincts screamed at her to slither out of this conversation. "I have to get back to what I was doing. The ambassador brought some attendants I mean to interrogate now that I know more about him. Would you like to accompany me?"

Brenn laid a hand over Freya's bouncing leg. "The queen will be safe for half an hour. She'll be safe for longer, too. She's got the most loyal guard in Torden. Nothing bad can happen to her here."

Freya made a conscious effort to keep her legs still. "What about the prediction from the goddess? The loss?"

Brenn shook her head. "I wish I hadn't told you the truth."

"What? Why?"

"Have you seen the bags under your eyes?"

"It's my duty to protect the queen and to keep her appraised of all pertinent information. Maybe, yes, if I don't have all of the information I need… Maybe not being able to perform my duty prevents me from sound sleeping. Is that so odd?"

"It's different, is all I'm saying." Brenn took back her hand and placed it primly in her lap. "From when you took care of me."

"Brenn," Freya said, "please be plain."

"You're so intense about Queen Astrid. I worry that you have an unhealthy attachment. Do you think your well-being is dependent on your proximity to the queen?"

"Why would I think that?" Freya asked.

"You notice your surroundings. Every detail," Brenn said. "I've seen you check the exits three times since you brought me here. But you don't notice *yourself*."

"You think I'm not self-aware."

"I think you could benefit from more introspection," Brenn agreed diplomatically.

Maybe it had been a mistake to invite Brenn to the castle. Any priestess would do for the purpose of conveying the goddess's visions, for the purpose of healing magic, illusion magic—but Brenn was the only priestess Freya trusted.

Or so she'd thought.

"I disagree," Freya said. "Can I show you to your rooms? I know the castle can be overwhelming."

"That's vicious, Freya."

Freya threw up her hands. "I am feeling defensive!"

Dryly, Brenn laughed. "I suppose you *are* self-aware. Have you given any thought to why you defend the queen so adamantly when she has entire armies at her disposal?"

"She needs my eye for defense. And you've told me something bad will happen to her."

"I didn't say that," Brenn said. "I said she'd experience loss. She could lose anything. Her favorite armband... Anything."

The suggestions did not convince Freya. "And I suppose the goddess cares to tell you when a queen loses her favorite armband but not when an ambassador has completely switched identities."

"I can't control that."

Freya sighed. "You and I were just two humans in a warzone. *Two* warzones. Protecting us was easier. Anything could be a threat to an orc queen. I have to remain vigilant."

"Right." Brenn shifted to face Freya. "You don't think there's any other reason? Have you ever felt the need to guard anyone else so closely?"

Comprehension dawned on Freya. She stood abruptly, scuffing her boots. "You think I care too deeply for her."

"She's unavailable." Brenn stood and faced Freya. She was taller, looking down, and Freya had the sense of being imposed upon. Not priestess magic, exactly, but a persuasive habit Brenn had picked up—leverage. "She's closed off from romantic opportunities, or else she'd have taken any number of lovers. And you can't be with someone who needs to care for an entire country. She won't have space for you. And...your life will end sooner."

That went without saying. It had taken a long time to become accustomed to the way orcs lived out their much longer lives, and Freya had maybe fifty years left if the stress of her lifestyle didn't age her heart sooner.

"I'm not in love with the queen," Freya protested.

"I didn't say you were," Brenn said. "You came to that assumption."

Freya remembered when she touched Astrid's hand. How she needed outlets for her frustration when they spent too much time together. Freya knew what that meant. She also knew what was possible and what wasn't.

But what about Astrid? She'd asked about Freya's hair. She was wrong that Freya had done anything different to it. When she'd asked, Freya's body had been charged like the moment before lightning strikes.

Too often, being close to Astrid made her feel like that.

Brenn took Freya's gloved hands in her own. Unblemished, perfect cuticles against golden skin. Hands unused to engaging directly in war, though Brenn had been complicit in some things.

Nothing as bad as Freya had done.

"You will get hurt," Brenn whispered, like it was one of her prophecies.

"Do you say this as my friend? Or did you see it in a vision?"

Brenn hesitated before answering, giving Freya the confirmation she needed.

Through the gloves, Brenn's fingers squeezed Freya's. Her dearest friend. No matter how many times they fought, Brenn was quick to forgive first. They'd forged their friendship in the darkest of circumstances—they knew each other better than they knew anyone else.

And Brenn knew, both within herself and with deific confirmation, that Freya would be hurt by her connection to Astrid.

Presented like this, the inevitability was undeniable. Freya's mouth was dry, unpleasant. She thought of lacing up Astrid's dress. The discomfort. The want.

"Fuck," she said.

"It's not too late to step back," Brenn assured her.

"Brenn, I have stepped back. I lost myself in my work. And I'm still..."

"It's not so easy to let go, is it?"

Freya huffed. "Said like you're talking from experience."

Brenn's expression darkened. "There are things about me you don't know."

"I'm not in love with her," Freya insisted.

"I believe you."

Freya looked into Brenn's eyes. What she wouldn't give to have the powers Brenn had—the ability to *know*. Brenn would say those abilities were only given to those chosen by the goddess.

Very well. Freya fought hard for everything she did know, and she would continue to do so, goddess or no goddess.

A commotion broke out down the hall back in the foyer. Freya readjusted her gloves as she took them out of Brenn's hands, tilting her head to listen.

Brenn's eyes widened first. It was her reaction that spurred Freya to action.

Freya broke into a run. She threw herself into the foyer with such force that she slammed directly into Hedda's burly chest. Hedda reached out to steady her, surprise and hurt registering on her face. One of the ambassador's bodyguards was beside her, looking rather more upset than the stoic exterior Freya noticed earlier.

"What's happened?" Freya demanded, clutching Hedda's leather armor with both hands.

"You have the priestess," Hedda said with relief. "The queen's been hurt."

CHAPTER EIGHT

One second, Astrid was descending the stairs, and the next, she was on the floor with bruises all over and an arm that didn't move the way it was supposed to.

Astrid was distracted. Trying to get the ambassador out of the castle, when all he'd wanted to do was see every room on every floor. She'd needed fresh air badly. She hadn't had Freya by her side.

She had tripped down an *entire* flight of stone stairs.

And now she was bedridden in the infirmary when she had important things to attend to.

"I am perfectly fine," she insisted to Brenn, who stood over her. "Not ambushed by enemies. Just some blasted stairs. Tell everyone to hold back the funeral bells."

"Your Majesty," Brenn said, "I insist. Please drink some of this."

Astrid allowed Brenn to tilt the concoction into her throat. The taste was pleasant, at least. The castle healer—not magical at all, merely an herbalist—usually forced Astrid to drink teas that tasted like something meant to exit the body, not enter. The magic tingled on her tongue.

"Is Freya here?" Astrid asked.

"Yes, Your Majesty," came Freya's voice from the other side of the room.

Astrid tried to guess at Freya's reaction, but her spymaster was stoic as ever. Freya wasn't likely to believe Astrid had taken a tumble down the stairs out of distraction and clumsiness.

"You'll be healed up in a week or so with the magic," Brenn said, but she wasn't looking at Astrid. "Don't move the arm unnecessarily, or else you may extend your healing time."

That wouldn't be a problem. Brenn had wound up Astrid's arm so tight in the sling, she couldn't move it if she wanted to.

The familiar soft scuff of Freya's boots trod to Astrid's bedside. "You're sure you didn't hit your head?" Freya leaned over her. "Your Majesty," she added belatedly.

"Yes, I'm sure. Just the arm. Have you checked on Hrothgar? They blunted my fall quite a bit with their body when I fell on them." Hrothgar had grabbed Astrid's arm, wrenched it out of its socket, then promptly fallen with her. The arm popped right back in, but a lingering ache told her the damage was more than superficial. She could only imagine how Hrothgar felt.

"Hrothgar is going to be fine. Your healer is looking after them." Brenn stepped back, allowing Freya to take up the space.

Freya had not exactly *asked* Astrid whether it was acceptable for Brenn to join them in the castle, but Astrid liked the way Brenn cooled hot attitudes anywhere she went. And, if Brenn hadn't been here, Astrid would be choking down some brutal, eye-watering tonic.

"My head is fine," Astrid said.

A conflicted look crossed Freya's face. "And you weren't pushed by—"

"*No*," Astrid said. She grabbed Freya's shoulder with her free hand. "Do *not* assume it's the ambassador, please. I tripped. I swear."

The muscles of Freya's shoulder were tense under Astrid's touch. Astrid released her and Freya's jaw clenched. "I am sorry I was not there."

Ah, stars. Freya was taking the tumble personally, as if she could save Astrid from the blunt impact of her own clumsiness.

"Her Majesty needs to rest," Brenn said to Freya.

"Very well. Rest away," said Freya, and pulled a chair up to the bed.

Astrid closed her eyes. She was awfully tired, and she was sure her exhaustion extended beyond the fatigue of the healing magic. Freya and Brenn continued to talk in hushed voices, lulling Astrid into a deep, pleasant slumber.

When Astrid woke, it took a moment for her to remember where she was. It was dark, her enclosed, curtained area in the infirmary lit by one tallow candle. At the edge of the curtains, Freya jabbed a finger into Hedda's breastbone.

"Thirsty," Astrid said weakly.

Freya rushed to her side and placed water into her good hand.

Greedily, Astrid drank. When she was finished, she said, "Why are you fighting with Hedda?"

"She has a problem with her demotion," Freya said.

Exhaustion swept over Astrid. "Let me speak with her."

"My Queen, she is quite angry, and you are vulnerable."

"Hedda?" Astrid called. "You can come in."

Hedda pushed past Freya. Freya looked as though she would protest, but she sulked back through the curtain, no doubt within earshot.

Hesitantly, Hedda took the seat where Freya had watched over Astrid. "Your Majesty."

This wasn't the Hedda Astrid knew. She was stiff, formal. Too formal for someone who had served at Astrid's side since the beginning of her reign.

It was Astrid's fault that Hedda was creating this distance. Astrid had put distance between them first.

"How are you feeling, Your Majesty?" Hedda asked.

Astrid's head was clogged from whatever magic or drug Brenn had given her, her sensations dulled. She took that to mean she had sustained a great deal of bruising. "I am feeling well."

Hedda nodded. She looked down into her clenched fists on her lap. "I have apologized before, and I will do it again," she said. "I am terribly sorry for my outburst at the midsummer festival and the negative perception it brought upon the félag, and the damage it did to your reputation as our queen. I did not mean the things I said, even under the influence of too much mead."

Astrid had heard this apology before. There was more hurt in it now than there was before—more remorse.

"I swore my loyalty to you all those fifty-two years ago," Hedda went on, her voice tight, anger barely held back. "I have never wavered except the once."

"Yes, Hedda. I know."

"Then why have you demoted me?" Hedda said. "I thought... I thought I had made it up to you. I did everything you asked me to. Every last demeaning task. I cleaned and took terribly long overnight shifts. I have labored day and night beyond the hours of my duties."

Astrid's sluggish brain worked hard to cycle through appropriate responses. "I appreciate the work you've put in. It is noticed. But Freya thought—"

"So this is Freya's fault," said Hedda. "Of course."

Stars, what a mess this had become. "No. That's not what I meant. Freya does not speak for me."

"Perhaps Freya has too much influence over *you*," Hedda said, and the anger finally leaked into her voice.

"Hedda," Astrid said delicately, "this is why we needed to remove you from being captain. You are at the whims of your fraught emotional state too often for someone with such great responsibility."

"I see," Hedda said, deflating. "Shall I look for employment elsewhere, Your Majesty? Is there no hope for me?"

"I would like to reinstate you. Hrothgar will perform your duties in the interim."

"The interim? Until what? What do I need to do to prove I can do this job well?"

Until what, indeed? Until Ulfur was defeated, if such a time ever came? Until this time of political turmoil was over, if such a thing could be measured? Astrid had no answer for her, and Hedda seemed to understand this, because she stood shakily.

"I was heartbroken when I denounced you." Hedda no longer faced Astrid but the curtains. "I am heartbroken again to hear how easily the trust of half a century has been ruined."

Astrid cleared her throat. "As am I."

Hedda wiped away the tears pooling in her eyes. "There is no chance at redemption, then."

"I don't know, Hedda," Astrid said. Her voice had gone weak.

"I am terribly sorry to bother you in such a state. I'll take my leave."

Hedda—fierce, brokenhearted Hedda—left Astrid, and Freya filtered back in. Astrid closed her eyes and pretended to be asleep, but Hedda's words played over in her head, a melancholic song whose rhythm she could not escape.

The next day, Astrid wandered in and out of sleep, spurred on by the effort of her healing body and the magic that kept her unconscious. At dusk, the healer's apprentices drew her a bath and sponged her down. The bruises were already a healed greenish hue, not purple and black. Brenn was a skilled priestess, Astrid conceded.

The apprentices helped her don a lightweight silk dress and wrapped her arm once more in a sling. It was easier to move, but not without pain. When Brenn and the healer agreed Astrid could go about her day, Freya joined Astrid at the exit from the infirmary with three guards.

Hrothgar filled Astrid in on the ambassador. Guthmar had taken to sitting in the kitchens, and was currently on a quest to bake the most perfect loaf of bread.

"Are the kitchen staff perturbed by his presence?" Astrid asked, and Hrothgar nodded.

"I'll get him away from them," said Freya.

"No," said Astrid. "I will do it myself."

Astrid spent the next half hour gently redirecting Guthmar to other pursuits which would distract him from the kitchens. His spouses caught on quickly and joined her, until finally they convinced him the outside of the castle was particularly beautiful, and he agreed he had not yet seen it from every angle. As he left, the kitchen staff rushed forward to clean up an absurd quantity of sticky clumps of dough.

At midday, Astrid finally returned to her rooms. They were redder than she was used to.

Her eyes adjusted to the sight. On her floor—under her bed, even, meaning someone had lifted it up—was an enormous rug woven with deep red wool.

The saturated color immediately bestowed upon Astrid a pulsing headache.

"What is this?" Astrid asked, more to herself than to Freya. She could not comprehend how a rug would make its way into her room, nor how a group of people had taken it upon themselves to rearrange the furniture. She had ordered no such thing.

She bent to examine the rug, running her fingers over the fine threads. It was woven well. Not the hasty, uneven threads one sometimes received from the priestesses which valued magic function over beauty. She looked up to find Freya wearing a guilty expression.

"What's this for? Does it have a protection spell woven into it, or...?"

"Since you are so clumsy," Freya said, "I have decided to cushion the floor, Your Majesty."

Astrid blinked at the rug. Was it a joke? Freya did sometimes have an odd sense of humor. Or did Freya really think Astrid would crack her skull open on the stone floors?

"I don't like it," Astrid said.

"That is a shame," Freya said, and left.

The ambassador called for Astrid, but she politely declined, pretending she needed to rest. A courier brought a message from Ruga, the response to Astrid's previous inquiry, and Astrid devoured the words hungrily—wishing her well, having heard of her injury.

How widespread was the news of Astrid's embarrassing fall down the stairs? She hardly wanted to know. A queen who'd survived a civil war could have been taken out by one misstep.

Astrid had not *just* been distracted. The truth was, she'd been looking over her shoulder every minute for Freya. She needed to know when Freya would be back, and instead of taking a step, her foot had landed on nothing, and she'd fallen.

Before Freya came to Vakker Castle, Astrid had relied on her félag without issue. It wasn't that she didn't trust them now. With Freya weeding out those who were not loyal since her first day as Astrid's spymaster, Astrid trusted the félag more than ever. And Freya was good with her dagger—when it was in someone's back, not in hand-to-hand combat. So, it was not that Freya served well as a physical protector, either.

Astrid sat in bed with a book, not reading the words. The magic began to wear off and an ache bloomed in her arm by the time Freya returned. The sun had lowered by then, washing the room in pink and orange.

"Dinner in an hour, My Queen," Freya said.

Astrid stood, considering Freya—all five feet of her. Was there some way to overcome this dependence she'd formed? She couldn't simply fall down the stairs every time Freya wasn't there. She had a country to run.

"What do you think of moving house?" Astrid asked.

"Pardon?"

"Of moving out of my rooms," Astrid clarified.

"I am your lady's maid. Lady's maids live in close quarters with the person they serve."

"Yes," Astrid said, "but you are not *really* my lady's maid."

Astrid turned to her wardrobe. Usually, she might change out a dress like this for a more appropriate dinner outfit, but she was not sure how she would accomplish that with her arm. She sat in front of her mirror and began to brush her hair awkwardly with her left hand.

The silence was less comfortable than usual. Astrid caught Freya's gaze in the mirror, and she held her breath.

"Do you want me gone, Your Majesty?" Freya asked. "Have I failed you in some way?"

Astrid had already done this to Hedda. She couldn't do it to Freya. She closed her eyes, wishing her braid was tight against her head, in control. The healer's apprentices had not offered to braid her hair, and she had not wanted to appear needy.

"Of course not," Astrid said. "I just wonder if you are better off with more space to yourself. You spend all your time here. Don't you want to go have fun once in a while?"

Like a spirit, Freya appeared in the mirror behind Astrid. "I am the knife at your side. I would not have it any other way."

Astrid found it hard to read Freya's expression, but she gathered that she'd upset her. Still, Astrid could not bring herself to explain why she thought they needed the distance.

"Very well," she said. She brushed her hair, tangling the strands and her brush in her horns several times, until it at least looked smoother.

But it was loose around her shoulders, undone, and she hated it.

"I can braid it," Freya offered. She set her gloves aside.

Astrid let Freya ease the hairbrush out of her hands. She watched her reflection as Freya brushed out the areas Astrid had missed, her smaller fingers gently untangling knots.

Soon, she was lulled into a state of half-sleep by Freya's gentle handling of her hair. If Astrid had real attendants, she would request someone do this for her every day. She had denied the need for personal attendants in her court, thinking it looked better for her image if everyone was self-sufficient. Ruler Lyn had done the same before her, and she liked the example.

It would not be the same, though, if someone other than Freya did her hair.

This concept haunted her. She opened her eyes. Freya bit her lip as she concentrated on her work, dividing Astrid's hair to make the plait, and then she deftly wove the parts together in a rhythm that told Astrid she'd done it thousands of times before.

Had she learned to do this on her own hair? Freya had come to the castle with longer hair, but she'd not kept it in a plait that Astrid knew of. The idea of Freya plaiting someone else's hair like this was too much.

Freya leaned over Astrid to reach the iron band that secured her plaits. Astrid was overcome by the smell of her, the whiff of citrus, the slight layer of sweat.

"What do you think?" Freya asked.

The plait was prettily done, tighter and more perfect than Astrid was used to. Freya had worked with more than three parts, braiding together an intricate pattern. Astrid turned to compliment the work, to see Freya in person, but when she looked upon her, all Astrid saw was a human. Small, vulnerable, soft. Maybe fifty years of life left—if they were lucky.

And Astrid had nearly six hundred to go.

"Lovely. Thank you," she managed.

Offended by the lack of enthusiasm, Freya stiffened, then bowed.

Astrid suppressed the urge to apologize. Her instincts told her she needed to be more aggressive about getting Freya out of her apartments before Astrid did something she would regret.

CHAPTER NINE

Freya stood in her corner by the staff table at dinner, lamenting that she had not thought to assert a position closer to the queen.

Her queen had *fallen down the stairs*. Every time Freya sighted the queen's sling, her own arm throbbed in sympathy. She didn't quite believe no one had pushed Astrid—but she did believe they had been subtle about it if they had. Astrid was not stupid, but there was still part of her that saw the best in people.

In the meantime, the ways Astrid could die haunted Freya. Stairs were an enemy she had never considered. It seemed the castle was made of knife-sharp edges and bone-crushing stone wherever she turned. A death trap, and there was little Freya could do.

Well. Not *little*. She had spent her time at Astrid's bedside in the infirmary thinking of all the ways Astrid could be additionally protected. All the ways Freya could step in and cushion a potential blow.

Though Freya could not hear the conversation at the queen's table, she gathered that the queen was closed off from the ambassador and looking quite tired, in spite of the beautiful dress the healer's apprentices had put her in and the plait Freya had constructed so carefully.

She was stunning. Almost impossible to look away from.

Freya gathered that the queen did suspect someone there of *something*. Or else she was too tired to talk, or in a foul mood about falling down the stairs. Astrid did not like to look weak; that she'd injured herself in such a simple way would plague her dreams for months to come.

With Freya at her side, seeing these new threats, Astrid would never so much as trip over uneven ground again.

The next night at dinner, Freya moved a little closer to the queen's table, and even closer the night after.

Over the next week, new people filed into the castle, setting Freya's nerves on edge. They were here for the history fair, and therefore mostly Vera's concern, but Freya insisted the guards work day and night, monitoring the newcomers and doubling the protection in any location the queen had even a small chance of visiting.

The ambassador continued to take up much of the queen's attention, but if he intended to harm her, he was biding his time. Putting himself in Astrid's good graces, perhaps, so when he finally struck, everyone would be taken by surprise.

Freya was not sure she believed it. Even with her penchant for seeing danger in everything, the ambassador's soft hands had never killed so much as an insect, and his countenance, if it really was put on, meant he had quite promising prospects if he ever considered a career in the theater rather than the field of spywork.

"It doesn't make sense for Sydlig to kill me outright," Astrid insisted whenever Freya brought up the ambassador. "Even if King Skarde sided with Lynby, Sydlig would lend Lynby their military, not assassinate me. They're much more likely to try to sway me politically into making a decision to gain their support."

"If you say so, Your Majesty," said Freya. They often had these conversations as Freya braided Astrid's hair. The sling would come off in a day, which was both good news and bad. The good side was that Astrid would be able to defend herself with both arms—or catch herself if, say, she happened to fall down the stairs again.

The bad news was that Freya would no longer have an excuse to braid Astrid's hair every evening before dinner.

Freya knew her enjoyment of this task went beyond what was appropriate for a lady's maid. Certainly beyond what was appropriate for a dutiful spymaster. She did more than she had to. She wove in extra bits, added a flourish, then pretended she didn't like the way it looked and started over.

Anything to delay the moment when she had to stop.

Whenever Freya ran her fingers through Astrid's silky hair, she remembered Brenn's warning. *I am not in love*, Freya said as she touched the soft strands, feeling the warmth of Astrid's scalp underneath. Sometimes, perhaps subconsciously, Astrid leaned her head farther into Freya's touch.

And Freya wanted her to. She wanted Astrid to feel totally comfortable in her presence. She wanted the warmth of Astrid under her bare hands.

She wanted, and she wanted, and she wanted some more.

This needed to end. Nothing could happen between them. Even if Freya admitted to herself she wouldn't mind if something did happen. Even if, when she closed her eyes to go to sleep every night—in her own room, as Astrid insisted—she saw Astrid's face, and wondered what it would be like to touch her lips and her muscled arms with gloveless fingers.

None of it mattered. Astrid wouldn't be interested. And it was a distraction from the things Freya needed to be worrying about, from the ambassador's entourage to the history fair, which was meant to take place tomorrow. The event had crept up on her; the enemy of time had bested her, as it always did.

Freya stepped back from her handiwork. She'd learned to plait her own hair from her mother many years ago, and the style was different from Astrid's typical, looser look. Five parts instead of three interwoven in a pattern that differed from the usual orcish plait.

Now, Freya didn't have enough hair of her own to braid. This was just one more way she had severed herself from her past.

"I have to admit, Freya, I'll miss when I don't need you to do this anymore," Astrid said.

"I'm happy to keep doing it if you like the style," Freya said before she could think better of it.

Astrid looked back at her, lips parted. Freya stared at Astrid's tusks before wrenching her gaze back to Astrid's surprised, blue eyes.

"Oh, I couldn't ask you to do that," Astrid said.

"If you insist, Your Majesty."

Astrid frowned.

Freya covered the awkwardness by beginning the process of pinning the crown in place atop Astrid's brunette hair. When Astrid stood from her vanity, her grand cloak brushed the floor at her feet. She looked every inch powerful, every inch a queen.

I am not in love, Freya told herself again.

Dinner was blissfully uneventful. When it was over, a courier waited at the door to Astrid's antechamber, surrounded by three guards and carrying a box determined to wriggle out of their hands.

"What is this?" Astrid asked.

"For Freya Wedd," the courier said. A grumbling noise came from the box.

Astrid raised her eyebrows significantly at Freya.

"Extra protection," Freya said. She accepted the box from the courier and brought it with her into the antechamber.

"Freya," said Astrid, "I think we need to talk about these precautionary measures you've been taking. I'd like you to ask me before you do anything drastic. I feel I can't take two steps without tripping over my own guards."

"I'd prefer if you didn't trip over them," Freya said.

"*Freya*," Astrid said.

"The castle is full of strangers. Anything could happen."

"Has something brought on this overabundance of caution?" Astrid could be just as perceptive as Freya. "It's not just the ambassador, is it?"

The box yowled at Freya. She set it on the floor, her mind working furiously. The last thing she wanted was to tell Astrid about Brenn's prediction. Brenn had no new information to share about the specifics, even though she was checking in every day with the goddess. Freya was going to wear Astrid's cloak thin with all the strings she pilfered.

"Of course not, Your Majesty," said Freya. "I simply could not bear to lose you."

Astrid's eyes widened at the admission.

Stars. That was far too honest. "I meant, I take my role seriously."

For a time, Astrid was quiet. "We should revisit the idea of you moving out of my apartments."

"I would love to," Freya lied, "only perhaps we can wait until the visitors for the history fair have left."

Unhappily, Astrid sat on her bed.

Freya had to invent a good reason to stay in the queen's rooms. The assertion of distance did not bode well for Astrid's impending loss.

"Show me whatever new precaution you've come up with," Astrid said, resigned.

Freya lifted the lid of the box. Out strolled the largest cat she'd ever seen. It was black with green-yellow eyes, and it was perfect. Promptly, it strutted over to Astrid and rubbed against her leg.

"What's this?" Astrid asked.

"Fenrir," said Freya. "He will alarm us first if something is amiss. I've been told by his previous owner that he is an excellent guard cat."

"Freya, I have my orcs guarding me, and you. Why do I need a cat?" Regardless of her protest, Astrid bent to scratch Fenrir between the ears.

"He comes all the way from Olwen," Freya said. "He used to guard their queen. She passed recently, and they had no use for him. Think of it as a charity case, if it helps, Your Majesty. He needs a home."

"I suppose this is not my first stray," Astrid said meaningfully.

Freya blushed.

"We can keep him for now. If he's a nuisance, though, please find him another home."

"Yes, Your Majesty."

A knock came at the door. Hrothgar stepped in, took notice of the cat, and quickly schooled their features. "The priestess for you."

"Let her in," Astrid said.

Brenn entered, eyes flickering between Astrid and Freya. She did not miss anything. She bowed quickly and said, "May I check your arm, Your Majesty?"

Astrid held it out for inspection. Brenn made quick work of applying pressure to the elbow, the wrist, the delicate bones of Astrid's hand. Freya watched in silence.

"The sling can come off. You should be able to use your arm for normal activities, but do be careful not to overwork it. I'll come check on your injury in one week."

Freya helped Astrid remove the sling once Brenn left. Astrid rolled her shoulder, straightened her arm, and let out a laugh.

"You have no idea how good it feels to be free again," said Astrid.

"I'm sure," Freya said, already missing the feel of Astrid's hair in her fingers.

CHAPTER TEN

The history fair was an annual source of dread to Astrid.

The fair had been Vera's idea shortly after she arrived in Torden. She'd proposed the event directly to Astrid, suggesting it would be good for morale. A reminder to Torden's people about their past and Astrid's role. Right away, Astrid had known how effective the idea would be.

She could not have predicted then how much she would grow to hate it.

The library was meticulously arranged for the event—rows and rows of tables brought in, important books and documents laid out, artifacts under glass so the visiting scholars could look but not touch.

Usually, Astrid endured the fair by mentally occupying herself with what she'd do when it was over—perhaps a luxurious bath of some sort to reward herself for making it through the day.

When anyone approached her with questions about the great feat that had won her the position of queen, she answered as curtly as she could and redirected attention to Vera.

Unfortunately for Astrid, Vera had taken a strong disliking to Guthmar. Vera ignored every one of Guthmar's probing questions.

"Is this the actual arrow you shot or a symbolic representation?" Guthmar asked, having dragged Astrid over to a table with a slightly bent iron arrow on prominent display. The placard read: *The arrow shot by Astrid Karrsdaughter which impaled Ulfur Rowansdaughter, thus ending the battle at Westgate and forcing Ulfur's troops to retreat.*

Astrid did not believe the display required further explanation.

"It is in such good condition, even after all this time," Guthmar went on, unable to read Astrid's cold expression. Or, maybe, unwilling to stop even though he had. "I can only imagine how clean a shot it was."

"It was a clean shot. I was there," Hedda cut in.

Until this year, Hedda only ever attended in official capacity as the captain of the félag, but Astrid had told her she was not worthy, and here Hedda was, ready to prove herself. She wore not her standby leathers, but her civilian clothes—present on her day off. Astrid let Hedda take over.

Once, Hedda and Astrid had been soldiers under Ruler Lyn. It was odd to think now of when they'd been equals. Their relationship had transformed since then.

Astrid had seen glory in the pursuit of becoming a soldier after her soft upbringing. Before becoming queen, the worst thing that had ever happened to her was her parents dying of natural causes. Back then, she'd thought it was her wyrd to become a strong, powerful, and admirable soldier like the heroes of old.

Of course, Ulfur murdering Ruler Lyn in cold blood had dashed Astrid's hopes for a life of battle-ready servitude, and Ulfur's rallying of a rebellion force had drawn even the regular castle guard into Torden's civil war. Once Astrid was crowned, she inherited a country cut in two: not just Torden, but Torden *and* Lynby. A fragile balance, sure to shatter at any random catalyst.

She'd been struggling ever since, leagues away from the person she'd hoped to become.

"Marvelous," Guthmar said as Hedda explained the setup of the battlefield on that day. Even thinking about that important event made Astrid queasy. She was beyond relieved Hedda had stepped in.

"Can you still shoot so well?" someone asked from Astrid's side. Astrid jumped. Guthmar's wife Alvor had snuck up nearly as silent as Freya.

"Likely not. That was a while ago," Astrid said. As long as the conversation was veering away from the event itself, she'd be fine. "When it came down to it, I was in the right place at the right time, that's all."

Alvor laughed. "I am sure Torden does not see it that way. Why would they elect a queen who just happened to be there?"

Astrid bit back a bitter response. Why indeed?

"Queen Astrid is a great ruler," Freya said.

Alvor jumped in surprise. Like most, she hadn't noticed Freya.

"She's hardworking and cares deeply about her people, and that would be true whether she'd shot the arrow which gravely injured Ulfur or not," said Freya.

"Of course," Alvor said, eyes flashing.

Tassi and Guthmar looked their way. Oh, stars, they'd been listening the whole time. Astrid shuffled her feet under the weight of their full attention.

"So humble, too," Guthmar said, and though Astrid was fairly certain he meant it genuinely, there was a sharpness to it she disliked. She took it that Guthmar was not generally one for humility.

Thankfully, Guthmar's interest turned to history and the rulers who'd served before Astrid. Time passed slowly, but it passed.

The longer Astrid was there, the more the bustle of bodies became too much. On another day, Astrid might have retreated to her favorite nook of the library as a peaceful sanctuary, but she could not escape there now. What a violation to make this sacred, quiet space so boisterous.

By the time most of the scholars had left, going back to their rooms to prepare for dinner, Astrid was left alone with Guthmar's retinue, her félag, Freya, and a few stragglers.

"What's this?" Guthmar was saying across the room.

"A recreation of the ceremonial crown," answered Hedda tightly. Astrid froze in horror as Hedda excused herself from the library.

"Well," Guthmar said to Tassi, "that was abrupt."

"Why a recreation?" Alvor asked Vera.

Vera smirked. They'd nearly been in the clear, but now Astrid wished more than ever that she could skip the rest of the day to hide in bed.

When Vera launched into a fictional account of how the original crown had been destroyed, Astrid had no energy left to stop her. They'd come up with a reason for its destruction that wasn't so inflammatory as the truth—the scholars would know the difference, and ultimately, it was not worth hiding from them.

Astrid slumped against a bookcase, allowing herself a moment of being Astrid, not Queen Astrid, if such a person existed anymore.

"My Queen," Freya said, so softly Astrid almost didn't hear.

Astrid turned her head a fraction. "Yes?"

"May we speak privately?"

Anything to get away from Guthmar and his curiosity. "Of course."

Astrid did not hear Freya leave her side, but she felt her absence, the coldness left in her wake.

She caught sight of Freya's boots turning the corner around a giant wall of bookshelves just in time. Excusing herself from a lingering scholar who attempted to engage her in conversation while clinging to his monocle, Astrid followed Freya into a small nook with a single chair surrounded by books.

"What is it?" Astrid asked. The enclosed space gave her a sudden sense of claustrophobia. She grabbed at the collar of her dress, tugging it loose from her sweat-drenched neck.

"Do you feel safe?" Freya asked.

Astrid examined her. Freya's eyes were open, earnest, curious. Concerned. A dangerous thing to be around Astrid, whose life was politics and people she'd never met both loving and hating her from faraway lands.

Freya was someone Astrid almost never needed to worry about. Why was she so concerned with Astrid's well-being of late? Astrid did not feel any more susceptible to danger than she usually did during these events.

"I am protected," Astrid said judiciously.

Freya scowled. "You've mentioned twice that I should move out of your rooms. Am I impeding your safety?"

This was nearly as bad as being interrogated by Guthmar. "Freya, *no*. Of course not. You are excellent at what you do. I wouldn't have anyone else."

What you do, Astrid had said, as though she did not want to put words to it. She knew well that she was taking advantage of military tactics Freya had gleaned from a questionable period of her life. Espionage, digging, pretending. She hadn't done any killing on Astrid's behalf, but Astrid knew Freya could. That she would.

"In case you decide to send me away, or you need extra defense," Freya said, "I want you to have this."

In one smooth motion, Freya dropped to her knee. She lifted the fabric of her tunic—so high, Astrid thought she would remove it entirely, but that was absurd, no matter how Astrid's eyes locked onto the strip of exposed skin—and extracted her bone-handled dagger from her side. Freya proffered it to Astrid, rolling the light blade on the tips of her gloved fingers.

"For your protection," Freya said.

"Freya—"

"Please take it, Your Majesty. And try your best not to fall down the stairs and impale yourself on it."

Astrid snorted. These were Freya's most disarming moments—when she could have a sense of humor about things that worried her half to death.

"Do you have other weapons with which to defend yourself?" Astrid asked. She knew a little about the history of the dagger. Namely, that Freya had commissioned it herself after her arrival to Vakker, that it had been carefully and deliberately forged by a silversmith who'd since retired. It was truly one of a kind.

The enormity of the gesture was not lost on Astrid.

In response, Freya reached down and peeled up her trousers to the ankle, revealing two shining knives packed closely into a strip of leather. She let the fabric drop, grasping the handle of the dagger with her other hand, and once more held it to Astrid, point-down.

"I want you to keep this on you in case something happens," Freya said. "And you must be bold enough to use it."

From anyone else, Astrid would have found an order presumptuous, but from Freya... Freya did not give orders to her queen often, even when she overstepped with her protections.

Astrid took the blade from Freya. It was surprisingly weightless. Freya was so nimble, she made everything seem light, but Astrid found that the dagger was almost brittle in her hands, like it wasn't as deadly as she knew it could be. She held it, and thought to put it away, but could not think of where it was supposed to go.

Freya understood Astrid's dilemma. She lifted her tunic again—flash of skin, smell of citrus—and unbuckled the leather belt around her waist with its scabbard, perfectly crafted to fit the dagger.

When Astrid touched the leather, the first thing she noticed was its warmth from the heat of Freya's body. She was overly conscious of the history of leather. Its past as skin, its proximity to Freya's skin. The two objects in her hands were flesh and bone and steel, and though it did not make sense, she thought of them as Freya's—an offering of Freya's body. Of the things she used to protect herself and those around her.

Freya got back to her feet and leaned forward as if to help Astrid buckle the belt. The idea of Freya's hands on Astrid's waist was too much, and Astrid stepped back, hastily buckling it herself and sliding the dagger into its scabbard like a hand into a tailored glove. Her eyes fell to Freya's gloves, perfectly fitted, and the warm fingers underneath.

Stars. What had her thinking like this? Had there ever been a point when Astrid knew how to behave around Freya? She had no problem distancing herself from her other subjects in the name of royal duty. People expected her to be the hero who'd shot the arrow that had subdued Ulfur, someone with godlike status. Not someone who had all these cravings of the flesh.

"Does it fit you?" Freya asked, breaking whatever spell handing over her prized weapon had caused.

"Yes," Astrid choked out. Freya's waist seemed particularly small, just then; it was a kind of magic that the same leather fit around Astrid's own. "It fits perfectly."

CHAPTER ELEVEN

Dinnertime came around sooner than Freya expected. She had spent her day monitoring the scholars' conversations, scouting out potential threats, and gradually feeling more secure in Astrid's safety. The scholars posed little danger, unless Astrid was at risk of dying of boredom.

Still, the dining hall was unsettlingly full of people. The staff had pulled in extra tables and benches to accommodate the many scholars, who were more used to poring over their books than they were socializing over drink, if the increased volume of voices over the course of the night was any indication. Some of the scholars were simply excited to be there among fellow intellectuals, but several heated discussions broke out over historical accuracy.

The skald's repertoire had changed for the new crowd. Often, she shared tales of heroics of times long past, stories of the goddess and her ravens, lovers reincarnated—the types of things Vakker Castle liked to hear. Legends, fantasy, romance. For the history fair, the skald orated tales specific to Torden and its factual past, which were less romantic but more appropriate for this crowd.

And yet, something was off.

Usually, the queen checked in visually with Freya at least a few times per meal, but Astrid hadn't looked up at all tonight. In fact, she'd been quiet since Freya had pulled her aside in the library. Her body language was rigid in response to Guthmar's jokes—enough that other people would notice, too obvious to be in her control.

Freya had to wonder if it was because of her gift. Presenting Astrid with her dagger had been a spur-of-the-moment decision. She had been thinking about the arrow and the broken weapons on display. Once, Astrid had defended all of Torden, and now she wore no weapon to defend herself. But what if someone snuck past the guards and Freya was not around? What if someone somehow got past Freya?

Freya had fretted until she decided gifting the dagger would give her some peace of mind. She had hoped, too, Astrid would glean some peace of mind having it.

But now Freya was fairly certain she had overstepped.

She wondered which action had tipped Astrid over the edge. Not the rug, surely. The cat? The increased guard? Never leaving Astrid's side, even for a minute? Maybe even earlier, when she'd brought Brenn to the castle for divine assistance?

It did not matter in the end. Freya would do what she thought necessary to protect her queen. She did not need anyone's approval to do so.

She had been overstepping since she'd landed this job at the queen's side. In fact, crossing boundaries was what had won her the position of spymaster in the first place. Everything Freya had was hard-earned, and this was no exception.

No matter how Freya consoled herself that this was the same way she'd behaved for years—it was hardly likely her behavior had gotten on Astrid's nerves *now*—she was bothered that she could not guess at Astrid's mind. They rarely discussed their feelings, but Freya liked to think she knew Astrid after a decade by her side.

Unless Freya did not know Astrid as well as she thought.

Over the last few weeks, Freya had gradually moved from standing by the staff table to approaching the queen's, and tonight, she was finally just a few feet away, close enough to hear their conversations and feel the splatter of spilled mead. She knew Astrid had noticed her gradual proximity, yet Astrid still did not look up to acknowledge her.

But why would Astrid be upset by *Freya*? If Freya had not overstepped more than usual... Maybe Freya had said something Astrid did not like, but Astrid was too polite to comment on it. She thought over their previous conversation, combing through the words. Was Astrid disturbed by how many hidden weapons Freya kept on her person? Being disarmed was easy, Freya knew from her time on battlefields. It was always a good idea to have a backup weapon or five.

The skald only served to strengthen Freya's convictions as she began the tale of Astrid shooting the warlord who'd murdered Torden's previous ruler. An orc Freya had briefly, unwillingly served—Ulfur. She shuddered to hear Ulfur's name, even in this context. The fateful arrow had pierced Ulfur's shoulder so cleanly it caused the severing of her arm.

At the table, Astrid's back was straight, tension straining the muscles in her neck. She'd stopped eating. Astrid had specifically requested the skalds never recite this particular tale, but Freya understood the need for the exception tonight.

Humility did not account for this level of discomfort.

Lost in thought as she was, Freya did not notice until too late the kitchen staff had returned with dessert. They were well into the room already. She scanned each orc and human, counting off their names in her head, and froze when she got to a smallish human she did not recognize.

Impossible. Freya planned for everything. She made a point of introducing herself to every new staff member and thoroughly researching each person's history. She was supposed to be notified when someone new was hired. She stared for too long, wondering if she had merely forgotten a name and a face all in one, then she blinked and the staff had reached the queen's table, dropping off a heavy platter of honey-soaked pastries.

Without thinking, Freya rushed forward, stopping right at the queen's side. Astrid picked up a pastry with the serving fork and set it onto her plate. She looked back at Freya with a question in her expression.

The table was quiet. All eyes were on Freya as she reached down to Astrid's plate, grabbed the sopping pastry between her forefinger and thumb, and brought it to her lips.

She took a bite and chewed.

Someone at the table gasped. Freya fought her embarrassment at the reaction—at the spectacle—but Astrid's own face was a sight to behold, an emotion Freya had never seen on her.

Mortification.

The steward cleared his throat. "There are plenty of pastries available from the serving platter, if you are hungry, Freya."

This garnered several laughs down the table, loosening the tension. Freya continued to hold the pastry as she counted to one hundred, while Astrid stared and stared at her, her eyes bulging.

Freya set the pastry back down at the hundredth count. If it was poisoned, it was a slow poison, she decided.

She needed to refresh her memory about orcish poisons. What if everyone at the queen's table was eating something that would make them sick in twenty-four hours? In a week? What if this stranger had infiltrated the castle and successfully offed all of its important players in one go?

Here, Freya had been worried about an accidental death and ordered rugs to Astrid's bedchamber; she had worried about the queen's need to defend herself, and so had given Astrid her own dagger; she had worried about intruders sneaking in, and had gotten a cat to alert Astrid. And yet she had never thought to hire a food taster.

Astrid looked to her bitten pastry and back at Freya, uncomprehending. It was another minute or so before she picked up the pastry and ate it like nothing had happened. Tension rolled off Astrid in waves, but Freya did not leave her queen's side.

People continued to notice Freya as the chatter at the table resumed. This was the most visible she had ever made herself. She saw curiosity in the orcs' faces, even Guthmar and his retinue, even those of the queen's own félag.

Freya stood tall and held her hands clasped like a soldier.

The kitchen staff delivered the next tray of desserts. Freya spied the same new staff member, but it was one thing to attack a stranger unprovoked in the middle of a crowded dining hall and another to merely bite into the queen's food.

Astrid reached for the tray of pastries, then hesitated and retracted her hand. Somehow, Freya was assured by understanding Astrid's thought process—she could tell Astrid wanted another, but Astrid did not know how Freya would react.

Don't do it, Freya willed her.

Astrid eyed the plate, then took another pastry.

She made as if to bring the pastry directly to her mouth before Freya could get to it, but Freya was quicker. Freya snatched the pastry right out of Astrid's hand.

"Freya," Astrid hissed. "What in the goddess's name are you doing?"

Freya did not answer. She turned the pastry over until she found a spot that looked particularly scrumptious, and then she took another bite.

Astrid put out her hand for the pastry. Freya held it farther away. She counted to one hundred, noting the reddening shade of Astrid's face, and lowered it to the plate.

Her gloves were going to become very sticky if she kept this up.

Astrid opened her mouth as if to speak. It was clear the things she wanted to say could not be said in polite company.

The steward leaned in. "Is she bothering you, Your Majesty?"

Hrothgar raised an eyebrow, wordlessly asking the same.

Freya stood still. If Astrid dismissed her, Freya couldn't defy her without incurring some kind of public punishment. She swallowed heavily, feeling the weight of everyone's stares once more.

Truthfully, she did not know how she would react if Astrid said yes.

"No," Astrid said. "Freya is my attendant. She does not act against my wishes."

The skald finished Astrid's tale. In the quiet, other tables took notice of the odd situation occurring at the head table. The scholars were paying attention.

Not good. Freya prayed desperately the meal would be over soon.

Just then, a boy brought out a new pitcher of mead. Freya stepped back; she recognized him. Down the table, everyone filled their goblets. The night was winding down. Some of the scholars were heading to bed already, excitedly discussing the artifacts they'd seen today and making plans for next year's travels.

Astrid took the pitcher to fill her goblet.

The cellar for the mead was under the kitchens, Freya remembered suddenly. If the human Freya didn't recognize had access to the kitchens, she had access to the cellar.

This could be the true method of delivery for the poison.

Freya nearly knocked the goblet out of Astrid's hand. The liquid poured out, spilling over Astrid's red woolen tunic and staining it an unseemly shade of purple. Of course—berry mead. Freya looked on in horror as Hrothgar rushed to get a cloth to wipe the queen down, but that did not stop her from taking the goblet from the queen's hand, where Astrid had been limply holding it in shock.

Freya brought the goblet to her lips and took two hearty gulps. There. If it was poison, Freya would go down first.

She clutched the goblet in her sticky fingers just as Hrothgar returned with the cloth. Numbly, Astrid accepted it from him, but she sat there stock-still and made no move to mop up the mess.

All along the great hall, everyone stared. Another tray of pastries came through the door, and the whole room tracked the kitchen staff with their eyes as they made their way to the queen's table first.

Nobody made a move to take from the communal platter this time. They waited. Astrid looked back up at Freya—just barely up, as Freya was only slightly taller standing than Astrid was sitting—and knitted her brow.

"Freya," she said again, and Freya heard her frustration, her embarrassment.

"I will not stop," Freya whispered back.

"You'd better."

"I can't."

Astrid lifted her hand to the pastry plate. Testing Freya. The test was whether Freya would stop her, but Freya could not fathom which outcome Astrid desired. Astrid looked back at her once more when her hand was halfway to the platter, daring her.

Freya couldn't breathe. Absurdly, she thought of the threat of poison, the way it could asphyxiate her, and this was not so different. Astrid inched her hand forward, and Freya swept in, grasping Astrid's wrist with her less sticky glove before either of them could blink.

Freya was leaning close, far too close, over the table, her other hand steadying her. The wool of Astrid's cloak grazed the back of Freya's thighs.

She was practically sitting in Astrid's lap.

Their eyes locked, and Freya caught the scent of Astrid's breath. Mead and the same honey treats that had touched Freya's lips first. The intimacy warmed Freya from head to toe.

The look in Astrid's eyes told Freya she felt the same. There was a want that Freya had never noticed before. A want directed right at Freya, right at her eyes and down into her soul.

Hope flared in Freya's thumping heart.

Astrid's lips stretched into an awkward smile. A rumbling sound emitted from her throat.

It took Freya a second to realize the queen was laughing.

Freya released Astrid's wrist and stepped out of her personal space. Astrid grabbed the table with both hands and threw her head back as she cackled. Her laugh was the loudest thing in the room, buoyant and heady. She laughed and laughed and laughed until tears streaked down her face, her entire body shaking.

A couple of sympathy laughs started around the room, but they were quickly stifled by the awkward duration of the laughter.

Just as suddenly as she had started, Astrid stopped, and her face sobered. Her features were perfectly subdued; the only evidence of the laughter was her damp cheeks.

"Excuse me," she said, and rushed out of the room.

Freya dashed after her, guilt clogging her throat.

CHAPTER TWELVE

The unmistakable sound of Freya's footsteps trailed behind as Astrid stormed from the great hall to the castle, her cloak billowing behind her.

How utterly humiliating. Not Freya herself, though it was hard to deny Freya'd started it. But Astrid had reacted poorly. She'd challenged Freya, knowing exactly what she was getting into. Together, they'd caused a spectacle Astrid had no doubt would be a source of gossip for some time to come.

Somewhere along the way, the absurdity had struck Astrid, and she'd been unable to hold in her laughter. She had laughed with reckless abandon, unable to stop. Everyone would think she was in hysterics—unfit to be queen any longer.

The guards at the castle doors moved aside for Astrid to enter, but she could hardly see them through her tears.

"Your Majesty!" Freya called.

The urge to retreat overwhelmed Astrid. There was too much attention focused on the two of them. When had the barrier Astrid put up between herself and her subjects become so thin when it came to Freya? Was there anything left keeping them apart?

Not if Freya was chasing Astrid down the castle halls.

Stars.

Astrid picked up speed. Freya was fast, but Astrid's legs were longer. Alarmed castle guards—not even of her félag—joined in her stampede, protecting her while she was unguarded.

She grabbed her cloak in her fist and leaped up the stairs two at a time until she was back at her own wing of the castle. Hedda stood at the top of the stairs. Right away, she jumped into action. Hedda dismissed the guards who followed Astrid, thanking them for their service. A responsibility for Astrid's captain.

More laughter bubbled up Astrid's throat. Only one orc was doing her job properly around here, and she'd openly expressed her distaste for Astrid. What a fine queen Astrid was, stomping out of dinners and throwing tantrums.

Astrid threw open the door to her antechamber. Down the hall, Freya shouted again. Damn her.

Stubbornly, Astrid slumped into one of the chairs and waited for everyone to catch up. A breathless Freya came in first, followed by Hrothgar and Hedda. Hrothgar looked sullenly at Hedda, but Astrid said nothing to dismiss anyone. She was tempted to tuck her head into her knees on the chair like when she was little. The simple life of merchants with little worry, a lifetime away, appealed to her more than ever.

How she wished for something like parental guidance now.

Astrid waited. The ensuing claustrophobic quiet enveloped the group. She measured the beats between Freya's frantic breathing until it evened out, then she said, "Leave us."

There was no question of who she meant by *us*. Hedda and Hrothgar bowed and exited the room.

"I need air," Astrid said, and pushed through the door to her bedchamber. The cat yowled as Astrid passed.

She didn't stop until she was on the balcony. The crisp air of autumn barely cut through her heavy wool, but she felt it on her cheeks and ears. She leaned against the stone railing into the breeze. It centered her to be on the precipice, looking down on the world. She closed her eyes and gulped down a lungful of cold air.

"Your Majesty?"

Astrid opened her eyes. Freya had taken the spot to her right.

Maybe it was not the balcony that centered Astrid after all.

"Please let me explain. I thought—"

"That the food could be poisoned," Astrid said. "I know."

"Then why did you…?"

Why indeed? Astrid thought she'd been in the mood to test Freya's limits after several weeks of Freya gently terrorizing her with unnecessary precautions. She shouldn't have done it in public.

She was so, so close to snapping.

"It wasn't poisoned," Astrid said. "I have trusted the kitchen staff with my life for fifty-two years, and I won't stop now."

"There was someone I didn't recognize."

Comprehension dawned on Astrid. She had to stifle another inappropriate bout of laughter. "The head chef's second daughter," she said. "They told me she'd be starting this week. She's old enough to work."

"Why wasn't I informed?" Freya asked, her voice tight.

"Must have slipped my mind." Like so many other things. Astrid felt a fresh wave of embarrassment at what the onlookers at dinner had perceived. She'd been so overwhelmed when Freya leaned over. That citrus smell. She had felt the heat of Freya's hand through her glove on her wrist, somehow more intimate than if Freya had touched her directly.

Freya swallowed audibly. "My Queen, I know I have been…overstepping lately."

Overstepping? Astrid wanted to laugh again, to cry. Freya had been overstepping since Astrid met her. She noticed things Astrid would never see and took action where it was needed, whether Astrid wanted her to or not. Astrid needed someone like that in her life.

But she couldn't tell Freya.

She couldn't tell Freya, either, that Freya didn't overstep enough. The truth was, Astrid ached for Freya's connection. Every time Freya involved herself too far in Astrid's business, Astrid was overwhelmed with how much Freya cared. How far she was willing to go.

Go farther, Astrid wanted to say. *Overstep right into my arms and into my bed.*

"Is there a reason for the increased precautions?" Astrid said instead. "Ambassador or not, you were not this concerned at the last history fair. I am in no more danger now than I was then."

This had bothered Astrid more than cats and rugs—not knowing the inner workings of Freya's mind.

Freya stood staring straight ahead, chewing her lip like she did when she was being thoughtful. Astrid hated that her heart swelled at the sight of Freya. If anything happened to Freya, Astrid would be beside herself.

The problem was that nothing had to happen to Freya for Astrid to lose her. She just had to live her life fully and die at an impossibly young eighty years old, and Astrid would be left alone for the rest of her long orcish life.

It wasn't fair.

"I'm afraid of losing you," Freya said, and Astrid wondered if Freya really could read her mind.

"Of losing *me*?" Astrid choked.

"I wasn't raised like you," Freya said. "I lost everything up there."

In the north, she meant, during the human wars. The last time they'd spoken of Freya's past before she'd escaped to Torden had been when she first arrived ten years ago.

"My family," Freya went on. "My mother and my father and my siblings. Smaller things, too, only a child would be upset by. A soft, hand-woven blanket. A rock with the indentations of a face. Those don't matter, but I remember them because of how it felt to lose them." She cleared her throat. "And I lost things you and I cannot see."

Astrid's chest was heavy. Condolences came to her tongue, but voicing them would be empty. It was not sympathy Freya searched for now.

"Brenn and I found each other. Helped each other. I kept her close, and we got out of there. Out of the frying pan," she said dryly, "and into the fire. When we reached orc country, I finally thought—" She clutched a hand to her cheek. "I finally thought we were free. We'd made it out of the north. But then we were on the wrong side of Torden, and Ulfur captured us. I thought it would go on forever."

"But it didn't. You made it here to me."

Surprised, Freya turned to her. Astrid bit down on her tongue, hard. She had not meant to imply Freya had come to Torden to be with Astrid. Back then, Freya hadn't known who Astrid was.

"I did," Freya said slowly. "I did make it to you. That's... I mean to say, the things I value, I hold close to me. Very close. Because I know how terrible it is to lose them."

Astrid could hardly handle the weight of Freya's gaze, but she forced herself to look into those stony gray eyes. The longer Astrid looked, the more watery Freya's eyes became. She had never witnessed this level of emotion in Freya. Her first instinct was to dismiss it as a trick of the moonlight.

There was no way Freya could be crying for *her*.

"Are you going to make me say it?" Freya shook her head, incredulous.

"Say what?" Astrid breathed.

"I value *you*, Your Majesty. I—"

"Just Astrid." Astrid wanted to rip off her cloak, rip off her skin. How stifling—*Your Majesty*.

Freya chewed her lip some more. "All right. I value you, Astrid, so I try to keep you close. And lately, I've been under the impression you felt the same."

Astrid did not know what had possessed her to tell Freya to dismiss the formality, but the usage of her name, however awkward on Freya's tongue, made her warm and dizzy, so dizzy she had to cling to the balcony's railing for support.

How long had she lied to herself about Freya's role in her life? Never had Freya acted solely as spymaster or bodyguard or handmaiden. She had been many things, everything, and Astrid relied on her more and more until Freya was of utmost importance to her. She could not imagine a future without Freya, and yet she had to. She wouldn't be given a choice.

Astrid clutched at her heart. "Freya, I can't discuss this right now."

"Why not?" Freya demanded. She rocked back on her heels, using the railing for support. "Do you not feel the same?"

"I can't answer," Astrid said honestly. "There are so many things wrong with... We can't do..." She swallowed. "You serve me, so the dynamic is unfair. I have my country to think about, and I can't indulge distractions. And you will be gone in a few decades, but I will be here."

"So many can'ts," Freya said. "Can't do this, can't do that. Do they sound like excuses to you as much as they do to me?"

Without Astrid realizing, Freya had stepped closer. Astrid glanced at Freya's hands. Those hands had braided her hair so delicately and touched the palm of her hand out of instinct. Everything Freya did occupied Astrid's mind much longer than it needed to.

She swallowed again.

"It's not a matter of excuses," she argued.

"Give me a better one, then." Freya's eyes were earnest. She genuinely wanted an answer.

Every reason Astrid came up with could be dismissed as an excuse. How silly, then, to hold herself back when they were just two people on a balcony. She didn't have to think about her duties as queen or Freya's impending mortality or a power imbalance just now.

If anyone had power here, it was Freya.

Astrid fought her one last time, but even when she spoke, she knew it was futile as resisting her wyrd: "I can't."

Freya sensed her weakness and met it with breathtaking tenderness in her tone. "What if you could? What would you do if you could?"

By this time, Freya was so close, Astrid could feel her breath against the skin of her neck. She looked down at Freya—really looked at her, with her sharp hair and her sharp eyes and her fierce stance—and crumbled to pieces.

Astrid bent down, and Freya stretched upward, and they collided in the middle. Freya's hand wound around the back of Astrid's neck, pinning her in place. Her lips were so warm, so surprisingly soft. She tasted like mead. Mead and loyalty and danger. All the things Astrid wanted but could not have.

Astrid clung to Freya like she always had, backing her against the railing. Nimble as ever, Freya hopped onto it, and then they were at eye level. The soft sound of leather falling against stone was followed by Freya's bare hands caressing Astrid's face. Astrid stepped closer—she needed to be closer, *closer*, closer even than this—and Freya's thighs wrapped around either side of her, squeezing her hips.

With the fervor of someone doing something she knew she shouldn't, Astrid kissed Freya, and she kissed her some more. She touched the soft, short hairs on the back of Freya's head. She clamped a hand onto Freya's thigh, and Freya made a sound Astrid had never heard before—something between an inhale and a moan.

And Astrid knew she could die happy here. Denying herself this was foolish. She was suddenly self-conscious of her enthusiasm—aware her observant spymaster would pick up on how long Astrid had harbored these feelings. With every movement, Astrid gave away a little more of herself and how much she truly cherished Freya.

But Freya was meeting her enthusiasm with every kiss. It was pure luck they'd felt the same way. Pure luck and, perhaps, a bit of a curse.

Astrid was overcome with the desire to *see* Freya's face, not just to feel her, and she pulled away. Two ragged lines tore down either side of Freya's lips, and it took Astrid a moment to place them—where her tusks had dragged against Freya's skin. Freya's lips were swollen, almost bloody, the skin scraped but not broken.

Astrid had not been careful. So much time had passed since she'd kissed someone. She should have considered Freya's soft, human skin.

Gently, Freya leaned her forehead against Astrid's and closed her eyes. The gesture was so tender, Astrid swallowed down bile.

There was no one in the world she trusted as much as she trusted Freya.

Back in Astrid's chambers, Fenrir yowled. The beating of wings sounded above them; then, a distinctive, rapid, repeating bird call. Freya's eyes flew open.

Something whizzed past them. It was dangerously close to Astrid's ear; she heard a whoosh and a clatter, and felt the wind move her hair.

Freya reacted first, unpinning Astrid from her grasp and landing lightly on the stone. She swore loudly.

Still overwhelmed by the kissing, Astrid did not register at first the tips of Freya's fingers, glistening red in the moonlight. She did not understand the broken arrow in her hand.

"Freya," she said, "you're bleeding."

Freya's hand went to her ear. Thank the goddess. Just her ear, though it was nicked pretty badly—Astrid could see the sky where skin should be.

"It's nothing," Freya said. Her voice was cold. She walked up to Astrid, grabbed her arm roughly, and forced her back against the wall. "Do you see this?"

Freya was waving the broken arrow in Astrid's face. Someone had been down below and seen them above and thought to kill them.

Someone had seen them *kissing* and thought to kill them. Someone who happened to have a weapon.

"An opportunist," Astrid said at once. Her first instinct was to alleviate Freya's concerns. "They missed."

"You need to get off this balcony *now*," Freya said. "Someone just tried to assassinate you."

Astrid followed Freya's orders to come inside and sat at the end of her bed. Fenrir curled up into her lap and she scratched his ears absently. From the antechamber, she heard Freya barking orders at the félag and the running of boots.

In her daze, Astrid was not worried about being assassinated. The arrow had come out of nowhere, so it was easy to imagine it as an act of the goddess and not an act of a mortal.

A sign Astrid shouldn't let herself be close to Freya.

Freya came back. Blood streamed down the side of her head, onto her neck, pooling at the collar of her jacket. Had they really kissed just minutes ago? How easily they went back to being themselves. If Astrid pretended they had never kissed, how would Freya respond?

"Varin is setting up a safe room for you within the castle," Freya said. "You have to follow me. We don't know who did this or when it will be safe for you to appear in public."

"Freya," Astrid said, but Freya was done talking, her singular focus shifted to Astrid's safety.

She so wished the arrow belonged to the goddess. If it belonged to someone here, and they really were intent on harming Astrid, and they'd seen her with Freya on the balcony...

They already knew how much Freya meant to her.

CHAPTER THIRTEEN

Freya stayed up all night making arrangements. The steward secured a windowless interior room for Astrid's protection, and Freya ordered the félag around as if she was queen herself, fortifying the area.

Scholars were moved to inns in the bordering towns, if they weren't asked to go home entirely. The excuse Freya and Varin had come up with was this: the air was dry, and so many people in one place posed a fire hazard. The goddess herself had warned Brenn a fire could happen if the scholars did not leave, they said.

The historians, remembering the great castle fire of four centuries past, moved quickly to outlying buildings. For the first time, Freya was grateful for the history fair.

Meanwhile, Guthmar was an inebriated pest. He was too drunk to nock an arrow, Freya knew, but she was more suspicious of his retinue than ever. As she made her demands, she was reminded of his astuteness.

"You have a lot of power here for a lady's maid," he said under his breath. He was there with one of his bodyguards, who shook her head at Freya apologetically.

"Please remove him while we deal with this fire hazard," she said to the bodyguard, and to her credit, the bodyguard maneuvered Guthmar away. Most of his staff was used to wrangling him like a lost puppy.

Just because Freya disliked Guthmar didn't mean he was the assassin. The castle was full of strangers. Any of them could be harboring secret hatred for the Torden queen and her reign.

Once Astrid's rooms were prepared, the félag escorted the queen to the doorway.

Freya watched for Astrid's reaction to the confined space. Astrid said nothing. She merely scooped up Fenrir, adjusted her crown, and entered the room.

Freya's shoulders relaxed. These rooms had only one entrance, and it was guarded by half a dozen guards who could easily take down any assassin. She'd not been surprised that Hedda volunteered to be one of the two additional guards within the antechamber that led to the main room.

Freya stood apart from the félag at the end of the hall. They'd cleared all the rooms in this wing. She was half-tempted to bar every window, too, so anyone who climbed the walls had no chance of getting in. How terribly ironic that castles had the reputation for being fortified structures and yet they were full of security failures.

Footsteps echoed loudly as someone ascended the stone steps leading to this wing. A singular, resounding thump accompanied each set of steps. Relieved, Freya leaned against the wall.

Brenn arrived seconds later, holding her staff and wearing a flowing set of priestess robes originally meant to impress the scholars with its authenticity. In contrast, her hair was all over the place from her rush to get up here.

"By the goddess, Freya. Where did all this blood come from?"

Freya touched her ear and winced. She'd nearly forgotten. A fire hazard didn't explain an ear wound.

"Let me heal you," Brenn said.

"I will not leave," Freya said.

"I can bring my supplies."

Freya's ear stung, and there was an indent where skin used to be, but the wound had mostly clotted. Her gloves were stained with the dried rust of her blood. "I don't think I'll be regrowing that skin," she joked.

"Freya," Brenn said. "Please."

Freya said nothing, which Brenn took as acceptance. The eyes of the queen's félag from down the hall weighed heavily on Freya. She did not want to be healed in front of anyone—to have this admission of her vulnerability. That she could be hurt, that she was just human.

By the time Brenn returned with her supplies, Freya was tired of standing and waiting, listening for anything that could take her by surprise.

The first swab of cleansing agent against her ear caused Freya a great deal of anguish, but she steeled her gaze. Sensing her pain, Brenn was gentler after, wrapping the ear and whispering something in a trance-like cadence, her eyes looking far away. When she was done, Freya's ear was admittedly less sore.

"You were right. I don't think the skin will grow back," Brenn said. "Wait, what's this?"

Freya turned away, but Brenn was too quick. Without warning, Brenn grabbed Freya's chin and dragged her close. Freya winced as Brenn dug her fingers into the sore, raised skin at either side of Freya's lips.

"I warned you." Brenn sounded so heartbroken that Freya felt a tinge of regret. "It's a bad idea, Freya."

Freya wrenched her chin out of Brenn's grip. "I can make my own decisions."

"Can you?" Brenn asked. "Or do you need to ask me what the goddess says first?"

Freya pursed her lips. "I don't care about the goddess, and I don't believe in wyrd."

"You are a contradictory woman, Freya Wedd." Brenn's eyes bored into Freya's. "I wonder whether you are lying to me or to yourself."

The argument was too public, but Brenn was less explosive than Freya, and she deflated at seeing her friend upset. The fight never lasted long in Brenn—something Freya had noticed early on, and part of the reason Freya had stood up for Brenn and gotten them both out of the human wars. For better or worse, Freya was drawn to people who *needed* somebody.

"Please be careful," Brenn said, gentler. Then she put her hand over Freya's collarbone, and Freya felt her heartbeat slow. She was more aware of her surroundings than she had been before.

Freya had the wherewithal now to acknowledge she'd fucked up. Not with Astrid—even if she never had the chance to kiss her again, she wouldn't take that back for the world—but with her immediate, terrified reaction to the assassination attempt. She'd seen the arrow and had narrowed in on eliminating every threat, no matter the cost. She'd had Varin evict the scholars, and she had been obvious about her level of influence.

The félag knew her true purpose here, but now outsiders to the castle might suspect that she was more than a mere handmaiden.

From their conversations at the dinners Freya had attended over the years, the scholars were not huge gossips, but an assassination was a big enough event to go down in the history books. Freya had to make sure they did not hear about the attempt.

Freya was slipping. She wanted to smack her head into the wall. How had she been so obtuse? The things she should have done would keep her up at night. She had to ensure Astrid's safety—her primary goal, now and always. She remembered the feeling of Astrid's lips on hers and shuddered. That was a problem. There had to be a balance between her feelings and her actions. A balance she had never struggled with before.

Another problem was that she could not dismiss Guthmar without causing some sort of international incident. Vakker Castle's court had seen more near-disasters this year than since before Astrid was elected queen. They did not need the Sydlig king upset with them. For all Freya's power, she was not willing to put her queen in deeper danger.

"I wish you hadn't done that," Freya said. "I needed the adrenaline to keep me from falling asleep."

Brenn's brow furrowed in concern. "You should rest to think clearly."

"About protecting the castle, or something else?"

Brenn didn't answer.

"I won't leave," Freya repeated.

"I'll set up rooms for you here, so you can be close," Brenn said, gesturing to the hallway.

"That won't be necessary," said Freya. "I'll need to be closer."

Freya nodded to Brenn as she left her, but she felt the weight of Brenn's judgment against her back like a warning.

CHAPTER FOURTEEN

Astrid was ordered to rest, even though she was not the one who'd been hurt. Emotional duress, Brenn had called it—and that much was true. The shock of seeing Freya's blood had worn off, and suspicion settled in, rendering Astrid unable to do more than cower under her bed covers.

An assassin roamed the castle somewhere. Astrid had been left out of the investigation entirely, locked away in her new rooms. To make matters worse, Fenrir prowled around with his sulky feline saunter, less like he was guarding Astrid and more like he was looking for a way to escape the small space.

Astrid couldn't help but feel panicked at the idea of being trapped. There was only one, heavily guarded exit. She gathered she would not be able to so much as piss alone for a while.

She did not bother speculating about *who* would assassinate her. Freya would have balked, but Astrid hardly cared. There were plenty of people—people Astrid had not even met—who would undoubtedly seek the notoriety that came with killing her, even if they didn't want to usurp her entirely.

But she worried Freya could be hurt, caught in the middle. She worried Ruga would be targeted over the channel, that Ruga's wife could be in danger, that Astrid would lose members of her beloved félag to the killer.

No, she amended. Not a killer yet. She had her loyal bodyguard to thank for that.

But how had someone ascertained the location of Astrid's rooms from outside? They'd picked out her balcony; they'd been good with their bow, or good enough to nearly hit Freya.

They knew Astrid had kissed Freya like she was the one thing Astrid truly wanted in the world.

Astrid was not worried about Freya physically—the cut had been superficial, and Brenn would heal it. But Freya would be distraught. Thinking of herself as a failure for not apprehending an attack she couldn't have possibly predicted.

As if summoned by Astrid's thoughts, Freya entered the room quietly, holding a small stool, and locked the door behind her. Astrid watched in silence as Freya set the stool next to the bed. The room was empty of most furniture. Once upon a time, long before Astrid's reign, it had been used as a holding space for political prisoners.

And now it was a prison for her, she thought wryly.

Freya sat atop the stool and extracted a book from inside her shirt. Fenrir stopped his prowling and pawed at Freya's leg, and Freya shifted to let the cat jump into her lap. Astrid's heart warmed as Freya removed one of her gloves to run her hands through Fenrir's fur. Freya was soft on animals. She was soft on anything she felt needed protection. Astrid had always admired that about her.

Was Freya going to sit there all night? Astrid held in her questions due to Freya's serious expression. Freya did not look nearly as distraught as Astrid thought she would be. Her ear was healed, albeit missing a chunk of skin, and her hair had been gently mussed—the way Freya styled it before dinner when she wanted to look good. To Astrid's dismay, Freya looked so good, it was hard to stop looking.

Astrid forced herself to avert her eyes before she got caught, down to the cover of Freya's book. The binding was leather, and the cover illustration displayed a rosy-cheeked orc woman held by another helmeted orc woman in chainmail. A memory surfaced: little Astrid, hardly more than a hundred and twenty years old, searching through her parents' cart of goods for reading material to pass the time while they traveled from one city to the other. She had wanted to be a soldier even then, and had picked it up because of the chainmail, thinking it to be an adventure story.

There had been adventure in the book, to be fair, but the things that kept Astrid awake into the night were not about battling evildoers and putting the kingdom to rights. Even now, Astrid could recall in explicit detail some of the phrasings about the creative positions the author had given the soldier and her sweetheart.

Her cheeks warmed. Why would Freya be reading *that*? Astrid had not known Freya to read fiction at all; Freya's time was always pared down, utilized in the most practical way possible, and when she picked up books they were about war, weaponry, politics, finance—things that would assist in her spymaster work.

Was it possible the book was meant to send a message to Astrid? That Freya was in an amorous mood? Or maybe they could experience this kind of relationship in erotic literature, but not in reality? Whatever the answer, Astrid fully planned on pretending the balcony had never happened, to push it as far from her mind as she could, and now she saw Freya as the soldier in the story, and somehow *Astrid* was the lover who needed rescuing, and the memory of their kiss merged with her memory of the story, and then she had to turn in bed to face the wall because the sight of Freya overwhelmed her.

There were so many reasons not to pursue Freya, and the only reason Astrid could think of to initiate anything now was *because I want to*, which was hardly good enough. The most pressing reason, which weighed on Astrid constantly, jumping ahead: the inevitable heartbreak of losing Freya when her short human lifespan ended. If Astrid wanted to be more pragmatic, she could admit it was messy for a queen to be involved with her attendant, spymaster or not, and it could jeopardize the whole country if something unpleasant happened between them, or if Astrid prioritized Freya over Torden's people.

If Astrid was being completely honest with herself, Freya's impending mortality and Astrid's queenly duties weren't the only things holding her back.

Astrid had no time or energy for romance since becoming queen—before then, even, when training to be a good soldier had required every ounce of her attention. Even if somehow she were to overcome every last one of her reservations, it had been so, so long since she'd been intimate with anyone. Quite literally longer than Freya had been alive. Astrid was not confident she knew what to do anymore.

At least like this—rationalizing, counting, compartmentalizing her reasons for not pursuing Freya—Astrid could make them real and remind herself why she could not act on her emotions. How any love for Freya could only end in heartbreak, one way or another. On the balcony, Astrid might have been able to pretend they were just two people. She had pretended there would be no consequences beyond, and now she was going to pay the price.

Fenrir leapt from Freya's lap, and Freya sighed, closing her book and standing. She lifted Fenrir gently and nudged open the door to the antechamber to let him out, to the dismay of the guards standing there.

"Was he putting you on edge too?" Astrid asked, and flinched. She had not meant to break the silence or open any doors that should remain closed.

"Yes," said Freya.

Astrid watched her closely as she cleaned her bare hands in the basin. Astrid had never asked where the scars on her hands came from, but she had asked, once, why Freya felt the need to cover them.

A lady's maid would not have these kinds of scars, Freya had said.

Astrid remembered thinking at the time that this was not quite true; many of the human refugees came to Torden with scars, physical or otherwise. What Freya really meant, Astrid realized much later, was that there were people who had been active in the war, who had engaged in the violence, and Freya was one of them. And she had not wanted anyone to know the role she'd played—not as one of the stragglers caught up in everything, but an active participant.

Her deadliness was now weaponized in Astrid's service.

Freya shook her hands dry and looked up. Her piercing gray eyes met Astrid's gaze, and Astrid suddenly admired Freya so much she thought her heart would give out. How did Freya know when to be quiet and when to be bold, when to disappear and when to make herself known? How did she know to assure Astrid with her eyes and her gestures that Astrid was safe under her care?

Freya did not sit back down on the stool when she returned to Astrid's side. Feeling awkward, Astrid pushed back the blankets and swung her legs over to face Freya.

"I think we should bring Hrothgar into this," Freya said, clearing her throat, "and maybe even Hedda."

The beginning of a laugh tickled the back of Astrid's throat. She couldn't make a fool of herself like she had at dinner, but what was Freya talking about? Bring Hrothgar and Hedda into their relationship? Did she mean to tell them, or was she imagining them being a part of it, all four of them? Hedda would never stand for that, and Hrothgar was spoken for—

And then Astrid's cheeks heated as Freya searched her expression, because of course Freya was not thinking of romance at all. As always, Freya was concerned foremost with Astrid's safety, with plans for dealing with the assassination attempt. Foolish, lovestruck Astrid had just been thinking about kissing Freya.

"Of course," said Astrid. Her voice sounded strange.

"I would like to analyze the angle of the arrow while my memory is fresh," Freya said, and started to pace. Just like the cat, Astrid thought. Freya was catlike in many ways—down to their claws. "I think the archer used a crossbow, not a longbow. The arrow was thick enough to be a crossbow bolt, and the strength of the trajectory suggests that weapon. This is assuming it came from the ground—it wouldn't have come straight-on like it did from within the castle walls, or another balcony, for example. But I will need to check the trees. There could be a vantage point I'm missing. With your permission, I would like to go look for tracks and see if we can replicate the trajectory of the arrow with one of our archers."

Freya turned to Astrid, waiting for her consent, as if Astrid would ever willingly tell Freya to leave her side.

"Do what you need to," Astrid made herself say. "I would like to start trusting Hedda again. I think... I think she is more liable to spill her own drunken secrets, not mine."

"I will defer to your judgment," said Freya.

Was she going to give in so easily? Freya followed Astrid's wishes before Astrid even knew, herself, what they were—and now she trusted Astrid to accept Hedda back into her good graces, even though Hedda was a hothead and sometimes unpredictable.

"I'll let Fenrir back in, then. I should get going."

"Freya, wait," Astrid said.

Freya stood by the door, arching her neck at Astrid's command, and Astrid jumped from the bed. The idea of being alone in this room, even with the cat, was unbearable.

Astrid approached without knowing what she would do when she reached Freya. If pressed, Astrid could've come up with a hundred more reasons why not to act on any urge that would get her deeper into this mess.

Want and *need*, not rationality, propelled her legs forward. Freya turned around, and Astrid stopped with her heart in her throat. It seemed time had come to a standstill—that the odd, isolated space they inhabited was separated not just from the castle, but from the universe itself.

Astrid was not a strong person. She had floated through queenhood with the support of her sister and her court and her félag, and then Freya had come along. Freya was the one who made Astrid feel safe.

Freya was the one who made her feel brave.

Astrid reached down and cupped Freya's face in her hands. Freya's cheeks were warm under Astrid's thumbs, and Freya's hands closed over Astrid's wrists, holding her there. Steady as her gaze.

What would you do if you could? Freya had asked, a question that resounded louder than any of Astrid's protests.

Astrid had her answer.

CHAPTER FIFTEEN

Freya had been refreshing her memory about orcish poisons. She'd been calculating trajectories of projectiles, contemplating arrows and plants and the kitchen staff and how many ways there were to die. Continually itching out of her skin, ready to burst from this room and apprehend every single person in the castle until she had some damn answers.

And then Astrid put her soft hands on Freya's face, and Freya's mind went completely empty. The only thought she had was to hold Astrid there in place the way Astrid was holding her. To ground each other the way only they knew how.

"My Queen," Freya whispered. The way Astrid was looking at her was almost unbearable. So soft and trusting and full of affection.

"Astrid," Astrid corrected gently.

"Astrid," said Freya. "Should we talk about...?"

The unfinished question hung between them.

"No," Astrid said. "Let's not."

This time, when Astrid leaned down, the kiss was soft and deliberate, not desperate. Freya closed her eyes and allowed herself to feel every inch of contact between them, her hands on Astrid's wrists and Astrid's lips on hers. Astrid was so careful with the kiss—Freya realized Astrid was trying hard not to graze Freya with her tusks, and Freya was touched by how much Astrid cared. They'd built their bond of trust for a little over a decade, and it had evolved to something deeper and impenetrable. A fortress within which only the two of them could reside.

Freya pulled Astrid closer, backing herself against the wall. She loved Astrid's hands enveloping her own and the feeling of Astrid's firm body against hers and the way Astrid's soft brown hair flowed around her ridged horns. She loved that Astrid was so tall and strong and solid. She admired her queen more than she could put into words, and the emotion filled her up.

I am not in love, Freya had told Brenn, and it was a lie.

She had been in love with Astrid for years. Maybe even as long as she had known her.

The first time Freya had seen Astrid was simultaneously forever ago and just yesterday. Beaten-down Freya, finally coming to a place that promised sanctuary and peace. And there Astrid had been, powerful and steady, the only leader to whom Freya had ever wanted to bend her knee.

And now Astrid was bending to reach Freya, and Freya was pushing off the wall and pressing the palm of her hand against Astrid's chest to direct her deeper into the room. When they backed into the bed, Astrid's knees gave out and she sat on the edge of the sheets, surprised to be there, blinking as though coming out of a trance.

Still standing, Freya reached toward Astrid as though her hands couldn't help themselves. She dropped them abruptly. "Do you need water? Or anything?" she asked, swallowing.

Astrid's eyes were flushed, alive, when she shook her head, when she put one firm hand on Freya's waist and dragged her onto her lap. Conscious of Astrid's warm thighs under her legs, Freya let her knees sink into the mattress on either side of Astrid's and leaned in to kiss Astrid's neck. Astrid arched her back against Freya's touch, and Freya had the thought that this was a kind of magic—the power to elicit this response, with Freya's lips on Astrid's long, soft neck. Astrid's pulse beat against Freya's mouth; Freya's fingers wrapped around Astrid's horn; Astrid's arm wound around Freya's waist.

Astrid's plait was undone, stray hairs askew, and Freya thought she had never looked more beautiful.

"Stars," Astrid murmured at Freya's kiss, then, "Wait, Freya."

Freya stopped. Astrid broke the contact between Freya's lips and her neck and rested her head on Freya's shoulder. Her breathing was deep, rattling.

After a moment frozen—Freya in Astrid's lap, Astrid on Freya's shoulder—Freya stroked Astrid's hair gently, and shifted to kiss the top of her head.

Freya waited in agony for Astrid's next words. She was impatient. Life had come at her hard and fast, and she had learned to expect the same from it.

This left her unmoored, unknowing, and she hated being unknowing. Freya had learned the way Astrid worked, her rules and her preferences and her needs, but none of it applied to romance. She did not know Astrid's boundaries, did not know what was acceptable and what was comfortable.

A pit formed in Freya's stomach: A desire to discover this, too, the way she'd figured out the workings of this castle when she'd first arrived. *Not knowing* was the thing that kept her awake at night.

I would do anything for you, she wanted to say. *I would be struck by a thousand arrows every day if it meant staying by your side.*

But Freya and Astrid had never been the type to use their words to say anything so powerful or true.

"You make me forget," said Astrid, "what a bad idea this is."

Freya squeezed her eyes shut. She would stay with Astrid in any way Astrid would have her, and yet it hurt to hear. Already, Freya had voiced why they should be together however they wanted, and why it was a waste of time to hold back.

When had this started? How far back did it go? The first name, given like a gift. The ease of communicating without words. The offering of the dagger. Everything had been a gesture of love, almost since the start.

Freya couldn't fathom how not to love her queen.

"What are you thinking?" Freya asked. Despite the care Astrid had taken, her tusks had still scraped Freya's chin, and the raw skin stung in the cold, stale air of the room.

Astrid lifted her head to look Freya in the eye. Shifting, Freya lifted her legs so they weren't touching Astrid's. The breaking of contact was like the breaking of a spell.

"We shouldn't touch each other," Astrid said. "Not like this."

"All right. Of course. As you wish," said Freya. She slid off the bed and back to her stool, with the poison book inside the romance book rested upon it. Before, she hadn't paid attention to the cover of the fictional book on the outside of her botanical research; now, the lovers in the illustration mocked her.

"I'm sorry," Astrid said.

"You have nothing to apologize for," Freya whispered, biting back the *My Queen* and the subsequent correction to *Astrid*. She would need to keep her mouth shut and stay in her place to maintain her proximity to Astrid. It was not fair to Astrid to engage in something she wasn't comfortable with, even if they both wanted it.

The want was present on Astrid's face in the concerned furrow of her brow.

"What would you like me to do?" Freya asked finally. "Should I leave?"

"Please don't," Astrid said. "I feel trapped in here, Freya. I do. Is there any other way to keep me safe where I can have a window and walk around?"

"This is safest." Varin had arranged the accommodations, and Freya trusted his wisdom after his many years of serving Astrid. He'd served the previous ruler, too, and helped Torden through its civil war. "I can bring something comforting in here to make you feel less trapped?"

Astrid did not look pleased at the prospect. Of course, Astrid's usual rooms were already austere. Stripped down to the essentials, like Astrid was stripped down to the essentials of what it meant to be a queen.

"Don't leave," Astrid said, because she did not need to say what Freya already knew. "But don't touch me. And I won't touch you."

Freya's gaze dropped to Astrid's hands in her lap, fidgeting, one of them rubbing the inside of Astrid's thigh.

Almost as if...

Something light and buoyant simmered through Freya's fingertips. Her original assumption about not knowing Astrid enough in this aspect was wrong.

Freya dropped the books on the floor and sat rigid in the stool, setting her feet apart ever so slightly. "Of course. We won't touch each other," she said carefully.

"Yes," Astrid said. Her fingers found the waist of her trousers, and she nudged them down an inch at a time. Freya merely watched as the fabric passed over Astrid's knees, then her calves, pleasantly toned, and finally past her ankles and onto the floor.

The hem of Astrid's tunic lifted as she rolled it up with her fingers. A slow reveal, like pulling back a curtain.

Her brown skin reflected the room's warm candlelight, and then the tunic was bunched around her waist, her smallclothes revealed. White cloth covered Astrid's softest parts, wisps of dark hair curling around the edges.

Astrid paused with her tunic rolled up to her hips. Her legs opened wider and then came to a stop. A second passed, then two.

She was waiting, Freya realized.

Freya fumbled with the laces of her trousers, stood to slide them down, left them at her ankles. Her bare legs were exposed, and Astrid was drinking in every inch of them in a way Freya rarely let anyone do. Freya raised her tunic and placed her fingers against the pin keeping her smallclothes in place. Astrid mirrored the movement.

Freya licked her lips. Should she say something? Were they really doing this?

"Astrid," she started, and Astrid unclipped the pin holding the cloth covering her in place, and Freya had no words left.

Astrid's eyes were intense, set on Freya's, as she parted her legs farther for Freya to see her. Between her legs, Astrid glistened in a way that made Freya's mouth water. How Freya yearned to drop to her knees, to touch and taste and satisfy her queen.

Instead, she sat back on her wooden stool and unraveled her own undergarment, revealing herself to Astrid in reciprocation. Their eyes met, blazing. Freya gave a slight nod; Astrid's hand drifted toward her inner thigh.

The division between them and the rest of the world, the realization of Freya's fantasies come true—all of it culminated in a sense of surreality. It was not hard to imagine the hand Freya placed against her hip was Astrid's and not hers. That the slow, circular movement Astrid began against her clit was something out of a dream.

Freya mimicked Astrid's movements, following her pace. She was overly conscious of every one of her senses, as if time had slowed down. A faltering on Astrid's face, so unlike her. Their breaths filling the tiny space, faster and faster. A squelching noise, almost embarrassing in volume.

A moan—Astrid's. They'd reached a frantic speed with their touching, and Freya leaned her head back and closed her eyes. She pretended her fingers were against Astrid's cunt and not her own; she pretended she was being touched by Astrid and not herself. She heard a hitched sigh, imagined the look on Astrid's face that she would make if Freya was the one to pleasure her. If Astrid could lie there and focus on her pleasure alone.

In her mind, Freya saw Astrid's head rolling back, her horns catching on the fabric and pulling it, her mouth parted in satisfaction. How it would feel to run her hands over Astrid's bare spine.

The change in breathing was Freya's only indication Astrid was close. Her eyes snapped open. Astrid was struggling to sit up. Her other hand twitched against her thigh, and Freya wanted to take it, to finish out together, but she didn't quite dare.

Astrid's eyes squeezed shut. Her body began to tremble. She let out a soft, "Oh," and shivered. Freya's body reacted more to Astrid than to her own movements, and she rode the crest of the wave coming on and held it back for as long as she could, until it overcame her all at once. She clamped her mouth shut to hold in a noise the guards outside would have heard.

Astrid's hand came to a stop, her fingertips wet in the candlelight.

Later, after they'd taken turns cleaning themselves up in silence, Freya returned to her stool, her body buzzing with energy.

She needed to discuss what this meant, where this was going, what to expect. And she was fairly certain Astrid had little intention of doing so. The conflicted look on Astrid's face when she stole glimpses of Freya from under her sheets left no doubt in Freya's mind about Astrid's internal struggle with what she wanted.

Freya knew what Astrid wanted. She would have to let Astrid come to that conclusion with finality on her own.

And so Freya kept her quiet. Her leg bounced with anxiety, and nothing would stop it. When she crossed her arms over her chest, she could not stop them from shaking a bit.

And Astrid noticed.

"Freya," she said, and Freya waited for the chastisement to come. Perhaps an order to leave. "Can you take out my plait?"

Rather than getting up, Astrid turned her back to Freya and shifted to the other side of the bed, like she wanted Freya to get in.

Freya was conscious of the smell of sweat clinging to her skin after this long day as she lifted the covers to join Astrid. She found the iron band holding Astrid's hair in place and twisted it free. They had no comb or hair oils. Instead, Freya used her bare hands to unwind Astrid's long hair. She raked her fingers through the soft brown strands and allowed herself to soak in Astrid's comforting smell.

"Thank you, Freya," Astrid said, and Freya could not stand the unknowing of it all.

"Did we take it too far?" she blurted.

Astrid took Freya's hand in hers and wrapped Freya's arm around her. Freya nestled into her back and waited for a response. For any confirmation or firm rejection.

She wouldn't get it. Astrid pressed Freya's fingers to her lips and sighed.

"Too far," Astrid said, "and somehow not far enough."

CHAPTER SIXTEEN

Astrid woke to a dark room with the warmth of a cat weighing down her ankles. She shook out her legs to bring the feeling back, upsetting Fenrir, and when she reached out to the other side of the bed, her fingers closed over a cold, empty blanket.

Freya.

What had happened last night could very well have been a dream, but Astrid remembered it vividly—the rapid beating of her heart, the sound of Freya's breathing, Freya leaning back in the stool with her neck extended. The vulnerable, blissful look Astrid never thought she would have the privilege to see.

No, it had been real. And Astrid was at once reduced to a girl with her first crush.

She felt under the pillow for the dagger Freya had gifted her. Her fingers wrapped around the bone handle. It was as much a part of Freya as Freya's own skin and flesh. Astrid imagined, by holding it, Freya was protecting her, even in her absence.

Would Astrid ever have to use it? Always, she was surrounded by guards, soldiers, protectors. She was good with her weapon—

better, even, than some of her most trusted guards—and yet she had no need for one. The irony put a bitter taste on her tongue, even as running her thumb over the handle soothed her.

Astrid did not regret acting on her urges—how could she, when she'd wanted this for so long?—but she needed to be rational, to proceed with caution. One way or another, this would end in heartbreak, and Astrid would have to accept that to accept the relationship itself.

It scared her, the willingness to sabotage her future self so readily. Would she be able to rule the country while dealing with the hurt? Would she slip up and make a mistake that would become immortal in the tales of skalds and shared for tawdry entertainment in taverns centuries down the line?

Astrid remained in the dark for an indeterminate amount of time before the thoughts began to circle, never reaching a conclusion. Uneasy, she went to the door and knocked. Hrothgar was waiting for her in the antechamber. They rushed in to light some candles. Someone had left a tray of food on the table. All cold foods; nothing fresh and hot like Astrid was used to.

Perhaps foods that were easier for Freya to prepare herself.

"Is it morning?" Astrid asked, realizing she had no way of telling the time.

"Midday," Hrothgar said, apologetic. "Is there anything I can do for you, Your Majesty?"

Astrid thought to beg Hrothgar to let her escape. They had to listen to her orders. She was queen, after all.

But if Freya was right, and Astrid's safety was at risk as much as Freya thought, then Astrid could wait a few days while they carried out an investigation.

Staying here was more a favor to Freya than to herself.

"No," said Astrid. "There is nothing."

In spite of Astrid's insistence on needing nothing, she was not left alone for most of the day.

She would have welcomed a bit of solitude. More time to think and decide what to do, and less time figuring out how to act around people now that they treated her like she couldn't defend herself.

Instead, Astrid was constantly interrupted by members of her félag. They brought her a stack of practical clothing. Someone replaced the water pitcher. Vera came by with a pile of books, blessedly free of any erotic content.

Astrid sat on the edge of her bed and read about Torden's history. In a way, it was grounding to revisit the past and be reminded why she ruled and how she would be remembered.

The candles burned down. People filtered in and out.

There was no sign of Freya.

On the second day, furniture began to appear.

First, a table for her bedside, where Astrid promptly put her books. Next, a wooden wardrobe to store the pile of clothes she'd been brought. After that, a writing desk and chair. Astrid's instincts were to question her félag. Under whose orders were these items appearing?

When the hideously red rug from her bedroom appeared, Astrid ascertained who was responsible.

And still Freya did not make herself known.

By the third day, Astrid began to worry. The room was looking too comfortable, even more homey than her old one. A stash of candles had been provided, enough to last weeks, and more clothes made an appearance along with stacks of paper. The only people Astrid saw were the orc guards of her félag and, occasionally, Vera. She guessed Freya would not allow anyone else near her.

Astrid asked Hrothgar for news of the assassin as they brought in her evening meal, and Hrothgar hesitated before answering.

"Freya has the full story for you. She will be here soon."

Once left alone, Astrid had trouble finishing her meal. The idea of seeing Freya again filled her with a contradictory blend of hope and apprehension. She longed to see the face she associated with comfort and love, but the conversation they needed to have filled her with dread. Some part of her wondered if Freya was keeping her distance because *she* was the one who regretted how far they'd come.

She needn't have worried. When Freya made her appearance, it was with her hair slicked back, leather freshly oiled, and a weapon bulging at her hip through her tunic.

Astrid's heart soared at the sight of her. She had to stop herself from rushing forward to hug Freya, but Freya took a comfortable seat on the stool and gestured for Astrid to sit across from her on the bed.

Astrid remembered, vividly, how Freya's legs had parted last time they'd been situated like this. The memory was so distracting, she did not at first register Freya's words.

"What?" she said.

"How have you been? Are you content?" said Freya. Astrid was not entirely sure this was the same thing Freya had said at first, but she swallowed down the urge to respond to questions with a question.

"You are preparing me to stay here for a long time," she said evenly.

"Only as long as necessary," Freya said, looking down at her gloves. She adjusted them with the squeak of settling leather. "We analyzed the angle of the arrow. It was shot from the ground by a skilled archer who knew the location of your rooms. From a crossbow, as I suspected."

"That's good news," Astrid said. The sentence lifted at the end like a question.

Freya raised an eyebrow. "Good and bad. There are many archery hobbyists within our staff."

That came as no surprise; even the mention of archery made Astrid's fingers itch to pull back a bow-string. In her experience, few things matched the thrill of an arrow making its shot.

"The truly skilled archers, as far as I know, are members of your félag and the armorer. Unless I run an archery competition, there is no way to tell who among them is skilled enough to follow through with such a shot."

Astrid bit down and tasted blood on her upper lip where her tusks had punctured the skin. Freya suspected a traitor. A spy.

The idea was almost a relief once she'd thought it. Freya was the best spy Astrid knew. She would sniff out another like her in no time.

"We interrogated the ambassador's bodyguards ruthlessly," said Freya. "Both were at dinner, as corroborated by eyewitnesses. It is harder to determine who was in the kitchens or elsewhere in the castle. My understanding is Tassi stayed behind with a stomachache." Her eyes flashed at this.

Surely, an assassination attempt was a good excuse to send the entire retinue from Sydlig home.

"Everyone knows, then, that I was nearly killed," said Astrid.

"No," said Freya. "Guthmar's retinue does not know a thing about this. They think you have fallen ill from some of the food." She swallowed. "They think it is related to my tasting."

"Ah. My absence has not been explained?"

Freya worried at her gloves. "It was suspicious of me to send the scholars home before the history fair had officially come to a close. Most did not question the fire excuse, though some rumors are circulating due to your lack of public appearance. Few approach the truth. One of them is that you are pregnant," she said, humor lighting her eyes.

Astrid did not find this so humorous. "Ill or pregnant," she repeated.

"Yes, in your old rooms."

This caught Astrid's attention. "Surely people suspect something. My félag is guarding *these* rooms, not those. There has been an influx of sizable furniture to this part of the castle."

"We are merely rearranging since our guests have left," Freya said. "And... We have some people guarding your old rooms, too. This part of the castle has been closed off for renovations."

Astrid found it hard to believe anyone would buy such a simple excuse, that there would need to be so many guards and food coming and going from this space and no one would bat an eye.

"We have a decoy," Freya admitted. "That is why I have not had all of your clothes delivered to you. Sigurd from the félag has been wearing your dresses and walking out on the balcony to bait a potential repeat attempt by an assassin. I have people on the ground, too, waiting for someone to take the bait."

"*Freya*," Astrid gasped. "That's too dangerous. I demand you put a stop to it at once."

Freya looked up at Astrid then. Astrid nearly faltered under the intensity of Freya's gaze. It was as though Freya had pierced Astrid with an arrow right through her heart.

"Astrid," she said firmly, "I will protect you at any cost. Your félag swore to serve you for the rest of their lives. Sigurd volunteered when I brought up the idea."

Astrid could be sick. When would queenhood stop risking others and start focusing on actual ruling, making important decisions, keeping the peace? All she'd done since ascending to the throne was climb on the backs of her friends and allies as she ground them into the dirt under her heel.

She was damned sick of it.

"I need to get out of here, Freya," she said. "Please."

Freya closed her eyes. Stood from her stool, walked to Astrid. She bent to press a kiss to Astrid's cheek.

Desperately, Astrid seized her arm. "Please," she repeated. From the corner of the room, the cat mewled as though pleading her case with her. "Freya."

"I think it's better if these become your permanent rooms," Freya said. "I will let you know when I think it's safe for you to leave. Can you do this for me? Can you stay here?"

"This is a cage," Astrid said. "I need a window. I need air, natural light. I need you."

Freya sat on the bed. Astrid found it hard to read her expression; her guard was up, her brows pinched.

"I can't focus on figuring this out unless you're safe," Freya said. "I know it's frustrating. I'm sorry you feel trapped. I'm trying everything I can to make this box welcoming." She threw up her hands, gesturing to the room.

She had done well, if one could make a prison feel like home. Someone had brought a tapestry earlier that day, and Astrid recognized her sister's handiwork. It made her miss Ruga so very much.

"I am the queen. I will not be stuffed in this prison. I don't care so much about an assassin. They failed, didn't they? The castle is only inhabited by people you know and approve of?"

Freya scowled. "Assassins are dedicated. Anyone could bide their time for years upon years, waiting for the right moment to strike. You can never really know someone."

"I know *you*," Astrid said, hurt.

Freya's mouth opened and closed. She reached for Astrid's horn and gently guided Astrid's head to her shoulder. "Do you have a solution that works for both of us?" Freya asked.

That odd laugh Astrid had been using lately nearly came back. A human who had only been here for ten years had so much influence over an orc queen who had ruled for fifty. It was funny, in a gallows-humor sort of way.

Freya placed a hand on Astrid's hair, gently pinning Astrid to her shoulder. Astrid felt warm inside and out. Secure. Held. Like Freya would always be there.

It was obvious they wouldn't come to a conclusion tonight. When Freya got up to leave, Astrid tugged Freya toward her, and Freya curled up under the covers, and for a little while, Astrid did not feel so trapped.

Over the next few days, Astrid began enticing members of her félag to keep her company. They engaged in the same activities the guards did to pass time in the barracks. Astrid remembered how to play the card games, and she was excellent at Tafl. It helped to pretend *she* was the soldier, defending someone else, playing games during an uneventful overnight shift.

She asked Hrothgar about the increased defenses; she sat across from a terse Hedda, who moved pieces around the Tafl board in silence.

At night, Freya would come and update Astrid. Nothing had changed. No more clues had been unearthed, and there were no new suspects. Freya had sent several of the staff she did not know well home on leave, and in doing so, had caused a bit of controversy. Worse, she had done it through Varin, who was bitter about the whole thing.

Astrid slept well with Freya at her side, but it was another thing during the day. She felt she was searching out one distraction after another to fill the time. Conversations with the guards grew bland fast. They did not dare to speak of certain things with their queen, not even those who had served with her as fellow soldiers. The books lost their luster or made her miss the outdoors. One description of a garden brought her nearly to tears.

It wasn't until Hrothgar stood from their stool and stretched their legs after a particularly grueling game of Tafl that the idea came to Astrid. She'd taken to playing with Hrothgar over the others. Some of them thought, because she was queen, she should win, and Hrothgar never let her off easy.

They were of nearly the same height and build. Standing next to them, Astrid was directly at eye level. Their hair was shorter, and their attire more masculine than Astrid sometimes wore, but it wasn't a bad idea.

After all, Freya had employed one decoy already.

CHAPTER SEVENTEEN

A week had passed since the assassination attempt, and Freya was no closer to finding the culprit.

When she'd served under human warlords, Freya had detected spies within hours of their appearance. Under Ulfur, she'd worked even harder to prove her place. Never in her career had she taken this long to detect and eradicate an intruder.

Here, when it mattered most, she was failing.

The queen's fake sickness could only last so long. Soon, even the most loyal staff would suspect Astrid of either hiding or dying.

All of Freya's initial suspicions were correct: An arrow shot via crossbow from the ground by someone who knew the layout of the castle. This barely narrowed down her suspect list. Many people down to the bakers in the kitchens liked to practice archery. The idea that someone in the castle was capable of hurting the queen raised the hairs on the back of her neck.

"She's safe," Brenn assured Freya for the millionth time.

Freya had taken to having Brenn around in case Brenn was struck by the odd vision from the goddess. Some guidance on where to go from here would be much appreciated from the heavens, no matter how little deference Freya displayed.

The problem was not just that it was rare for Brenn to be overcome with a prophetic vision. Within the castle close, Brenn's magic was intermingled with those around her. She could perform her usual seer ceremony, but everyone's wyrd would intermingle, confusing her and clouding her visions. It was part of the reason she lived isolated from society.

As far as Freya knew, this feature was unique to Brenn. Brenn had never meshed well with the priestesses in Vakker's temple. The orcish magic was too dissimilar from what Brenn had been taught. It did not sit well with the orc priestesses that Brenn's magic still worked despite its vast differences.

Brenn had not been struck by any visions, mixed wyrd or not, but Freya had to admit she still appreciated the company. Freya was a gale, sweeping through the castle; Brenn was a cool breeze, calm and steady.

Freya stood at the balcony of a previous Mara rendezvous site, watching her breath puff out into the chill air of the night. Answers would not come to her from the skies. She had exhausted every option she could think of, short of sending everyone away from Astrid or relocating Astrid to an abandoned island.

Brenn cleared her throat, and Freya's thoughts scattered.

"I have a hunch," Brenn said. "Something has happened outside of the castle."

Freya stiffened. "What kind of something?"

"Something you'll want to investigate."

Brenn's eyes were sad in the dim light of the moon. Freya could ascertain why: Brenn had warned Freya against her feelings for the queen, and she knew Freya had acted on them.

But she hadn't acted on them since. Not unless holding the queen at night counted. Freya suspected that Brenn would, indeed, count this.

Freya huffed in one last frigid breath of air and turned on her heel.

When Freya and Brenn reached the castle's outer wall, Freya wanted nothing more than to turn around. Sitting in the grass just beyond the gates were Guthmar and his husband. Guthmar swayed as if pushed by the wind.

"Shadow!" he slurred when he caught sight of Freya.

Brenn's hand brushed the bare skin above Freya's wrist, and Freya forced herself to focus. *This* was what Brenn wanted her to investigate? She would have been better off moping on the balcony.

"Sorry," Tassi said. There was a clarity to his expression Freya had never seen on Guthmar—something akin to guilt. "He's bored."

"Did you know a shadow can exist without the object which casts it?" said Guthmar.

"What is he babbling about?" Freya's gloved fist tightened. She forced her fingers to relax.

"It's nothing," Tassi said. "He has had some mead."

"So I see."

"Queen's shadow. The shadow's queen," Guthmar went on. "The queen without her shadow."

Brenn stepped forward and reached for Guthmar's hand, where he'd been guzzling from a great drinking horn. Freya recognized it as one of the ornamental ones from the meadery—stolen.

Sheepishly, Guthmar surrendered it to Brenn. With more grace than the gesture deserved, Brenn poured the mead out onto the dead grass.

Guthmar blinked at Brenn, then hung his head. "I am homesick."

"How long must you stay?" said Freya.

The ambassador looked to his husband, who shook his head. "Indefinitely."

"Surely the king doesn't mean to keep his important cousin away from home forever?" Brenn asked.

Guthmar began to sob.

Tassi wrapped an arm around Guthmar. "Would you mind giving us some privacy?"

"No," said Guthmar. "Please, sit with us. I could use the company of friends."

There were a hundred things Freya would rather do than sit on the icy cold ground with the Sydlig ambassador, several of which involved sticking her hands in boiling water.

Brenn sat down across from Guthmar with a warm smile.

"I never wanted to come here," he said.

Pathetic. The display put a bad taste in Freya's mouth. She had never seen a leader so un-leader-like.

"The king did not like his report," said Tassi.

"Was there something unpleasant to put in the report?" Freya said, so sharply Brenn put a hand over her knee to admonish her. Huffing, Freya joined them all on the ground. The cold soaked through her leather trousers.

Guthmar wiped his nose on his sleeve, leaving behind a shiny smear. "Of course not. It's so pleasant here, and you've treated me well. I just... My letters get all jumbled, you see. I have never been much for reading or writing. He said it was"—Guthmar hiccupped—"like a *child* had written it. Uninformative and riddled with errors."

In spite of herself, Freya felt angry toward the Sydlig king. Why had he sent someone who he knew struggled with writing and reading to correspond about Torden? Not for the first time, she was struck by how little sense it made for Guthmar to be here at all. It was as if he'd been set up for failure.

"Perhaps there is someone else the king could send?" Brenn said. "You could switch places with a courtier whose skills more closely align with King Skarde's goals."

Freya wasn't sure if she would prefer Guthmar's kind inquisitiveness over someone who was trained to do an ambassador's job. As it was, Guthmar had proven himself to be observant enough.

"There is no one," Guthmar said. He put his chin in his hands and sighed. "Do you suppose the consuls in the other cities are as miserable as I am?"

This question was aimed at Tassi, who shrugged. "They have similar responsibilities, I suppose."

"Stupid Elgir had to go and get himself sick," Guthmar muttered.

This was a waste of Freya's time. She began to stand and was overwhelmed by something like intuition. Her eyes snapped to Brenn's, whose mouth had fallen open in surprise.

It took Freya a moment to understand why Brenn would respond that way. When she did, a chill took over her body.

"He was sick?" asked Freya.

"Oh, yes," Guthmar said, at the same time Tassi said, "No."

"That's not what you told us when you came here. You said the king had had an argument with him." Freya paid closer attention to Tassi, who grew pale. He was the one with the answers. "Was that untrue?"

"He fell ill," Guthmar said. "What? It's the truth, is it not? I never saw the point in pretending. He fell ill, and he is likely ill still. Or dead. A sickly rash all down his torso, pustules around his eyes. Vomiting. So much vomiting. They had to quarantine him."

"Guthie," warned Tassi.

"Why would you lie?" Brenn asked. "An illness sounds better than an argument from our end of things. An argument is volatile, a sign of trouble. An illness is a good excuse not to embark on a hard month of travel."

"We cannot presume to know the minds of royals," Guthmar said. There was a cheekiness to him, a glint in his eye. "Elgir is sick, but your queen is not."

Blood roared in Freya's ears. "Pardon me?"

"I saw her," he said.

Guthmar was always wandering the castle. Perhaps he spotted the decoy from Astrid's old balcony and recognized the fraud.

"He did not see her," Tassi said, wrapping his hand around Guthmar's elbow. "He has had too much to drink."

"She was with the burly orc," Guthmar insisted. He shook Tassi off his arm and glared at him, then tapped his nose. "The one with the scar."

"Hedda?" Brenn asked.

"You saw Hedda?" Freya said, still not processing.

Tassi looked as though he wished to cover Guthmar's mouth. "He saw two of the félag leaving the castle. But it does not mean anything. Right, Guthie? Tell them that's all you saw."

No one from the félag should have left the castle. They were all working double shifts, covering Astrid's old rooms and her new ones. Heat licked up Freya's spine. The first sign of alarm—delayed, like all her other instincts had been delayed.

"You saw Hedda leave the castle?" she said.

"Freya, let's listen to him," Brenn whispered.

"Where did she go?"

Guthmar pointed. "She was with the queen. I told you. The queen was dressed like..." He stopped, hiccupped, visibly lost his thought trail, blinked twice.

"Dressed like?" Freya said. She had jumped to her feet, though she did not remember doing so, and she had the neck of Guthmar's doublet gathered in her fists. Tassi stepped forward as if to intervene, then he let his hands fall to his sides.

"Dressed like a soldier," Guthmar finished weakly. He did not resist Freya's anger, but leaned into it, gazing into her eyes like he was really seeing her for the first time. "The queen without her shadow," he concluded.

The first thing he'd said when he'd seen her. He told her right away, and she had missed it.

Freya released Guthmar with such force, he fell back and Tassi had to catch him. She stormed away, feet pounding the dirt.

The guards at the castle gates greeted her and faltered when they saw the thunderous look on Freya's face. Brenn followed quietly, making pleas Freya could not hear through her fury.

This was all Hedda. It had to be. She had unrestricted access to the queen, and she had kidnapped Astrid for how she'd been treated. So stupid on Freya's part to not talk it over with Hedda first before making the marriage arrangement which ended Hedda and Ruga's relationship; stupid, also, to not have known the resentment building up behind Hedda's stony exterior; and stupider yet to not understand how such resentment would manifest even more harshly once punished.

People were so unknowable. Every time Freya thought she had them figured out, she was taken aback by something new. Nobody was like her.

The félag guarding the queen's new rooms parted for Freya with practiced precision, as though she wasn't about to barrel them down if they didn't move. She flung open the door to the antechamber.

"Freya, really," Brenn said from down the hallway, out of breath.

The antechamber was empty. Unguarded. Where in the goddess's name was Hrothgar? Of all people, she had trusted them to protect their queen.

The door to the inner chamber opened before Freya reached it.

Astrid was on the other side. Freya's heart began to calm, taking in the crown and the familiar fabric of her cloak.

No, not Astrid: An impostor in Astrid's clothes. Freya's hand was empty one second and armed the next. She shoved the blade of her knife up at Hrothgar and they leaped back to avoid the blow.

"How long have you been planning to betray us?" she shouted, swinging at them. She wished she had her dagger. "Where is Hedda? Where the *fuck* is the queen?"

A hand closed firmly around Freya's wrist, and she lashed out with her elbow, which Brenn caught in her other hand. Brenn looked into her eyes, calmly, and waited. Freya loosened her grip on the knife. It fell to the plush red carpet with an unsatisfying noise next to the cat.

Calmly, Fenrir lifted a leg and began to lick himself.

"Please be gentle with Hrothgar," Brenn urged.

Freya was not feeling particularly gentle. She was like the blades of her knives, sharp as steel.

"I don't know where she's gone," Hrothgar said from a safe distance. They removed the crown as gently as one would handle a newborn and set it on the side table. "I cannot disobey a direct order from my queen."

It came to Freya all at once. Her brain had jumped to the worst possible scenario—betrayal within the court, Astrid gone forever at the hands of those she trusted the most.

But Astrid had left on her own. And Freya had pushed her there.

Freya slumped onto the bed. Hrothgar took several sizable steps backward.

Was there a way Freya could have prevented this? She'd known Astrid felt trapped in here, and she had thought Astrid would be willing to put up with it. Was it her own fault for taking away the queen's agency? Freya couldn't shake the feeling she had finally gone one step too far.

Maybe it was not being trapped that bothered Astrid the most. Maybe it was Freya herself and the intimacy they'd shared. At the time, Astrid had assured Freya it was something they both wanted. But being something they both wanted didn't mean it was immune to regret.

Freya was not prone to crying, but an itch built behind her eyes.

"Brenn." Her voice cracked; she tried again. "Brenn. Can you do something to make sure she is safe?"

"Of course." Brenn stepped lightly to the nightstand, still winded from the mad dash upstairs. She set the staff against the wall and lifted the crown.

"You'll want to close your eyes," she warned.

A strong breeze swept through the room. Freya's hair whipped around her ears, the unseasonable smell of summer grass filling her nose. A light, brighter than anything she could properly shield herself from with merely her closed eyelids. A sound like back in Brenn's house—the clanking of keys, the cawing of a raven, the yowl of Fenrir. And then the light disappeared, the breeze went away, and it was like the room was completely devoid of air, stale as it had ever been, and Freya could not entirely blame Astrid for leaving.

"She is safe," Brenn said. "With Hedda. She's still disguised as Hrothgar."

"Where is she?" asked Freya.

She sensed Brenn's response before the priestess could speak, how Brenn tamped down the instinct to deter Freya. "I saw docks and the sea."

"She's been gone for several hours," Hrothgar added, a bit guiltily.

"I know where she is," Freya said. "Will you join me?"

This was Freya's fault. She'd locked Astrid away without thorough consideration for her feelings. She hadn't properly conveyed to Astrid what she meant to Freya, or perhaps she had told her too much. She hoped the queen would give her the chance to apologize—and that Astrid would still want her around, in one capacity or another. Whichever way she would allow Freya to serve her.

Brenn was fast on Freya's heels when Freya arrived at the stables and demanded a horse. A startled stable boy, half-asleep, jumped up at once and brought her two.

As Freya mounted the horse, her muscles moved, but her mind had stilled. Above, her falcon cawed.

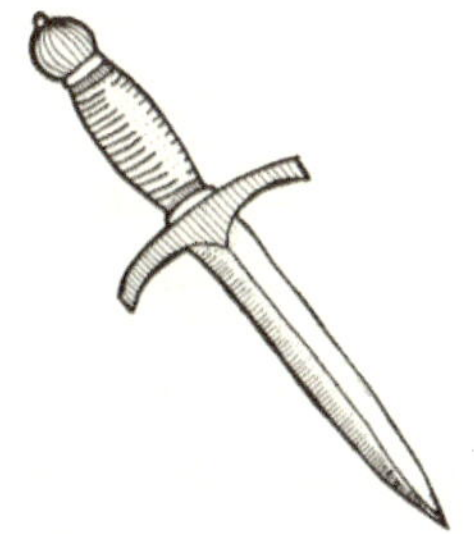

CHAPTER EIGHTEEN

In a port town several hours' ride away, Astrid and Hedda sat across from each other at the Rosebriar Inn with two steins of mead between them.

The smell of this place was like coming home. Fish and yeast and the sweet notes of fruit. The ceiling bore the same slightly hideous and ill-woven tapestry of a woman playing the lyre. It was so old that it frayed around every edge, red strings dangling down. Worn, ugly, and familiar.

When Astrid was younger, her family had stopped in Rosebriar more often than the city of Vakker, though it was barely notable enough to mark on a map. Trading hubs in Torden were plentiful, but there was something about this town that had endeared her parents to its fishers.

The creaking of leather followed Astrid when she shifted to face Hedda. Hrothgar's leather armor was a tad oversized on her, in spite of her perception that they were the same height. Hrothgar was back in Astrid's room, sulking in her clothes. The narrative they'd come up with was quite simple: Hedda and Hrothgar had left the castle to celebrate their night off.

As long as no one knew the félag did not currently have nights off, they would be fine.

Astrid imagined if it were Hrothgar here and not herself, Hedda would be warmer toward them.

Hedda glowered at Astrid impressively. Once, when Hedda and Astrid had trained to be soldiers together, Hedda would have gladly accepted any alcohol gifted to her, perhaps even challenged Astrid to a drinking contest. Now, reserved, Hedda sipped as daintily as any earl in polite company.

Astrid couldn't stand it any longer. "I am still your friend," she said.

Their cloaks were wet from the rain, and they both smelled faintly of horse. Astrid had not reserved a room yet, but she was considering it. She needed to know if Hedda was comfortable staying overnight. Initially, she'd thought Hedda would sneak out with her as part of the plan and then leave, but Hedda had insisted on joining her. Astrid wondered if Hedda considered herself on-duty or if her role was more like watching over an unruly child.

"Can you be friends with someone you've sworn fealty to?" Hedda swirled her mead, staring into its murky depths.

"I meant, I am on your side," said Astrid. "And I forgive you for your behavior at the midsummer festival, whatever that means to you."

Hedda looked up sharply. "What about me? I have to forgive *you*."

Astrid's next sip was bitter. Just like before—she was stepping on others to help her rule rather than relying on her own skills. Choosing who sacrificed what.

"I know," said Astrid.

"May we speak about you and Freya?" asked Hedda.

Goosebumps spread over Astrid's arms. "Pardon?"

"It's a little hypocritical, isn't it?" Hedda huffed. "You and Freya, sneaking around like lovers when you know you shouldn't be. But I have to be the mature one who can handle losing a relationship."

Astrid closed her eyes. The resentment leveled in her direction, boiling right under the surface of Hedda's skin, was a lot to take in. "Ruga needed to get away from Torden."

"That's not your choice."

"It was hers. And she made it." Astrid opened her eyes, gathered her courage. "It's my fault. She was miserable here, Hedda. She needed to get away, and we needed the alliance with Branwen. It worked out for all of us. Can't you see how much happier she is there?"

Hedda was quiet. Even when they were soldiers-in-arms, she had never been adept at swallowing harsh truths. "We were good together."

"Would you have gone with her?" Astrid asked, gently as she could. "I'm telling you she needed to leave. Would you have left Torden to stay by her side?"

The question was rhetorical. Hedda stood from the table, shoved it away, and stalked to the other side of the room.

Having her gone was a relief. Someone ordered stew, and it smelled incredible. When the server came by Astrid's table, she asked for two bowls.

Alone with her thoughts, in the anonymity of a soldier's disguise, Astrid realized how much she needed this. She would give up her queenhood in a heartbeat to drink in this little inn on the sea forever. How little pressure it was to just be a normal person, not to have to make any tough decisions that hurt the people around her. She was inept as queen.

All of the books in the world could instruct her in strategy, but they could not prevent the country she ruled from going to war. They could not teach her how you were supposed to care for an entire country and also value people as individuals.

The tales of rulers who played favorites were never flattering.

Hedda returned to the table in time to eat the stew while it was warm. Astrid waited for her to finish. When she was done, Hedda wiped her mouth on her sleeve and threw back the rest of her mead in three loud gulps.

"You're right," Hedda said, gruff. "It was for the best. I just wish we had the kind of relationship where you could tell me before acting on something that impacts my life. I don't know how queens work, but I thought I knew you. Queen Astrid is a stranger to me after all these years."

Astrid's heart ached. She and Hedda had been friends. Close friends, even. They had trusted and relied on each other, laughed together and shared food over fire at the soldiers' camp. It was one part of their relationship Astrid had to mourn when she became queen, like so many others.

You could not be queen and be close to anyone.

"You are right, too," Astrid said. "About Freya. Do many people know?"

"I brought it up to Hrothgar. We were in your antechamber together these past few nights. Just something about the way you look at each other." Hedda waved her hand in a somewhat lewd gesture. "I assume you coupled. We both noticed the shift."

Astrid nodded solemnly. "And you resent me for it."

"I resent that my own relationship was not allowed to succeed or fail on its own merits," Hedda said. "I do not resent love itself. And she clearly does love you."

Astrid hardly dared to join the word *love* with her feelings toward Freya, as though voicing it would doom them even more. It was one thing to have felt Freya's skin under her hands and against her lips. It was another to hear Hedda call out what was so clear to others.

"It cannot last, even if it was appropriate for me to court my..." Attendant, spymaster? No single word described Freya's role. "She'll live for eighty years, like all humans do."

"Even if I knew I only had twenty years with Ruga, I would not shy away. And I don't regret it now that it's over."

Tears lined Astrid's eyes. How could she overcome the constant feeling of dread toward her future? Wyrd was its own ever-looming threat. All things came to an end—life, her rule, this queendom. One day all would be nothing.

"Oh, Hedda," Astrid said, putting her face in her hands. "Why did I let it go so far?"

"You get so few of the things you want," Hedda said, which Astrid found generous, considering Hedda's own life, sacrificing in the name of her queen. "How long have you been...?"

"Only recently," Astrid said. Her cheeks were warm; she blamed it on the fire roaring in the hearth. "Right before the arrow."

Hedda tilted her head. "We should go back."

"Why?"

"Freya will be worried sick about you. She'll know you're missing."

"Not until morning. None of the félag know," Astrid said.

"She has a sixth sense for you," said Hedda, "and its name is Brenn."

Astrid liked Brenn. Brenn was rational and steady where Astrid was not, and Astrid trusted Brenn's discretion. If Brenn knew Astrid was gone, then she also knew there was no danger to her.

"I want more time," Astrid said. It seemed they would not be staying the night after all, but the idea of getting back on their horses and leaving was less appealing than jumping into the ocean and letting the water take her where it would.

"Must I say it?" Hedda set her stein on the table hard enough to draw eyes from the next group over. "It was foolish of you to come all the way out here when there's been a threat on your life. You do not have the luxury of running away when your feelings get in the way of your ability to rule."

"Hedda..."

Hedda's voice became low and dangerous. "When you put yourself at risk, you put us all at risk. I am the only one here to protect you now."

"Thank you for joining me, Hedda."

Hedda stiffened. "I will serve you, no matter how little sense I think you have. I hope we can go back soon, if you don't mind my saying so. Freya will tear the castle apart searching for you."

Did Hedda really think Astrid so out of her wits? Astrid was well aware of how irrational her actions were, but Hedda couldn't understand what it was like to be trapped in that room. Astrid was already trapped in so many ways. She could not handle one more if it killed her.

In one aspect, Hedda was right: whenever Freya discovered her missing, she would think the worst. Astrid hoped Brenn would be around to reassure her, then felt a pang of guilt that she was relying on other people to pay the price for her actions once more.

"I wish Freya was here," she mumbled into her stein.

Hedda snorted. "Lovesick is what you are." She looked over Astrid's shoulder, and her eyes widened.

"What?" Astrid hissed, suddenly alert. "Do we have to—?"

A familiar pattern of footsteps perked Astrid's ears like a dog's. A soft squelching accompanied every near-silent step alongside the stride of a much larger person.

Slowly, she turned. Freya's face was unreadable and calculated, but her fists were clenched, her stance ready for combat. At her side, Hrothgar walked with their head down. Traveling with an angry Freya Wedd would do that to a person.

When they reached the table, Astrid noted the blaze in Freya's eyes, but also the relief. She had undoubtedly caused Freya an immense amount of worry.

"I thought something bad had happened to you," Freya said. She wiped wet hair out of her eyes and sat lightly on the bench beside Astrid. Their thighs just touched.

Hrothgar sat next to Hedda on the other side. The two exchanged a look, and Hedda nodded. Astrid had put them in the awkward position of obeying her while protecting her, and they had done so.

Astrid struggled to formulate an appropriate response under Freya's burning gaze. "I'm so sorry," she tried.

"I wish you had told me what you were planning." Freya took the stein from Astrid and drank it down to the bottom.

"It was an impulsive decision," Hedda chimed in. "Wrangle your queen for us, shadow. We've done our part."

Freya shot her a dark look.

A musician chose that moment to play a jaunty tune. As one, their heads turned toward the noise. Someone stomped on the floor, and then a lot of someones stomped, and several people stood to engage in a drunken dance.

"I am sorry you felt trapped," Freya said under the cover of the noise. "I should have asked how you were feeling. I was only considering your safety, not your emotions."

Astrid's jaw dropped.

Freya leaned in to speak softer. Her hand hovered over Astrid's knee and came back to her side. "What is the matter?"

"I feel strange tonight," Astrid said evasively. "Restless."

This close, she could see the drops of rain clinging to Freya's lashes. She was overcome with the urge to lean in and kiss her again, wet hair and all.

"What do you need?" Freya asked.

Instead of responding, Astrid found Freya's hand and placed it on her thigh.

Her skin hummed under the leather. Maybe it was the general impulsiveness of the night, or something in the air, or the mead, or the soldier's clothes.

"Dance with me," Astrid said.

CHAPTER NINETEEN

Freya had observed others dancing many times, but she could not recall ever dancing herself.

The sailors swayed, haphazard and without rhythm. The variety of dances had no technique to them—they were dances not of skill but of joy.

And yet Freya's nerves were on edge as Astrid stood and offered her hands.

There was a dreamlike quality to the place as Freya took hold of Astrid. The height difference was comical, but no one gave either of them a second glance. Freya was not the only human in the common area of this inn; several elves were present as well, and sailor danced with soldier danced with server danced with merchant. The drink had leveled them all.

In her disguise, Astrid was just another soldier.

The perception of Astrid as something other than queen unsettled Freya's stomach. Her feet struggled to keep up with this new side of her queen. Astrid swung Freya around, and her face broke into a huge, beautiful smile like Freya had never seen. It was enough to stop Freya's heart.

Astrid had never looked so free. Her hair was loose, tumbling out in curls that sometimes smacked into Freya's face and tickled her. Freya picked up the pace of the dance, paid attention to the beat of the music. She danced, and she did not feel for her knives even once.

The song came to a crescendo. Somewhere, someone shrieked with delight, and Astrid laughed, throwing back her head and exposing her neck to Freya. Freya was dizzy with giddiness, but also with the knowledge that she was entirely out of her element.

Hollers filled the room. Sweat built on the back of Freya's neck and under her breasts and between her palms and Astrid's. Astrid spun her with flushed cheeks. Clapping, stomping, spinning. Freya was an observer, not a participant, and her mind struggled to keep up with the activity through the noise. She clung to Astrid like a lifeline.

At the end of the song, Astrid lifted Freya off the ground and spun her in a large circle. Freya stumbled back to her feet when Astrid set her down and looked back at the table, where Hedda was leaned over whispering something to Hrothgar.

Both were staring.

Astrid's smile faded as she took in Freya's face. Freya wasn't sure exactly what expression she wore. All she knew was that she was extremely overwhelmed and had no control over this situation.

"Sorry for lifting you," said Astrid. "I got carried away."

The phantom touch of Astrid's hands on Freya's hips made Freya's mouth dry. "No, I..."

How could Freya understand so little of what was happening? Here Astrid was, away from the castle and enjoying herself greatly. While Brenn had assured Freya that Astrid was safe, Freya had not considered Astrid would be happier here. She'd thought Astrid had run away on the verge of a mental breakdown.

She did not know Astrid to be the kind of person who could be cheered with drink and dance and music in a social setting.

"Can we talk?" Astrid asked.

The music started up again, less boisterous. A few people swayed drunkenly, but Astrid made no move to pull Freya back into the group. Dazed, Freya remembered she'd been asked a question and nodded.

Astrid led her back to the table with Hedda and Hrothgar. Freya felt herself clam up. She could not say the things she wanted to in front of the félag. The other tables were full, leaving them with little choice. She wished Astrid had never run away, that they could have had this conversation privately in her rooms.

"They know," Astrid said, gesturing to Hrothgar and Hedda. Reading Freya's mind. But surely she didn't mean it the way it sounded.

"They know what?"

"About... About us."

Freya flushed with embarrassment. Slipping, always slipping lately. She spent too much time around Hedda and Hrothgar for them to not pick up on these things. If they were truly good enough to be part of the félag, of course they would know the depth of her connection to her queen. Just because she was more observant than the average person didn't mean no one else could notice things.

The orc server stopped by their table. "Any more for our valiant soldiers of Torden?" the server asked, winking.

Freya glanced down at herself. The leather she wore was darker than the others', but she supposed compared to everyone else in the inn, she did most resemble a soldier.

"Yes, please. Appreciate it." Astrid answered with such comfort, Freya was taken aback once more. It was easy to forget Astrid had not always been the queen. Once upon a time, she had ordered drinks at many establishments with her fellow soldiers on their nights off.

A sick feeling crawled over Freya's skin—comprehension. Running away had given Astrid the opportunity to relive a life she no longer had. Tonight, Astrid was a soldier again, out with friends. No responsibilities, no making tough choices.

Astrid turned to Freya and smiled. Was this how Astrid had been back then, too? A happier person?

"Excuse me," Freya said, and bolted for the door.

The fresh, biting air calmed her just a little. She was scared she might have vomited right in front of everyone if she didn't escape. She ran her tongue over her teeth, counting them, then took several deep breaths, like Brenn had taught her to.

The door to the building squealed open. Freya recognized the cadence of Astrid's footsteps before she saw her.

"We can go back," Astrid said. "I'm sorry for causing you so much distress."

If only she knew.

"You need to be better guarded than this," Freya said. "Someone could have followed you. Guthmar recognized you when you left, you know. It's possible he wasn't the only one."

"I have Hedda, and Hrothgar, and you." She leaned against a barrel printed with the inn's insignia. "I am perfectly safe here."

But you weren't before, Freya wanted to say. Hedda had been the only protection on the journey here. And Freya was sure Hedda had insisted on joining Astrid, and that Astrid had meant to be alone.

She tried not to feel hurt that Astrid had tried to get away from her. She failed.

Astrid reached for Freya's shoulder. Freya let Astrid touch the leather and forced her body to be still.

"Is there anything else bothering you?" Astrid asked.

Funny, how Freya did not know Astrid as well as she thought, but Astrid knew Freya just fine.

A million things bothered Freya all the time. The things she wanted, the things she could not have. Blood on her hands, her scars an ever-present reminder of how far she'd gone in contributing to the violence of the human territories.

What bothered her now was this: She had dedicated her life to protecting Queen Astrid, but she had not once thought to try to make her happy.

Happiness was an experience for other people. It wasn't meant for someone who had poisoned entire camps' water supplies for a warlord. It wasn't meant for someone who had made herself into a weapon. Weapons could not be happy.

But... Freya remembered the unshakable smiles of Ruga and Elketh on their wedding day. A delighted laugh from Vera, newly appointed as Torden's librarian, as she discovered her favorite text in the collection. Brenn, greeting Freya thousands of times over with a smile because she was pleased to see her friend.

Maybe Freya wanted happiness too.

"Stars, I've made you cry," Astrid said. "I'm so sorry, Freya. I'll go back to the castle. You were right. It was foolish for me to come here. I just needed a break so badly."

Freya brushed away tears on the back of her gloves and looked up at Astrid. The queen's eyes were watery in the dim light of the evening. Guilty about hurting those around her by running away, and guiltier for enjoying herself so much once she had.

Freya took Astrid's hands in her own. "Let's stay here."

"What?" Astrid asked, blinking.

"We'll stay for the night. You can continue to drink and dance."

"Are you serious?"

"Yes." Freya was frantic now—she would give Astrid this one night off. How many more would Astrid be able to have? She was a good queen, a good friend. She deserved this.

Freya herself had encouraged Astrid to seize the moment when it came to acting on her feelings. It would be hypocritical to take that back now.

Astrid's expression was full of hope. "It will give Hedda a heart attack."

"And Hrothgar," Freya reminded her gently.

"Do you think we can get them to relax?"

"No," Freya said, laughing.

"Well, I am going to try."

Freya let Astrid lead her back into the inn.

With new expectations set for the evening, Freya was able to stuff down her discomfort with a bit of stew. She kept her examination of the room subtle, searching out sharp weapons and sharper eyes. Dourly, Hedda sat by her side, drinking more mead than a guard on-duty reasonably should. Freya considered saying something.

She decided not to.

Astrid convinced Hrothgar to dance with her. Freya wondered at this side of Hrothgar, too—serious Hrothgar, sipping from a passerby's offered ale to cool down. Freya had never observed them drinking before.

When the stranger offered the same tankard to Astrid, Astrid met Freya's eyes and shook her head, and Freya nodded.

Freya did not care so much if Hrothgar was poisoned over the queen, she noted dryly.

As time passed, and no one keeled over from poisoned mead or pointed steel, Freya started to relax. She was not enjoying herself—not exactly—but she couldn't deny the openness on Astrid's face as she looped Hrothgar into yet another dance. This was not a place where anyone would be looking for their queen. Hedda was smart enough to have done everything she could to ensure they were not followed to the Rosebriar Inn.

Hedda was quiet throughout the night, only the slurps of her drink keeping Freya company. Freya was just getting used to it when Hedda finally spoke.

"'Reya," she slurred.

Freya glanced to the side. Drunk Hedda had made quite a spectacle of herself the last time Freya had seen her like this. Freya needed to tread lightly. "Yes?"

"Next time you do one of your *schemes*," Hedda said, spitting the last word, "I want to be in the know."

Freya bit back a retort about how her schemes kept the queen and country safe. "What do you mean?" she asked instead.

"I want to be involved." Hedda peered into her drink, morose. "When there is the chance to be involved. The queen does not trust me. I need to prove myself."

"I don't trust you either," Freya said, unable to help herself.

"I don't care about your damn trust, Freya."

Freya considered what Hedda was really asking for. She didn't want to be screwed over again without notice. Or did she want extra assignments? She was already working extra.

"Very well," Freya said, thinking she understood, but wondering if she would actually be able to give Hedda what she wanted. "I will let you in on my next...scheme."

Hedda grunted. "Weird that someone who wasn't alive at the start of Astrid's reign has so much power." She stood from the table as Freya's face blazed red.

As if Freya had not earned her place here, just like Hedda felt she had. And Freya had not done anything to sabotage her position, either. She was always perfect. She had to be perfect.

"Did you reserve the rooms yet?" Hedda asked.

Freya shook her head, still fuming.

"How do you know they have vacancies? They could be full. Then where would we go? We'll be sleeping in the streets, or dead asleep on our horses," Hedda said, condescending. "I'll go ask the innkeeper."

She stormed off, leaving Freya to stew in the wake of her anger.

Freya kept her focus on a few notches in the table that looked vaguely like a bird. She did not know how or when to order rooms at an inn—just another skill she lacked. Freya had not been raised in a place where you could hop over to entertainment after a long day of work. It would have been unfathomable to her just yesterday that this was something she needed to know to protect her queen.

Hedda came back, and her jaw was looser than it had been. She sat on the bench next to Freya and pushed the tankard away from them.

"Two rooms, four baths," she said.

"Four baths," Freya repeated, not understanding.

Hedda looked like she was about to tell Freya off. She swallowed and spoke. "They have a tub in the back, and they fill it for each customer who buys a bath. Four baths."

"Ah," Freya said. She smelled like horses and rain, but she did not like the idea of removing her clothes and weapons in an unknown venue. "And the rooms?"

"Hrothgar and I in one, and you and Astrid in the other. Hrothgar and I will take turns sleeping and pretending to be drunk in front of your door to guard Astrid."

Freya wet her lips. "You can share a room with Astrid. I'll take the shift."

"Astrid," Hedda started, turning to Freya, "is my friend, and has been for many, many years. She does not allow herself many opportunities for indulgence."

"Hedda—"

But Hedda shook her head, cutting Freya off. The idea of Hedda helping Freya and Astrid have a night to themselves was more than slightly humiliating.

"We may be her félag," Hedda said, "but you are her true bodyguard. So, guard her."

CHAPTER TWENTY

By the time Astrid's feet grew sore and her eyes had begun to droop, she sought out Freya's watchful gaze from the table—and didn't find it.

Maybe Freya had gone back after all, knowing Astrid would be safe under Hedda and Hrothgar's protection. Astrid's heart hurt to think of the possibility. She wanted to spend time with Freya. They had so much to discuss.

Hedda offered no answers as to Freya's whereabouts as she guided Astrid to a hot bath. She turned her back to guard the doorway.

The water was hot and refreshing against Astrid's skin. It was one thing to bathe in her own rooms back in the castle, but it was another to do it in the soft candlelight of somewhere different. The castle had undoubtedly nicer facilities, but the luxury of the experience wasn't lost on Astrid. It reminded her of days past. Summers with her parents, stopping at inns and taverns when she'd been too young to participate in the drink and dance, smuggling a book up to the rented rooms and reading them by candlelight until, exhausted and happy, her parents had come up to join them.

She thought of the past often lately. Perhaps, in Ruga's absence, the memories came quicker, tied hand-in-hand with missing her. The two had exchanged letters, but where Ruga shared much about her time in Branwen, Astrid found it hard to put her feelings and experiences into words, and so she kept her responses brief. Ruga was busy adjusting to her new life; Astrid did not want to burden her more than she already had.

Perhaps, also, Astrid's evolving relationship to Freya made her wish she was better positioned to woo her properly.

Astrid imagined how she would have courted someone back when she wasn't queen: Flowers. A night on the town. Taking Freya to Astrid's favorite spots. Traveling together, showing off the skills she'd learned from her childhood for navigation, for finding hidden gems where no one knew to look.

Astrid mourned the experiences she could not have, even as she acknowledged Freya would not be in her life had Astrid never become queen.

When the bath was over, and Astrid had donned a clean robe, Hedda escorted Astrid up to the rooms. Though it was cool and wet outside, the inside was warm, and Astrid looked forward to whatever soft, worn mattress the room would have.

"We will take turns guarding you tonight," Hedda said. "Freya is aware of the plan."

"Did she leave long ago?" Astrid asked.

Hedda blinked. "Leave?"

There was noise from within the room. Astrid's heart raced; her body warmed. "She's here?"

In response, Hedda knocked on the door.

"Did you clear the hall?" Freya's muffled voice called from within.

"Yes. All clear," Hedda answered.

Astrid swallowed. She turned to Hedda with wide eyes.

For Hedda's part, she swayed a bit with the drink, but she held her own. She gestured toward the door, all business.

Astrid opened it. Freya stood by the single window in the room, adorned in the same inn-provided robe and holding something in her fist. Her hair was wet but slicked away from her face.

She was not wearing her gloves.

Astrid turned back to Hedda once more. Hedda wore a conflicted look that cleared when she noticed Astrid staring.

"Good night," Hedda said.

She closed the door, shutting them in.

Astrid stepped into the room tentatively, as if afraid to spook Freya. She brought herself close enough to see the water dripping from the end of Freya's hair, the damp on her shoulders.

"Letter from Brenn," Freya clarified. Huginn, Freya's falcon, preened in the window, magnificently reflecting the warm orange glow from the hearth. "Varin wanted to send a search party after you, but Brenn assured him we were safe."

"That was kind of her," Astrid said carefully. She had decided hours ago she would worry about the consequences of her ride into the distance later.

"Can I get you anything, My Queen?" Freya asked. She stood soundlessly as a snake. "Water?"

"Water would be nice," Astrid said.

Freya poured her some from the pitcher next to the bed. The water was cold, the pitcher beaded with moisture. Astrid tilted the cup back to get every last drop.

When she put the cup down, she caught Freya staring at her neck.

"I'm glad you didn't leave," Astrid said. "There's something I would like to talk to you about."

Freya remained standing. Astrid sat to allow them to talk at eye level.

"What is it?" Freya asked.

Astrid worked a circle into the eiderdown blanket with her thumb. What had started as an impulsive move to leave had turned into the best evening she'd had in recent memory. And it had the potential to be even better—

But she had no idea how Freya would react.

"I have grown very fond of you, Freya."

Fond didn't cover the depth of her investment, but *I would go to war for you* was a cliché—a line right out of the saucy romance with the soldier and the maiden.

"I noticed," Freya said. The corner of her mouth turned up. Astrid couldn't help but smile back.

"What do you want out of this? Out of..." She gestured between them, signifying whatever was there. Whatever they had not defined.

Freya considered this. "Anything. I mean... Everything."

Astrid tried not to show her disappointment at the ambiguity in Freya's answer.

"I told you before," said Freya, "that I try to take what I can while I can. So maybe the question is not what we want, but what we can have?"

"What can we have?" Astrid asked, desperation creeping into her voice.

Freya was quiet for several beats. "We can't present to the public as a couple," she said bluntly. "It would undo all of my spy work, and show my importance to those who we may need to hide it from."

Astrid knew this answer—had expected it, even—but if anyone could have come up with a solution, Freya would have been able to. The disappointment clogged her throat some more. She wanted to show Freya off to the world; she wanted everyone to know how much Freya meant to her.

If only Astrid could be someone else.

"All right," Astrid said. "What would you have from me in private, then?"

Freya took a step closer. Their knees were almost touching. A flash of sun-kissed skin peeped out of the slit in Freya's robe and then vanished. Her gaze was steady and serious, unblinking and unflinching.

"I am yours, Astrid. Completely. My body is yours, to shield you and to serve you. I would have whatever you want from me in private, and I offer you the same."

Astrid looked away, blinking rapidly to prevent the unshed tears in her eyes from making their descent. Freya's intensity was hard to stare at for too long. She was a star, brightly scorching, and Astrid wanted to plunge her hands into the core of her, even if they burned.

Another step closer. Their knees touched. Astrid moved hers slightly apart to make room for Freya's leg. Her skin seared where they made contact. Astrid wanted more, more, more, no matter what it cost her.

"May I…?" Astrid asked, and Freya was already nodding. Astrid lifted one shaking hand to the knot of Freya's robe and hesitated. She had stopped herself from going as far as she'd wanted last time.

She would not do either of them that disservice again.

Astrid tugged at the knot. The ribbon holding Freya's robe fell to the floor. With hungry hands, Astrid skirted over the exposed skin of Freya's stomach, the divot between her breasts. Her fingers found Freya's shoulders underneath the robe. Freya's skin was unbelievably warm and soft.

Astrid paused and looked up into Freya's cool gray eyes. Freya was watching her with something between apprehension and desire—taking in how Astrid took her in. Astrid waited, not breaking Freya's gaze, and then Freya nodded, and Astrid flicked her wrists.

The robe pooled around Freya's feet. She stepped back and straightened her posture.

It was easy to forget how short Freya was. Her presence could be so large and overpowering. She was like something out of a painting—fierce, an animal that couldn't be trapped if you wanted to keep your fingers.

Astrid started at the column of her throat and worked her way down with her eyes. Freya's skin was marred with old scars, shining in the light of the fire. Her shoulders were square and she tensed with the shifting of her muscles as she clenched and unclenched one of her fists.

Astrid gathered that Freya was uncomfortable like this. Exposed to the world without her weapons to protect her. As if reading her mind, Freya walked over to the nightstand on her side of the bed and rearranged two small knives.

Astrid found her own dagger from her pile of folded clothes and brought them to Freya, setting them next to the knives on the table. Freya looked up at her. Goddess, but she was *short*. Standing side-by-side, the idea of them together was laughable. Astrid's ears burned. She was quite sure she looked ridiculous.

"I haven't done this in a long time," Astrid said, licking her lips. "And never... Never with a human. So I don't know how it will go. I don't want to hurt you."

The corner of Freya's lips twitched. "I have a high pain tolerance," she said.

Unable to stop herself, Astrid's eyes dropped to Freya's scarred hands. Freya saw her looking and lifted her hands to place them on Astrid's torso. The fabric of the robe crinkled around Freya's fingers.

"It seems a bit unfair," said Freya, "that only one of us is naked."

And even though Freya had seen Astrid naked thousands of times, watching over her as she changed, Astrid may as well have unwrapped a present for Freya. As if unable to stop herself, Freya bent to kiss Astrid's bare torso.

And then, gently, Freya gave Astrid a shove that landed her back on the bed.

Astrid swallowed. "Freya, I'm not sure I know what to do. I really haven't... It's been since before I was queen."

The admission made Astrid's ears hot, but Freya just looked at her thoughtfully. "Do you want to stop?"

"I... No."

Freya's hand went to her waist, where her knives would have been if she was clothed, and then paused, clenching and unclenching her fingers. It was the same reassuring gesture Astrid had seen thousands of times across the great hall. The one that meant *you are safe*. The one that meant *I will take care of you*.

Freya lifted Astrid's chin with one finger. "You have to be responsible every day," she said. "Why don't you let me take control for once?"

"Please," Astrid choked out.

Freya leaned in until her lips were practically touching Astrid's ear. Her voice dropped to a whisper. "Did you know 'please' is my favorite word?"

Astrid flushed down to her toes. The room was warm with the fire blazing in the hearth; it was warmer still with Freya leaning over her, her breasts grazing Astrid's skin.

Freya shifted her head, and then they were kissing—a slow, building kiss that grew deeper as Freya pushed Astrid back, back, back and joined her on the bed. Astrid's hands found Freya's hips, and Freya's hands found Astrid's horns. Astrid loved that Freya's first instinct was to go for the part of Astrid that was different, fully accepting who she was down to the base of her. There was nothing quite like Freya's care.

Freya pushed Astrid down into the sheets by her shoulders and climbed on top of her. With Freya above her, Astrid was dizzy with the anticipation and the realization of a dream she'd had for years coming to fruition. She felt the plane of Freya's back, the bumps of her spine, and then Freya's mouth was on Astrid's neck, her collarbone, her chest.

"What do you like?" Freya breathed against Astrid's skin.

"This," Astrid said, panting. "I like this."

Freya smiled, dazzling, and took Astrid's nipple into her mouth.

Freya's touch was nothing short of magic. Her mouth, her hands, her gentle repositioning of Astrid—all of it was perfect, an act she must have done many times to many people. A knot of jealousy formed in Astrid's stomach at the thought that, all these years, Freya had found her pleasure elsewhere when she could have found it with her.

If only Astrid had been bolder, had said something sooner or opened the door for them. She'd been cold and cut off from everything and everyone. She could only imagine how that had looked to Freya.

Freya slipped lower, kissed Astrid's navel, then lower still, leaving a string of kisses along Astrid's hip. She nudged one of Astrid's legs up so her knee was facing the ceiling and then did the same with the other. Astrid found herself holding her breath, wanting to experience every little detail in full. She wanted to savor it all. She wanted this memory branded onto her brain forever.

"More?" Freya asked. Astrid propped herself on her elbows to look down at her. Freya had a hand wrapped around each of Astrid's thighs, holding her open. The warmth of her mouth caressed Astrid's skin.

"Please," Astrid said, and Freya grinned.

She lowered her face until all Astrid could see of her was the top of her head, her shiny black hair reflecting the light of the fire, and the profile of her nose. And then her tongue touched Astrid, and Astrid bucked.

Freya held her in place, surprisingly strong, as she tasted Astrid with slow, languorous strokes of her tongue. Pressure built in Astrid's body, primed for release, and Freya's tongue quickened, more desperate, at a tantalizing pace. Astrid's hands found Freya's hair, and Freya moaned against Astrid, and the vibrations of her throat nearly took Astrid over the edge, nearly made her—

The tense hold slipped from one of Astrid's thighs. Her leg fell to the side—she'd been doing nothing herself to hold it up—and then Freya's fingers were teasing her, poised under her skilled tongue. Astrid licked her lips then licked them again. Her shaking hands clutched at the sheets so hard she thought the fabric might rip.

Freya's fingers filled her, arching, and Astrid let out a sound more animal than anything—something primal she hadn't known she had in her, something between a wail and a moan, a hiss, and her legs shook in Freya's grip, and Freya—ever-perfect Freya, ever-wonderful Freya—held Astrid down with her one hand, pinning her there with mouth and fingers and sheer force of will as Astrid burst against her face.

"Stars, Freya," Astrid said when it was over. Her voice was hoarse.

Freya lifted her face from Astrid's cunt and smiled. Her chin was shiny with the labors of her love. Astrid's heart surged at the sight of her.

"You're so beautiful from down here," Freya said. "I wish you could see."

Tears sprang to Astrid's eyes. She wouldn't trade this for anything. If she died now, if the queendom burned, none of it would matter. Being with Freya was worth every second.

"I am guessing," Astrid said, wrenching her mind from the inevitability of the future, "that you know about our tongues."

Freya's brows shot up surprise. "Yes."

"Would you like to try?"

"What is it like?" Freya asked, resting her head against Astrid's inner thigh. Her hair tickled Astrid's skin. "I don't always enjoy being on the receiving end of penetration."

"It's gentler than you might think," Astrid said. But there was part of her that wondered if she had enough control to give Freya what she wanted. She truly was out of practice.

"You're nervous," Freya pointed out.

"Sorry," Astrid said instinctively.

Freya rolled to Astrid's side. "Did you want to try?"

"I do want to," said Astrid. She reached down to cup Freya's face in her hand. Freya closed her eyes and leaned in to kiss the palm of her hand.

"Are you scared because of how long it's been for you?" Freya asked.

The question shot through Astrid like an arrow. Stars, it was embarrassing to open up to people.

Freya sidled up close to Astrid's face and leaned in to kiss her. "You forgot something important."

"What is that?" Astrid asked.

Mischievous and radiant, Freya smiled. "I am in control tonight."

Freya repositioned herself, swinging one leg over Astrid's other side so she was straddling her.

Astrid was surprised by two things: the first, that she knew she was ready to try this, that she would not embarrass herself; and the second, that she felt comfortable doing it, even if she failed. Freya would not judge her.

There would be room for improvement later.

Freya inched herself higher over Astrid, passing her breasts, her neck. Her cunt hovered over Astrid, and unbidden, Astrid licked her lips.

Freya's hair covered her eyes. From below, she was even more beautiful. Muscular save for the soft curves of her belly and her breasts. Her collarbones shifted as she eased herself directly over Astrid's face and lowered.

Astrid's tongue unfurled. Tentatively, she pressed the tip to Freya's inner thigh, just off-center.

Freya shuddered. She brought her hand to the crest of her lips and parted them. She was wet—gleaming.

Astrid wanted so badly to taste her.

Astrid's tongue found Freya's clit and swirled. Controlled, clockwise. A high-pitched noise came from Freya's throat as she settled onto Astrid's mouth, helping Astrid move, guiding her to Freya's pleasure.

She tasted like everything Astrid had ever wanted in her life. If Astrid could stay here forever, she would.

"More," Freya said.

Astrid unfurled more of the length of her tongue. How much could Freya take? Human tongues were so small, though Freya had had no problem pleasuring Astrid with hers. Astrid filled Freya, and Freya bobbed, up and down, and released little moans with each movement.

Astrid grabbed Freya's waist to anchor her, and Freya gently knocked Astrid's hand away. Freya's fingers wound around Astrid's horns, firm but not painful, and she thrust at Astrid's face.

"More," Freya grunted.

Astrid filled her more, following her quick movements. A sheen of sweat glistened on Freya's toned stomach, drops beading. Astrid had to close her eyes. The sight of Freya like this was too much—Astrid thought her heart might explode.

Freya's thrusts quickened. "More," she said, and then, "More," and then Astrid had reached the full length of her tongue, feeling Freya's soft insides all around, pulsing with their heartbeats.

Freya's grip on Astrid's horns tightened; her muscles clenched; her breathing came faster and faster.

All at once, Freya's full body quaked, and Astrid's eyes flew open, wanting to see her like this. Head thrown back, her arms straining to hold on. Astrid plunged fully inside of her and out and then again. Freya shrieked, a sound Astrid had never heard before but very badly wanted to hear again.

And then Freya slumped down. Astrid curled her tongue back in on itself, back into her mouth. Freya's cunt was pink and engorged, used and drained.

"Did I hurt you?" Astrid said, suddenly worried.

Freya wiped her sweaty hair out of her eyes. "I told you," she said, "that I have a high pain tolerance."

Astrid swallowed. The tantalizing taste of Freya lingered on her tongue. She could have done it again, many times, but she was scared to break her.

Freya covered Astrid's cheek in kisses, and then down under her ear, and into her hair, her horns, her forehead, her eyes. "That was lovely," she said.

"I love you, Freya," Astrid said. "I really do."

Freya curled into Astrid's side. "I love you, too," she said.

CHAPTER TWENTY-ONE

The fire crackling in the hearth and the even breathing of Astrid's sleep were the only two noises in the room. Astrid was nestled into the nook of Freya's arm. It was so comfortable—more comfortable than Freya had been in a long time.

And yet Freya could not sleep.

Without a doubt, this was the most surreal night of Freya's life. She could not believe she'd finally had the chance to be with Astrid. Her fingers flexed at Astrid's side, remembering the sensation of Astrid around them. She'd been unbelievably soft. Perfect in every way.

Freya feared the possibility that, once they returned to Vakker Castle, everything she'd done tonight would become a far-off dream. How easy it was to engage in this romance when they were separated from everything they knew. When they came back home and settled into their old roles... Keeping up this sort of relationship might not be possible.

Astrid might not want this in the long-term.

As a lover, Freya was a distraction. She felt a hypocrite for hoping Astrid would keep her around exactly like they were tonight. If Freya wanted Astrid to be a good queen, shouldn't she support her however she could?

The problem was not the matter of support. No matter how Astrid chose to keep Freya in her life, Freya would stay.

But after she'd had a taste of this, it would break her to lose it.

Freya's stomach roiled as she watched the peaceful look on Astrid's face. This was the most untroubled she'd ever seen her. Freya yearned to shut down her worries, to close her eyes and fall asleep at Astrid's side and have a long, dreamless night.

If she fell asleep, she would lose precious seconds of their time together. She couldn't bear to waste it, not knowing what the future might hold. *Loss*, Brenn had said. Maybe she had meant the loss of this. The best scenario for both of them was if Brenn's prediction meant the loss of their relationship and not the loss of Astrid's life.

Astrid shifted in her sleep. Not wanting to disturb her, Freya held as still as she could. Dawn would break in a few hours, and then they would have to go back. Astrid deserved a good night of sleep.

"Freya?" Astrid mumbled.

"I'm here," said Freya.

Astrid blinked at her blearily. "Is it time to get up?"

"No," said Freya. "Go back to sleep."

"Have you slept?"

"No," said Freya again.

More mumbling noises came from Freya's armpit as Astrid shifted, peeling her skin from the blankets. Neither of them had bothered to dress after they'd made love. Freya was luxuriating in the skin-to-skin contact. When Astrid leaned back far enough to see Freya, the places where their skin had been touching raised goosebumps.

"Is everything all right?" Astrid asked. Her hair was looped haphazardly through her horns. Freya reached out to rearrange her hair, biting down a smile at how casually they could touch now. The awkward encounter when Freya had handed Astrid her own fingers seemed long ago, like it happened to someone else.

"Can't sleep. This bed is very different from mine," Freya said, opting for a half-truth.

Astrid rubbed the sleep from her eyes. "You've slept on my floor," she pointed out.

Freya shrugged. "You can go back to sleep. Here." She held out her arm for Astrid to return to. Astrid did return, settling her horns into the open spaces so they didn't press into Freya too harshly. Freya's chin burned from the trails left behind from Astrid's tusks during all of the kissing. She didn't mind, but she appreciated the thoughtfulness.

"I want to stay up with you," said Astrid. "What are you thinking about?"

Freya chewed her lip. "The future, I suppose."

"Oh." Astrid ran a finger over Freya's clavicle, making her shudder. "What about it?"

Freya had half a mind to speak the truth. It would press at her until she knew the answer. "What it holds for us," she said.

Astrid cleared her throat. "Actually," she said, "I had something similar on my mind."

"Really?" asked Freya.

"I was thinking... You and I talk strategy and politics and money, but we don't talk about us. Who we were before this. I don't know much about your past." Astrid moved her head to look up at Freya with her warm eyes. "I would like to, though."

Freya's lips pressed into a thin line. This seemed to be about the past, not the future, but she decided not to voice this thought. "What would you like to know?" she asked.

"What were you like before all this?" Astrid asked.

Freya's breath caught. Before? She couldn't discuss the person she was before coming to Torden. Part of her was always afraid she had too much of the old Freya inside of her—the one who had done what she had to in order to survive, and maybe worse. She had wrung out her old self, salvaged the parts that made her useful to her queen, and tamped down the rest.

"Ask me something else, please," she said, strained.

Astrid's eyes softened in understanding. Her fingertips brushed the back of Freya's hand. "Would you tell me how you got the scars?"

Freya flexed her scarred hands. In the dim light of the room, she could just see the shadows of irregularly raised skin, unnaturally shiny. In daylight, her scars were paler than the rest of her, just faintly pink against her tan skin. She closed her eyes, remembering.

"Poison plants," Freya said. "We had to pick them. When you were too little to be useful for anything else, the warlords would put you to work how they could. I collected the plants with my bare hands. I'd get sick for days afterward. The plants were poisonous even to the touch. Blisters and all that, and it had thorns. I was always scraping my skin against them, over and over." She lifted her hand to her face, turned it. "The marks don't go away."

Freya looked up at Astrid. Her queen's eyes were watery, her lips parted in surprise. But where had she thought the scars were from? There was a reason Freya hid them most of the time.

"Oh, Freya," Astrid said.

The sympathy discomfited Freya. She cleared her throat as the room blurred in her vision. "What about you? You've been so at home here. I imagine your life was pretty different before becoming queen."

Astrid's eyes lit up. "You have no idea," she said. "All the traveling with our parents. Learning the merchant trade, but so many other things, too. Ruga and I were thick as thieves. I was always getting in trouble and she was always getting me out of it."

"That hasn't changed," Freya pointed out lightly.

"No, it hasn't. Stars, but I miss her," Astrid said. "I loved traveling. Every place had something new. People thought I was so cute as a child. They indulged me when I wanted to see how the blacksmith forged swords, how the archer nocked an arrow, how the falconers trained their birds. I was so hungry for it all. Learning new things made me feel alive. I was good at them, too."

She didn't have to be humble, Freya knew. Part of the reason she'd been elected queen was her skill in nearly everything she tried her hand at.

The more Astrid spoke, though, the more Freya realized how limiting queenhood was to her. For someone who wanted to try new things, much of her time was spent on diplomacy and bureaucracy and running the country. Freya had never seen her go to the archery range or forge a sword.

"You never wanted to be queen," Freya whispered.

Astrid jolted upright in the bed.

Of course. It had been at the tip of her tongue, the side of her brain, an ever-present feeling. But if Astrid, who never wanted to be queen but was so good at it, who had the queenly traits Freya admired so much, didn't like that side of herself... How could Freya say she really appreciated the whole of her?

"No," Astrid said. "I never wanted to be queen." She swallowed. "I wanted to be a soldier. Soldiers have lots of free time to do whatever they please when they're off-duty. And I liked things that were physical. All the training and whatnot. It made me feel strong. It made me feel like I was contributing to Ruler Lyn's success by being able to protect what they had created."

Freya touched Astrid's arm. She might not have been as strong as she once was, but she had plenty of muscle left.

"And then you shot Ulfur," Freya filled in.

"Right time and right place, I suppose," Astrid said. A darkness came over her face.

Instantly, Freya regretted mentioning Ulfur's name. "I'm sure there was more to it than that."

"Can I tell you something, Freya? And will you promise not to share it with anyone?"

"What is it?" Freya asked, concerned. She searched Astrid's face for what had caused the sudden emotion, and she could not read what was there.

"It wasn't merely a lucky shot. Ulfur had already murdered Ruler Lyn in combat, and Varin was running things as best as he could. The castle was a disaster. We were divided up, trying to hunt Ulfur down and stop her once and for all."

Dread clawed its way up Freya's throat. She had the sense that once Astrid was done speaking, Freya would never see Torden the same.

"There was a brutal skirmish," she said. Her eyes were wide, frantic, desperate to get the story out. "It was outside Ravn. Hedda and I were posted there under our captain's command. We fought all day long until both parties had to retreat. We were sore, and injured, and mentally drained." Astrid's chest heaved as she caught her breath.

Freya waited. Her fingers itched toward Astrid's sternum and rested there. Without a word, Astrid closed her hand over Freya's.

"What I did was cowardly. We were so sick of everything, Freya. All of the fighting, all of the death. I convinced Hedda to sneak with me into the other camp. We donned the slipshod armor of Ulfur's dead warriors and made our way in. Everyone was asleep or caring for their injuries." She stopped, looked out the window. "There was no moon that night."

Freya kept herself completely still. She thought she would be sick.

"We dispatched the guards around Ulfur's tent. It was almost too easy. They didn't make a noise, and her tent was larger than the others to show her importance. I think she wasn't used to it yet. She had only just broken away from Torden and hadn't developed her strategy. She had killed the head of the country and hoped, in the bedlam, she would become the new queen."

The way Astrid spoke of Ulfur, like she understood the inner workings of her brain, made Freya's pulse quicken.

After all, Astrid had had the same idea. To cut off the head of the beast.

"I got into her tent. She had someone with her...in bed. And I killed them first." She licked her lips. "It wasn't clean. The gurgling, the thrashing—it awoke Ulfur. She jumped to her feet and swung at me with everything she had. I was able to strike her bicep with my axe. She was incapacitated by it—nearly immobilized. Because..." Astrid put her head in her hands.

Freya let her hand fall back to her side. "Because the blade was coated in poison."

"Yes," Astrid said, like she was sick with herself. "It was poisoned."

"What happened then?" Freya asked. Her mind couldn't keep up with the pace of the story, with this restructuring of everything she thought she knew about the queen she loved.

"We escaped somehow. Well. Not without running into some people who saw the fresh blood on us. Perhaps the goddess watched over us, because we made it out of there. And Ulfur lost the arm, as you know."

"There was no arrow," Freya said, keeping her voice even.

"No," said Astrid. "There was no arrow. When I got back to Varin... He was furious, as you might guess. He said, next time I tried to assassinate someone in their sleep, I'd better not miss. We spun a story about meeting with Ulfur in a skirmish. Me, atop a horse, valiantly nocking the fateful arrow that would strike Ulfur dead if only it had been a few inches to the right."

"Ulfur knows the truth," Freya said. "But she does not speak of it." Freya had worked for Ulfur for half of a year, and not once had this come up in Ulfur's inner circle. Ulfur hardly talked of Astrid at all.

"I imagine she wouldn't. Even if she did, it would be spun as a false story to turn people against me. She has enough people turned against me already, in any case."

"Why not just tell the truth?" Freya asked. More than anything, the lie did not sit well with her. All this glory afforded to Astrid when it had happened so differently—the results would be devastating if people found out. Freya would have shared the true story from the start, shameful or not.

"I was craven," Astrid whispered. "Cowardice led us to go after her in her sleep. To use poison. That is not the making of a queen. I have lived with the guilt all these years."

Freya choked down a dry laugh.

It was funny, in a way. Astrid's greatest shame had been Freya's lifestyle for over fifteen years, ever since she was old enough to wield a blade and strike true. She had encroached upon countless camps and killed hundreds of people in their sleep to prove her place in multiple warbands. To keep them from deciding she was just another mouth to feed and getting rid of her the way they'd done to so many.

"Who else knows?" Freya asked instead.

"I don't know who in Ulfur's circle knows," Astrid said. "On our side, only Hedda and Varin know. I think some of the félag suspect it did not happen quite how we said, but they are too loyal to question it publicly. Many people have pretended to witness the act to retain some of the glory for themselves. It's how myths are formed."

Varin deserved some credit. He'd fed the tale to those who hadn't been there, and then they'd fed it to the skalds hungry for stories, and those skalds had gone and spread the word about Astrid's near-victory as if it had truly happened.

The historians, Freya remembered. None of them had questioned the arrow. Briefly, she wondered if Vera suspected anything.

Astrid cleared her throat. "Do you think less of me?" she asked.

Less was impossible. Freya had given her full self to Astrid as best as she knew how—but *differently* might have applied.

All of the things about Astrid that Freya looked up to had given her something to which she could aspire. That the two of them might be more similar than Freya'd thought was more than a little odd. This new perception sat sourly in Freya's stomach, but she had to admit, deep down, part of her was thrilled.

If Astrid could have done this and still be considered good, there was hope for Freya.

"Of course I don't think less of you, My Queen," Freya said absently, realizing she had paused for too long.

Astrid wove her fingers with Freya's and pressed her face into Freya's collarbone. "Thank you, Freya. I am not sure I deserve your loyalty, but I always appreciate it."

They settled back into silence. The crackling of the fire began to feel like the ticking of a clock. Freya stroked Astrid's hair, and Astrid held onto Freya like an anchor at sea.

Loyalty... Freya had always been good at loyalty, when it came to those she cared about—Brenn, Astrid. She had been true to the warlords she'd served until a stronger one came around and took over, and then she was true to the new one.

She did not feel loyal now. A terrible thought occurred to her: Could she still be loyal while keeping secrets from the queen?

"Astrid," Freya said urgently.

"Hmm?" said Astrid.

"I have to tell you something. Since you trusted me with your secret." She watched Astrid's head bob with her chest. "It's something Brenn saw in your future. It's... It's not good."

Astrid lifted her head and cupped Freya's cheek in her hand. "I don't want to hear it," she said, gentle but firm.

Freya balked. "You don't want to...? Are you certain?"

A tear trailed down Astrid's cheek and plipped off the end of her nose. "I know what it is, I think."

"What is it?" Freya asked, tightening her grip around Astrid's shoulder.

Astrid smiled sadly. "Something inevitable."

Once more, Freya searched Astrid's face for answers and found none. She opened her mouth to speak.

Someone knocked on the door. Three sharp, urgent raps.

Freya jumped to her feet. Her tunic was over her head, legs bare, a knife in each hand by the time the door opened just a crack.

Hrothgar's eye appeared in the opening.

"What is it?" Astrid asked, tired. She made no move to cover herself.

"Varin is here," Hrothgar said. "Sorry to, ah, interrupt."

"You are not interrupting," Freya said. She had donned her trousers and her leather doublet. "Why would Varin come? I received correspondence that he had been mollified."

Hrothgar opened their mouth to reply, but they were shoved out of the way by someone else. The door flew open, banging against the wall. Someone from the next room shouted at them for being too loud.

Varin stood in the doorway, professional as ever despite the early hour and his posture, slumped by age. "Your—" He seemed to remember where they were and lowered his voice. "You need to come back to the castle at once," he said, unusually direct.

Astrid stood. The grooves of her bare muscles and curves were shadowed in dark contrast, making her look like a queen from the myths. "Has something happened?" she demanded.

"The king has arrived, and he is looking for you," Varin said.

"The king?" Freya asked, but a moment later, she understood. The king of Sydlig had come to Torden.

CHAPTER TWENTY-TWO

Though Varin had been in a panic—or as much of a panic as he ever was—the castle was strangely ordinary when Astrid returned.

By contrast, the difference within her was stark. Now, Astrid had had a taste of the person she was back in the day, and she meant to indulge in that side of herself more, no matter what it took.

This new understanding of herself stole her focus.

The tall horses of Sydlig whinnied restlessly as two young orcs who worked in the stables tended to them. The horses looked worn, travel-weary; Astrid tried to remember how long the journey from Sydlig to Torden was. A month, at least.

"Their hooves have been magicked," Freya murmured to her as they handed off their own horses to the stables.

Astrid thought the hooves looked normal, but she trusted Freya's instinct toward magic. Magic was one thing Astrid had not particularly bothered to learn about, seeing as she did not have the ability to perform it.

"I've left King Skarde in the grandest rooms I could find," Varin said. "He is not pleased. He only wished to speak with you and Guthmar."

"Where is Guthmar?" asked Astrid.

Varin sighed. "Probably getting an earful."

"Take us to him," Astrid ordered.

"Yes, Your Majesty."

They left the main hall, where the eyes of the guards and staff gazed upon them.

Freya cleared her throat. "I will check in with Brenn."

Stars. Astrid had not thought of that. How could King Skarde have visited without Brenn knowing? Had Astrid left the goddess's favor for fighting her wyrd?

Unease swirled within Astrid, made worse by Freya's disappearance.

Two of the félag joined Astrid and Varin: Sigurd, who had served as her double while Astrid was in hiding, and Norga, who Astrid had known since her own training back in the day. She'd have preferred Hrothgar, or even Hedda, but both of them were exhausted after the night guarding her, so she had told them to catch up on sleep.

Freya's quiet steps slid in behind Astrid as she began to ascend the stairs.

"Brenn?" Astrid asked.

"Sent her home," Freya said.

Astrid stopped and faced Freya on the stairs.

Perhaps Freya needed to sleep as well. The whites of her eyes were red around her gray irises.

"Brenn's magic is much weaker surrounded by all these people," Freya said. "She admitted she'd been having nightmares since coming here, but they were useless to parse through. All they did was scare her."

Astrid continued up the stairs. Though Freya had tried to explain before how Brenn's magic was different from that of the orcs who served as priestesses in Torden's temples, Astrid had little understanding of magic in general. Brenn was more sensitive—more empathetic, perhaps, than was entirely useful.

Sigurd and Freya reached out to grab each of Astrid's arms as she faltered on the steps.

When had Astrid started thinking of people in terms of how *useful* they were to her?

That was something she needed to work on while she was being conscious of incorporating the old version of herself. The old Astrid would never have thought of Brenn in such a way. Where was her compassion?

Freya's voice was tight when she released Astrid's arm. "I am begging you not to bludgeon yourself on the stairs again, Your Majesty."

"You're right. Yes. Sorry," said Astrid.

A guard waited at the top of the stairs. He took Varin's arm when they got close and whispered something in his ear.

"Back down the stairs," Varin said. "They're in the library."

"I thought King Skarde would be in our guest apartments," said Astrid.

"Guthmar is hiding in the library, and King Skarde has caught word."

Down the stairs again they went, Freya boring holes in Astrid's back with her eyes.

For an older orc, Varin's pace was brisk. Never a good sign, when it came to Varin. The closer they got, the more audible the yelling became. Astrid held the end of her cloak so as not to trip as she rushed through the open library doors.

"You're not my king," Vera was saying. "I don't bow to you."

"I demand you hand over my cousin right this second," King Skarde boomed.

He was surrounded by his retinue—attendants and soldiers, most of whom looked like they would rather be somewhere else, and two bedraggled priestesses. The soldiers had swords extended in Vera's direction, which she was understandably not taking well to. She shoved the weapons out of her face, only for them to be pointed at her with renewed vehemence.

Vera would certainly be injured soon if Astrid did not intervene.

"King Skarde," Astrid said. "I insist you refrain from skewering my favorite librarian."

The king jolted. "Queen Astrid," he said, cloying. "In Sydlig, we are usually present to greet our guests."

"Yes, well, perhaps you forgot to send word you were coming."

King Skarde stared. Astrid stared back, cocking her head in challenge.

The king was a muscular orc who might have seen some battle on his own. Unlike Astrid's, his crown was quite elaborate, littered with jewels that sent cascades of light in every direction from the morning sunlight that streamed through the windows. He was dressed in fine velvet, richly colored.

"I need to speak with my cousin, but your librarian is hiding him," King Skarde said.

"I am a scholar," said Vera, "not a babysitter."

Astrid turned on her heel. "Vera, where is Guthmar?"

Vera sneered. She had told King Skarde she would not bow to him, but in truth, she did not bow to Astrid, either. "In the back with his spouses. I should mention he does not seem fond of His Royal Majesty."

"Noted," Astrid said. She gestured for King Skarde to stay and headed to the private nook of the library that had served as her sanctuary over her years of ruling.

Guthmar was seated in the cozy reading chair. Tassi stood stoically behind him while Alvor kneeled at his feet, holding Guthmar's hand and muttering reassurances. His face was puffy and red from crying.

"Hello, Guthmar," Astrid said pleasantly. "Do you have any idea what your king wants from us that would warrant an uninvited and unannounced visit?"

Guthmar sniffled into a notably damp kerchief. "His brother's dead, I'd wager."

"His brother," Astrid repeated.

"The one who was supposed to be the ambassador," Freya supplied. "He'd fallen ill."

"Ill," Guthmar repeated, and laughed sadly. "If only. 'Tis a shame. His brother was a better man, though the standard is not high."

"Queen Astrid!" King Skarde shouted from the front desk. "You are being rather rude."

Astrid returned to the desk, where Vera stood glowering impressively at the entire retinue all at once.

"Your steward has been inhospitable and refused to answer my questions," said King Skarde. "Your librarian is impossible. You are a terrible hostess."

Astrid forced her trembling hands to be still. "And is it not rude to arrive in my queendom unannounced?"

The king's face turned an impressive shade of chartreuse. He responded by charging past Sigurd, bumping her on his way to Guthmar.

Astrid followed. Tassi and Alvor now stood protectively before Guthmar, who sobbed anew.

"Move," King Skarde ordered.

"You must be kind to him," Tassi said, voice shaking. "He has done nothing wrong."

"Both of you, leave."

Neither of Guthmar's spouses budged.

"That is an order from your king," he added darkly.

"We will protect him," Astrid promised them.

There was a clatter at the entrance to the small alcove as Sigurd and Norga held Skarde's guards back from joining him. This area was crowded enough already, the least peaceful Astrid had ever seen it.

Alvor and Tassi parted around Skarde to exit the library.

"Stand up for your king, you sniveling piece of shit," Skarde yelled down to Guthmar.

Anger rose in Astrid. She had become fond of Guthmar in his time at Vakker Castle, fonder than she thought possible.

"King Skarde," Astrid said, "I *really* must insist you do not accost my guests in my home."

"This guest is only here because I sent him."

Freya slid in behind Guthmar's chair. She patted the blade at her hip, and Astrid nodded.

"You never clarified why you sent your ambassador, not to mention the consuls in every major city. You've never offered to help us before, so I have to assume you're spying on us," Astrid said. "Why get involved now? Have you taken up with Ulfur's people?"

The king unsheathed his sword. Sigurd and Norga surged forward, blocking Astrid with their arms. No longer held off by Astrid's félag, King Skarde's guards came through, packing in like a mound of dead fish at the market.

Astrid shuddered. "Am I to take this as a yes, King Skarde? Are we at war?"

Skarde's chest heaved. The point of his sword descended and scraped against the floor.

Vera would have something to say about that, Astrid thought.

"We are not at war," King Skarde said, "but if you do not allow me to reclaim my useless cousin, I may reconsider."

Useless. Too similar to how Astrid had caught herself thinking about Brenn. She looked at King Skarde and saw how cold he had made himself, how calculating he had become as king. Maybe he had always been like this.

But Astrid hadn't.

"Consider Guthmar officially under my protection until you can tell me exactly what's going on here," said Astrid.

"My brother," King Skarde said, spittle flying, "is dead. Guthmar poisoned him."

"Poison?" Astrid said. The idea of Guthmar poisoning someone was so absurd, she wanted to laugh. "Do you really think this kind man is capable of poisoning someone?"

"Yes," said King Skarde. "My brother told me so, right before he died. He and Guthmar shared mead the night before he became violently ill. We had the mead tested."

Which meant Skarde had forcibly made someone else drink it, Astrid guessed.

"And it was poisoned," King Skarde went on, like he thought Astrid was slow to understand. "So Guthmar has done it."

Guthmar cried some more. "Did he really think...? He died thinking that I killed him?"

"Didn't you?" King Skarde said. "You've always been unpredictable, Guthmar. Unfit to do anything that required more than picking daisies in the garden."

"I like daisies," Guthmar said weakly. "They are beautiful."

"Do you have any proof Guthmar did this?" Astrid asked. "Did he ferment the mead himself?"

"I do like mead," Guthmar said. "Though I know not how to make it."

Astrid fought back a sigh. Of course, during the one night she took away from her responsibilities, the entire queendom would fall apart. "King Skarde, what is your plan if I do give you Guthmar?"

"*Give* me my own cousin," King Skarde said, snorting. "The plan is to take him home and behead him, of course."

"That is where we are at odds, Your Majesty," said Astrid. "I would like him alive."

"You are a terrible queen and a worse woman," King Skarde said. "I do not trust you to defend yourself from Ulfur's warbands any more than I would trust a horse to be my treasurer."

"I had a horse that could count, once," Guthmar offered.

Astrid and Skarde glared at him.

"Have I done something to make you lose faith in my competence, Skarde?" Astrid asked, forgoing his title deliberately. He puffed up like he was going to say something, but she cut him off again. "The last time we spoke, we treated each other as equals. What's changed?"

Astrid waited with her heart in her throat. If Skarde had news about Ulfur moving in... She didn't know how she could preserve her old self and defend the country from active war. It wouldn't be possible.

"I received word from a reliable source," the king began, "that you planned to redirect Ulfur to us first to buy yourself time after the alliance with Branwen."

"Your source is wrong," Astrid said. Her mind felt jumbled, unsure. What did Branwen have to do with this? The alliance between Torden and Branwen—cemented with the marriage of Ruga to Princess Elketh of Branwen—had been supposed to deter war, not encourage Skarde to act. Was Ruga safe there, or would Skarde come after her, too?

"My source is incredibly reliable and verifiable. Guthmar, tell your new queen."

Guthmar threw up his hands. "I cannot say," he said.

"Why, you—"

"If we could refrain from name calling, please," Astrid said, suddenly feeling very tired. "I have never spoken ill of you in court, Skarde, nor have I thought you wanted to be involved after my many pleas for Sydlig's help were ignored. I do not understand how it has possibly been turned against me like this."

"Who is your source?" Freya asked from her corner.

Everyone turned to face her. Freya was serious, her knife on display. She did not look like the meek servant who blended into the background.

She looked like a threat.

"I would just like to say," Guthmar interjected, "that I do not think this is true any longer, Skarde. As I said to you in my letter, I believe the source was mistaken."

"Damn your useless letters."

"*Who is your source?*" Freya repeated.

And then Freya looked up, up, up, and her eyes widened in horror.

CHAPTER TWENTY-THREE

Someone was feeding bad information to King Skarde.

Freya was determined to figure out who. It was clear King Skarde was not the kind of person who would let a conversation go anywhere meaningful. She found her interjection important and necessary, or else she would not have made it.

If they could not trust King Skarde, and they had a threat to every side of them but the sea, Torden was doomed.

As the accusations flung back and forth, Freya caught onto one thing—the poisoned brother. Guthmar had mentioned that Elgir, the original ambassador, was sick. Pustules, he'd said, a symptom Freya recognized from her research at Astrid's bedside. And he'd said it like he knew there had been some foul play afoot.

Was it possible Guthmar was the poisoner? Freya had seen him talk his husband out of killing a spider once. Maybe the king was setting Guthmar up to take this fall, while ridding himself of a brother who he thought was going to kill him and steal his throne like in the old days of orc country. King Skarde would need someone to take the blame, and Freya fully believed this king who waved his sword around like he didn't care who caught the pointy end was capable of cold-blooded murder.

The sound of scraping stone drew Freya's attention from the king. A sound from above. In the calamity, no one had thought to look up, not the félag and not Freya.

She tilted her head back to seek out the source of the noise. There—past the corbels, on the ledge, a silhouette against the morning sun. A figure, crouched. Freya only caught a glimpse when the figure's arm twitched.

"Get down!" Freya screamed.

She had time to register Norga and Sigurd throw their bodies over the queen, tackling her. King Skarde stood in the middle, dumbfounded as his soldiers at Freya's demand.

It was one of those times where being invisible did not come in handy.

She leaped over the chair, where Guthmar huddled with his hands over his head, and shoved the king squarely in the chest, knocking him back.

The head of the arrow landed thickly in the rug—just barely snicking the leather of Freya's boot. If King Skarde hadn't moved, he would have been shot.

"Out!" she screamed. "Everyone out!"

The Sydlig soldiers bottlenecked the narrow exit. Between them, too much armor, too many broad shoulders. Norga and Sigurd crouched and shuffled Astrid away from danger.

Guthmar jumped out of the chair and hid on the side opposite the window.

Freya chucked one of her knives at the archer just as another arrow whizzed past her and landed in the shoulder of one of King Skarde's guards. Right in the chink of his armor.

Stars. They were a good shot. The archer caught Freya's knife under their boot and kicked it away.

The archer was too high up. Freya didn't have the momentum she needed to be as deadly as she wanted. The arrows would kill anyone in this trapped space.

One of the panicked soldiers pushed through the bottleneck. A bookshelf fell in a clatter. There was a shout from Vera on the other side of the room, and then an arrow thunked into the king's shoulder, and he screamed.

Freya darted between Norga and Sigurd and took Astrid's hand. She tugged her to the thin space between two shelves and pushed with all her might, knocking an entire shelf of books down to clear a path. Astrid's eyes were wide, her hands trembling, as she slipped left and right over the sliding pages.

"The king!" someone yelled. "The king's been shot!"

A second time? The archer was targeting royals.

Freya would not let the archer take Astrid from her.

Freya shoved and shoved at Astrid. Someone slammed into the back of a bookshelf and it began to tilt, threatening to crush them. Astrid dodged; Freya rolled. The top of the shelf scraped the back of her calf, and she bit back a scream. She hobbled away and took half a second to check on Astrid.

They were too exposed. They were going to die.

Astrid hauled Freya up by her hands. "Are you all right?" Astrid wheezed.

Something slammed into Freya from behind, winding her. She jolted forward, crashing into Astrid. Astrid stood steady, held Freya's shoulders.

Astrid's midsection was splattered in blood.

Freya reached a tentative hand to Astrid. Where was the wound? Freya's pulse came quick. She couldn't find the point of entry, her fingers were slick with hot blood brighter than anything she'd ever seen, and—

"Oh, Freya," Astrid said. Tears welled in her eyes.

"I'm not losing you," Freya said. She tasted copper. "I will keep you safe." Something warm oozed from the side of her mouth. "You are going to be all right."

She coughed. Over the ringing in her ears, Vera shrieked. An onslaught of armed guards entered the library. A volley of arrows ensued—too many to be shot by one person. Most hit the stone and bounced off pathetically.

Freya's heart felt weak. She clutched at it and pricked her finger on the sharp tip of the arrow protruding from her chest.

"No," she said, as if disbelieving would make the arrow disappear. "No, no, no."

"Help!" Astrid said. "Send for a healer!"

Freya's legs gave out under her. She clung to the fabric of Astrid's cloak, sinking to her knees even as Astrid tried to hold her up.

"I'll get Brenn," Vera's clear voice called back.

Astrid sobbed. "She sent her away. She's not here! Do something, quick!"

Spots filled Freya's vision. She steadied her breathing. Look normal for Astrid, she told herself. Look like you can make it through this.

I've been shot.

The admission was like cold water coming over her. How bitter, to have survived everything she'd endured, only to go out like this. She knew better.

Freya couldn't feel the tips of her fingers. Astrid's bellowed orders rang against Freya's ears like the beating of a drum. Freya's head tilted back—too far back, against her will—and she caught a blurry glimpse of the mullioned window up high, showing an unobstructed view of a beautiful orange sky with a rising sun.

Someone was lifting her, then, touching her wound. She winced in pain. She winced again when someone broke the arrow in half.

Faces above her. Hedda, hands slicked with blood, a black-feathered fletching between her fingers. Wasn't she supposed to be resting? Where had she come from? And there was Vera, calm and steady, her cool palm against Freya's forehead.

Astrid, like her world had ended. Her wet tears fell over Freya.

Freya could not feel her fingers, but she moved them. Brushed them against Astrid's hand. An attempt to push her away.

"Don't touch," she gasped. "Poison."

And then she said nothing at all.

CHAPTER TWENTY-FOUR

Astrid couldn't breathe.

Freya's body was limp in her arms, practically weightless. As though the goddess had already claimed her soul and reincarnated her into her next body.

Someone took hold of Astrid's shoulders and gave her a good shake. Vera, her lips moving. She was saying something.

Astrid could not hear anything.

She was screaming.

An armored hand reached for Astrid. With wild abandon, Astrid unsheathed Freya's dagger and slashed.

Hedda only just moved her hand in time. She shouted, waving people back.

Astrid rose. Her fingers were slick with Freya's blood. She released a wordless wail of agony.

Hands up in defense, Vera stepped toward Astrid. Astrid lunged at her with the dagger, and Vera staggered back, stunned.

Blood pounded in Astrid's ears. She was aware of only two things—the crumpled body at her feet, and the need to protect Freya the way Freya had protected her these last ten years.

The faces in front of her blurred, unrecognizable. A few dared to come closer. Astrid stood her ground for what felt like hours, years: a tireless guard, a devotee to her deity, a mourner standing vigil.

She stared down at Freya's face. The skin was beginning to turn purple, bruised and sickly.

Astrid had pictured Freya dying a thousand ways: from stress, prematurely aged, or else sick, like humans tended to become. She had known Freya would be gone too soon from her life—had felt it in every interaction—but she could never have imagined losing Freya *now*.

It was unthinkable. Unreal. And yet here she was, standing over Freya's dying body.

The few guards left in the room parted as someone new arrived. Astrid's thoughts moved like sludge, not recognizing their face but instead the distinctive staff and the priestess robes.

Brenn approached, staff held in front of her as if herding a scared animal. Astrid returned to her body, grounded by the recognition.

The dagger clattered out of her grasp.

"Please let me care for her, Your Majesty," Brenn said. "I turned back as soon as I was far away enough to receive the goddess's messages. She needs my help. I can heal her."

Astrid's feet were leaden as she dragged herself to the side.

Brenn's face, usually so controlled, fell when she saw Freya. Astrid's heart lurched. She had feared the worst, but she always feared the worst. If Brenn thought Freya looked bad...

Freya really could die.

"I need you to summon the priestesses from Vakker's temple," Brenn said to Varin. When he didn't move, she added, "Now!"

Varin scrambled away, calling directions to the guards.

Astrid tried to speak, but her throat was hoarse from screaming. "You always work alone," she rasped. "She told me. You can't do magic with others."

"Your Majesty," Brenn said, and Astrid saw she was crying—of course she was, because Astrid was being selfish as always, and Brenn loved Freya too. "I cannot heal a wound this severe by myself."

Nonetheless, Brenn knelt next to her friend and pressed a hand to her chest. The sound of chanting filled the room as everyone waited in silence. Freya's chest glowed under Brenn's touch, and then began to rise and fall steadily.

Freya was alive. For now.

Astrid stepped back, and her fingers caught on Hedda's armor.

"We should give her privacy to work, Your Majesty," said Hedda, and Astrid numbly nodded her assent.

When Brenn had done what she could, she had Sigurd bring Freya to Astrid's temporary, secure rooms and set her on the bed over Astrid's plush blankets. Sigurd helped Astrid out of her blood-soaked tunic and into fresh garments. Dimly, Astrid registered Sigurd telling her that they'd scoured the area, but the assailant had gotten away.

Someone handed Astrid a cup of hot tea. The cat rubbed against Astrid's legs, but she could not bring herself to pet him. Meanwhile, Brenn kneeled at Freya's side, occasionally murmuring a chant that made the crease between Freya's eyebrows lessen for a few minutes.

After Astrid's tea had long grown cold and bitter, a herd of orc priestesses flooded the small room. They muttered to each other as Brenn explained the situation. One of them unscrewed the lid of a jar of pungent herbs, and then they surrounded Freya so Astrid could not see.

A trembling hand pressed into Astrid's shoulder through her cloak. She looked up. Varin watched her, grave-faced. She had not seen him come in. She had barely noticed anything but Freya and her care for the last several hours.

"You have a visitor, Queen Astrid," he said. "It will be better for the priestesses to not feel the pressure of their monarch's scrutiny."

What poor timing. "Send them away. I do not wish to leave."

"I will watch her, Your Majesty," Brenn promised. The look in Brenn's face—the wariness toward the other priestesses—soothed Astrid, if only briefly. Brenn would make sure the priestesses did not do anything Astrid disapproved of.

And queens always had to greet visitors.

"Very well," Astrid said. Her voice was still thin. "Send for me immediately if there are any changes."

"Yes, Your Majesty."

Astrid made no effort to move. Gently, Varin lifted her arm over his shoulder and got her back on her feet.

"I've sent out search parties to find the assassin. We do not know much about their appearance—only eyewitness accounts of a silhouette in a window. We have no idea of clothing, gender, or the type of bow used. They have horns, from several recollections, so we are only suspecting orcs."

Varin had to repeat himself three times before Astrid understood. When she did, she blinked at him in surprise. Of course, it was nice to have Varin's help, but Freya would investigate this and neutralize the threat.

The revelation hit her like a blacksmith's hammer. Freya could not investigate. She might never investigate again.

To Astrid's dismay, she could not remember a time before relying on Freya to take care of such matters. How would Astrid live if Freya didn't?

She staggered, but Varin had come to a stop in front of the félag guardroom. Astrid did not remember the path she'd walked to get here.

"Who is the visitor?" Astrid remembered to ask. Her heart had been clawed from her chest; she hardly cared to entertain a guest.

Varin pushed the door open. Daylight streamed into the room over a series of bunk beds. At one of the tables where the guards played cards and Tafl, an orc with silky purple hair in a flower-patterned dress paused, her fingers clenching a game piece.

She dropped the piece onto the board, eliciting a gentle swear from her opponent—Hrothgar, Astrid realized.

"Oh, Astrid!" the orc exclaimed, and rushed to throw her arms around her.

"Ruga," Astrid said, delayed. She could not bring herself to return the hug.

"How is she?" Ruga asked. She searched Astrid's face, and her expression grew somber. "Oh, never mind. Shall we find somewhere private?"

Astrid allowed herself to be led to one of the guest apartments on the floor below as if in a trance. The room was sparsely decorated and stale and the sun was abnormally bright against Astrid's dour mood.

"It is nice to see you," Astrid forced herself to say. She was not sure if it was true. Normally, she would be elated. It was hard to feel anything.

"Varin sent for me," Ruga said. "I took the first ferry over from the island. Is there anything I can do?"

Astrid snorted. Ruga knew her well—well enough to not ask how she was doing.

"The priestesses will have to heal her," Astrid said, voice cold. She was echoing what Varin told her, she knew from some deep part of her brain, but she could not recall when he had said it. "There's nothing else to be done."

Ruga sat on the end of the bed next to Astrid. "How long have you been together?"

"What?" Astrid asked, jerking her head.

"I'm happy you acted on your feelings, truly," Ruga said. "You held off for far too long."

Astrid knew Ruga well, too—well enough to know when the subject was being changed. Ruga was good at things like this. Distracting people to help them, or delving deeper into the bad feelings when that helped more. All Astrid did was hurt the people around her. Cause others to suffer, like Freya was now.

The truth was, Astrid and Freya had been acting on their feelings for years. Every time Freya patted her weapon from across the room to assure Astrid she was protected, she displayed her love. Every time Astrid waited for Freya to go to sleep before falling asleep herself, it was an act of love. This had been going on for a long, long time—and Astrid did not know how to determine its origin, the point at which Freya had tipped from an employee who had proven competent to the most important person in Astrid's life.

"Is it good to have acted on them?" Astrid asked, voice cracking. "Even though I could lose her?"

"Even so," said Ruga. Her lips turned up in a rueful smile. "You deny yourself everything, Astrid. You deserve to indulge where you can."

To hear Ruga affirm Astrid's feelings brought tears to her eyes. Naturally, her feelings brought her to this mental state in the first place. She had allowed herself too much.

"Was it obvious?" she asked, thinking of Hedda and Hrothgar. Astrid supposed you could only exchange so many meaningful glances across a room before someone noticed. She had been careful to hold all her other emotions close, and yet this one came through clear as day.

"Yes," said Ruga. "More so from Freya than from you, if you don't mind my saying so. I do not see her protecting the other Torden citizens—or Brenn, even—the way she does you. She cares for you deeply. I would wager she has done so for a very long time."

"Queens cannot have love like this," Astrid said. "I was beastly today."

She could only imagine how she had looked, not only to her own people, but to the Sydlig retinue. Like she could not be controlled. Lashing out at her own félag. She would have to issue an apology to anyone whose head she had nearly taken off. The embarrassment would set in later.

"Everything ends," Ruga said. "That does not mean it is not worth experiencing." She set her head on Astrid's shoulder lightly. The circlet she wore, signifying her as Queen Consort of Branwen, tickled Astrid's ear.

"You were sweet to come, Ruga, but I think you should leave," Astrid said. It was about time she started behaving like a queen again. "There is an assassin on the loose, and they have targeted both me and King Skarde. I cannot promise your safety."

She had completely forgotten about him until she said his name. He might be dead, for all she knew. She did not care if he was. She did not care about Sydlig, or Ulfur's battle-worn Lynby, or her own country.

Her only concern was her human handmaiden.

Someone knocked gently on the door. Ruga answered.

"Hello, Brenn," Ruga said. Kindness seeped from her voice, and empathy. Two things Astrid was not capable of at the moment.

"Hello, Ruga. You're looking lovely. Things are going well with Elketh, I take it?"

Astrid looked up in time to see her sister blush.

"*Very* well," said Ruga. "She certainly keeps me busy."

"I have heard much about her," said Brenn. "I do not doubt it."

"Is there an update?" Astrid croaked from the bed, feeling like she was the only one worrying, even though it couldn't possibly be true. "How is the healing process?"

Brenn turned to Astrid and gave her an awkward bow. "King Skarde does not fare well, Your Majesty. We do not expect him to survive the day. I spoke with Varin, who is concerned about retaliation from Sydlig. It does not look good for us. He thinks certain nobility left behind in Sydlig could view the assassination as your doing. It would mean more war."

Astrid could not convey enough how little she cared about this. "And Freya?"

"Freya is..." Brenn cleared her throat, and Ruga gave her shoulder a reassuring squeeze. "We are keeping a close eye on her. The arrow was poisoned, as you may have ascertained. The poison is in her blood. We are doing what we can."

"What you can," Astrid repeated. "Brenn, please be honest with me."

"I don't know," she said, and she threw up her hands. "I don't know, Your Majesty. I am so sorry. We have everyone working as hard as they can. Some people cannot be saved."

Astrid stood from the bed. She set back her shoulders, pushed out her chest. The change in her posture changed her mindset too, made her voice stable where it had been hoarse.

"I want you to leave," she said, "and do whatever convening with the goddess you must do to determine whether she will live. And if you see that she will not, you must stop it."

"Astrid, you can't ask that of her," Ruga said. "Only so much can be done."

"No, that's all right, Ruga," said Brenn. "I will leave and see what I can find out. I'll come back to check on her as soon as I can."

"Thank you, Brenn," Ruga said, because Astrid wasn't going to.

CHAPTER TWENTY-FIVE

Freya awoke on a cold stone floor to the coppery smell of blood.

She lifted her head and blinked at her surroundings. She recognized this place, though she had only been here once, well over a decade ago. The crumbling stone walls. Blood smeared on every surface, handprints and splatter from the slaughter that took place here.

This was the temple where she'd found Brenn. Brenn had been one of two survivors, and the warlord Freya served at the time had taken both priestesses into his warband. Priestesses were a valuable resource in war. They could make you hallucinate your commander telling you to turn on your own, or convince you your loved ones are in peril, drawing you into danger. Visions so real you could smell them.

Freya touched her scalp. Her hair was short, and she was wearing the leathers she preferred in Torden. Her senses were too vivid. Not one of her sick dreams in which she had to repeat the past, then.

"Brenn?" she called.

As if summoned, Brenn appeared in the middle of the room in a raised chair. This place was transient, everything and nothing at once. Freya would have sworn Brenn had not been there a moment ago, but the other part of her brain warred with her, telling her Brenn had been watching since she arrived.

The vision could come from any priestess, not necessarily Brenn. A tactic used against other warbands who also had magic on their side.

"Where are the bodies?" Freya asked.

Brenn touched a hand to her throat. In the wake of the massacre of Brenn's temple, bodies had been strewn everywhere. The blood was here, and so was the stench of death, but the bodies were now gone.

"I could not bear to see them," Brenn said.

Freya approached the raised chair. "Do you remember the name of the warlord we served?" she asked. "The one who did this?" Freya had served so many warlords, she'd lost count. She couldn't recall their faces now, the people she had murdered for over and over again, until someone usurped the leader and the cycle began anew.

"Of course I remember," said Brenn. "He ruined my life."

"He's gone now," Freya said, thinking it must be true.

"Yes," Brenn agreed.

"Why are we here?" Freya asked. Something faint came to her as if through a tunnel—she'd been wounded. An arrow, she remembered. An arrow had run her right through. "Am I dying?"

Brenn's eyes filled with tears. "I hope not."

"Have they found the archer?" Freya asked.

"We know very little. I don't know how we would identify him."

"It was a woman," said Freya.

"A woman?" repeated Brenn.

Another memory came to Freya—a glimpse of the archer in a window. Freya hallucinated her now in a shattered window of the temple. A flash, and then gone. "Just a feeling I have," she said, but she could not specify how she knew.

"Sometimes the goddess gives us answers when we need them," Brenn said.

Freya scoffed. "The goddess hasn't given me shit." Everything she'd earned had been on her own. All the goddess was good for, to Freya, were vague omens about bad things happening, or else no news at all. What use was that to Freya, who needed to know everything to feel safe?

"It is a little ironic, don't you think? That you are named for her, but you do not trust her power."

The only explanation Freya could come up with was that her mother had had a wicked sense of humor, or, perhaps, she, too, had had some unrefined foresight into the trajectory of Freya's life.

Freya Wedd had been named for the goddess, but destined for the shadows. Ironic indeed.

"She has not seen fit to show you if I will die?" Freya asked.

"You will die," Brenn said. "I know that to be true. But I do not know when."

"It will happen violently? A murder?" Freya asked. It was only fair, she supposed. She had taken her share of lives.

"I don't know, Freya. I'm sorry." Brenn placed her head in her hand. "I do not think your time has come yet."

"This was the queen's loss you mentioned," Freya said, and she was suddenly sure. She had been worried about other factors, like Astrid losing her own life or her reign or their love for one another, but she had not considered that the prophecy referred to herself.

"Yes, this could be a loss," said Brenn. "But I was mistaken to tell you so soon. It feels far away. Very far."

"So I won't die," Freya said, feeling frustration creep over her. "This is why I don't trust the goddess. It would be nice if, for once, she could give you a clear signal."

"Like the assassin's gender?" Brenn asked.

Freya reached for her weapons out of instinct, like she could take on the goddess with just her dagger and her audacity, but it was missing from the belt at her hip. She had, after all, gifted it to someone else.

"Is she all right?" Freya asked. She did not have to specify who.

"She is uninjured," said Brenn. "And quite worried about you."

"You have to heal me," Freya said, "or figure out a way to keep me around longer. She needs me."

"Yes," Brenn agreed. "But Freya, you will need time to heal properly. Months or years. You've been badly poisoned. You may not regain your full strength for some time."

She'd been unconscious, she realized. Of course. It was hard to remember reality in this strange place. "How long have I been gone? Is she protected? Is there anything I can—"

Brenn held up a hand to silence her. "You have been asleep for two weeks. We have the Vakker priestesses healing you in addition to my own talents. I suggested I could reach out to you in a vision to see if that would help. Sometimes waking the mind awakens the body."

"Stars," Freya said. It was no good if Brenn had called on the Vakker priestesses. They had made their contempt for the way the temples in the human territories conducted their magic clear from the day Brenn arrived in Vakker.

Being out for two weeks was even worse news. The archer would have had time to leave Torden or else, if they were determined enough, make a new plan of attack.

Freya could not stop letting everyone down.

Brenn shifted her staff to her other hand. "Keep healing, Freya. You are right. She does need you. I think the goddess smiles on you, however much you reject her. You will make it through this." She wiped a tear from her cheek. "You are too stubborn not to."

"Can I see her?" Freya asked suddenly. "Can I see Astrid here?"

"She wouldn't be real," Brenn said. "You'll have to wake up."

"Stars, are you serious? If I could, I would."

Wake up, Freya.

The voice surrounded them. Brenn's lips moved, but the voice was too powerful to be hers. The walls of the temple shook. Stone cracked and crumbled. Freya slipped and landed on her face. She was aware of the temple falling around them, giant chunks of stone blocking her view of Brenn.

Wake up, Freya!

CHAPTER TWENTY-SIX

Eight priestesses hunched over Freya's bed, and all Astrid wanted to do was scream at them to leave her alone. At the center stood Brenn, eyes closed, clutching her staff tightly. The chanting of the other eight priestesses made goosebumps rise over Astrid's skin.

Ruga patted Astrid's back to remind her she had support. Blessedly, against Astrid's advice, Ruga had remained with her through these last two impossible weeks. Astrid could not sleep, but without Ruga, she would not have eaten either. She would not have had a shoulder to cry on, her sisterly love to hang to like a lifeline.

On the bed, Freya's forehead broke out into a sheen of sweat, and her eyes moved rapidly under her eyelids, as if experiencing a vivid dream.

Brenn staggered back just as Freya gasped to life. Freya thrust herself upright. The priestesses moved as one, pinning her down, still chanting.

"Let go of her!" Astrid screamed. "Can't you see it worked?"

The priestesses did not listen to their queen. Instead, they finished the chant. Ruga took hold of Astrid's elbow, keeping her in place so she would not jump forward and start stabbing at them the way she had slashed at her own guard when Freya had been shot.

"Water," Freya croaked.

Brenn scrambled to bring her the pitcher. The chanting softened and petered out to nothing. Its absence was somehow more chilling than its presence had been.

Freya's trembling hands grasped the pitcher, and Brenn held the base as Freya drank directly from the lip in greedy gulps.

Astrid broke free of Ruga's grip and threw her arms around Freya. Her bodyguard was sweaty, and she smelled sour, but she was *alive.* Stars, she was alive. Grateful tears landed on the collar of Freya's borrowed priestess robe.

Freya's hands rose to hug Astrid back, but her grip was weak and wavering, feather-like.

"Don't you dare die on me, Freya Wedd," Astrid murmured into her collarbone.

"Not just yet," Freya promised.

Someone cleared their throat, and the patter of the priestesses' sandal-clad feet left the room.

Astrid had forgotten they were there. She pressed into the skin of Freya's neck and felt the warmth of her—proof that she could survive anything.

"Do you need space?" Brenn asked over Astrid's head.

"No," said Freya. "It's all right."

Astrid pulled back and knelt at the side of the bed. She took Freya's hand in her own.

"Hello, Ruga," Freya said. "I am flattered that my near-death is important enough to summon you all the way over the channel."

Her gray eyes were bright in the light of the evening sun. Astrid leaned in and pressed a kiss to her temple, and Freya flashed her a smile.

"I am glad you are awake and well, Freya," Ruga said.

Freya snorted. She always had liked to get under Ruga's skin, and when she couldn't, it bothered her. It was impossible to needle someone so pure of heart as Ruga—the only reason Astrid did not intervene in their dynamic.

"We are narrowing our assassin search to orc women," Brenn announced. "Freya caught better sight of the assassin than anyone else."

"Two weeks and not even a lead," Freya said dryly. "You people really do need me here."

"Yes, we do," said Astrid.

"Is there anyone who raised your suspicions in the past?" Ruga asked.

"Everyone does. We've had many strangers in the castle lately," Freya said. "And, the last time we had an arrow shot at us, someone saw us together."

"Intimately, you mean," said Ruga.

"There may have been some intimacy, yes," said Freya, unashamed.

Astrid had been so useless during all of this. Here they were, questioning Freya right after she'd woken, and Astrid had completely forgotten the circumstances of the first attempt. Their first kiss, interrupted. "I'm so sorry. I've had a lot on my mind."

"I knew," Brenn admitted.

"So it's not necessarily someone close to you." Ruga's shoulders slumped with relief. "I feared it was someone in the félag."

"It might have been better if it was, no?" Brenn said. "We have not narrowed down an identity or a location or a motive. At least we would have something to go off."

"I do not like to think of spies in my midst," Astrid said. She stroked the side of Freya's face, and Freya let her. "The assassin did target the Sydlig king. He died of his wounds."

"Can we rule out the Sydlig retinue, then?" asked Brenn.

"A country's people can surely turn against their own," said Astrid.

"I wouldn't rule out anyone," Freya said, stretching. "I need to pee, badly, and then I will look into it straight away. It does not bode well for us that the assassin has such a strong lead. She could be anywhere."

The room was silent. Brenn and Ruga looked to Astrid, and only when Astrid felt their burning glares did she speak. "You need to heal. I won't allow you to overexert yourself with an investigation."

"What?" Freya asked. "Where are my knives?"

"Freya, no," said Astrid. "I am having you sent to the priestesses' temple. They will be able to watch over you and track your healing progress. You'll be much safer there from any assassination attempts."

"Only the people in this room know about the plan," Brenn assured Freya.

"You want to keep me out of trouble, you mean." Freya's features cooled from frustration to something calculating. "You're getting rid of me because you're scared."

"Freya—" started Astrid.

"No," Freya said. "You've pushed other people away." She swallowed, clearly considering her next words before saying them. "You pushed Ruga away."

"That's vicious," Ruga chided. "Astrid is only part of the reason I left Torden. It wasn't Astrid's idea to betroth me to an elvish princess. It was yours."

"You agreed to it, though. Happily," Freya said.

Astrid pushed down a wave of guilt. "I want you to be safe. I can't lose you."

"I'm the one who advised the rest period," Brenn added. "This is my idea. Nobody else's. I'll check on you often. Keep you posted on how everything is going."

"I cannot find an assassin from inside the temple walls," Freya protested. "Where is Varin? I need to speak with him."

"He's busy with interrogations," Ruga said. "He has it handled."

"Does he?" Freya scoffed. "Two weeks, no answers. He *must* move faster."

"Please leave us," Astrid said. Sorrow nearly choked her. "Get out."

Ruga took Brenn's arm and escorted her from the room.

"You don't mean what you said," Astrid said. It was hopeful more than anything.

"I do. You shut yourself off from people because you think you cannot be close. It was something I admired about you," Freya said, "until it applied to me."

Astrid licked her lips. "I am sending you to the temple. Please rest, Freya. If you love me at all, please rest."

Freya turned away from her. Astrid tried to be understanding. Once, Freya had locked Astrid too in a room for her safety, and it had broken Astrid down. Astrid understood; she had been in the same position. The resistance was not unreasonable.

But Freya's words still hurt.

"Would you like your dagger back?" Astrid asked.

"No," Freya said quickly. "Keep it on you at all times."

Knees aching from where she'd knelt on the floor, Astrid stood. "I will have Ruga draw a bath for you, and then Hrothgar will escort you to the temple. Please, as my subject and my...friend, follow my orders just this once."

Freya said nothing. Astrid gathered her emotions to face Ruga and Brenn, whose muttering she could hear in the antechamber, and left Freya to sulk.

Ruga and Brenn were quiet when Astrid entered the antechamber. She was grateful, and fairly certain she could not speak without crying. Two weeks, she'd spent worrying, sleepless nights by Ruga, who stayed awake and told Astrid tales of Branwen and Elketh and her new rose garden and the delightful things that now occupied her days. Two weeks of torturous waiting, only for Freya to wake up and cut Astrid with her words.

There was part of Astrid that thought Freya was right. Astrid was protecting Freya by sending her away—protecting her from assassins and political enemies, but also from Astrid herself. And maybe Astrid was guarding her own heart. She'd had time to think about death and love and the roles they played in her life, and she knew they'd been taking higher precedence than a queen should allow. There was little energy to spend on ruling a country when the person she cared for most had nearly died.

Freya was right. And Astrid was a coward.

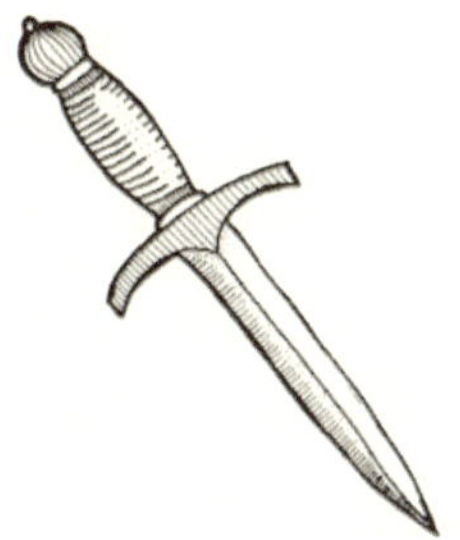

CHAPTER TWENTY-SEVEN

The queen really meant to send Freya away.

Freya dragged her feet down the hall, closed in on either side by members of the guard who had confiscated her weapons. Not the queen's félag, but ordinary guards. Somehow this hurt, too, the insult of not needing the higher rank to keep her from running off.

As she was escorted out, Freya played over her last conversation with Astrid. She'd meant to hurt Astrid, to cut into the raw parts of her, and she had seen the hurt on her queen's face, clear as day.

The memory made Freya sick. She shook as she walked, perhaps with regret and perhaps with anger. The things she'd said had been true, but she hadn't needed to say them. Astrid knew already.

Freya had been fooled. She'd really thought Astrid had gotten over the things that made her push Freya away. Sending Freya to the temple was a breach of the trust they had cultivated over the years—trust in Freya to take care of her queen and herself.

The guards stopped at the stables. Freya looked up at the imposing horses built more for tall orcs than smallish humans. She had become accustomed to riding them in Torden with the queen's retinue, but it wasn't going to be easy with her still healing. She considered which of them would be the most reliable for an escape.

Freya's falcon circled overhead, screeching her support. At least Freya would still be able to send messages to Brenn, wherever she ended up.

She had decided on a horse she rode with some regularity and half-plotted her escape from the guards when Hrothgar showed up.

They stood tall in the doorway. Their clothing was nondescript: not the leather armor the félag wore in downtime, nor the casual tunic that identified them as part of the queen's trusted guard.

This was to be secret, then. Did they anticipate she could be assassinated on the way to the temple? The idea was laughable. Who would target Freya over a queen? She was not convinced of her importance.

"I will take you to the temple," Hrothgar said solemnly. Long gone was the orc who had danced with Astrid at the inn.

"Should I have my weapons, Hrothgar?" she asked. "If we are facing such a big threat that I need a skilled escort."

Hrothgar flushed at the compliment. They never were good at taking praise. "It is a short trip, Freya. I am here to defend against your escape, not to protect you."

This made Freya feel a bit better. She turned to the horse she had chosen. "I will take Shadow."

The stable hand—a human boy who could not have been more than fifteen years of age—paled.

Hrothgar patted the neck of a much larger horse already equipped for travel. "We will both take Wodin."

So that was how it was going to be. Freya should have noticed when she'd walked in that she had no choice. The level of agency offered to her in the past had distracted her.

She swallowed her pride and allowed Hrothgar to lift her onto Wodin's back. Getting onto a horse alone was hard enough, and though her physical wounds were healed, her body was weak, recovering from trauma and the effects of poison in her blood. Hrothgar settled in behind her, grabbing the reins.

"Thank you," they said to the guards and the stable boy. Then they were off.

The ride was so short, Freya hardly thought it worth the horse. The horse was there to give her one more obstacle to her escape. She had let these people know her too well.

"I don't suppose you'll let me run off and lie to the queen that I've arrived safely," Freya said when the temple appeared in the distance.

"No," said Hrothgar. "And if you do flee, I would prefer you do so when you are not under my care."

There would be no escape, in any case. They reached the temple, where a group of priestesses waited for Freya in the orange light of the evening. Freya was bundled from the horse and handed directly to them like goods at the market.

She glanced back at Hrothgar as they left. Hrothgar stood still, statue-like, watching. So she was still under their care, Freya thought wryly.

"We have set up accommodations for you," one of the priestesses said. The call of Freya's falcon drowned out their voices, and then everyone was quiet as they looked up in awe at Huginn's broad wingspan.

Huginn was a companion to Freya but an omen to the priestesses. Freya had to admit she did like the idea of unsettling them.

Unfortunately, they only paused for an interval before shuffling Freya forward in a newly uncomfortable silence. Freya had a moment to take in the outside of the temple with its grand but simple stone arches, surrounded on either side by trees shedding their leaves. The sunset lent the stone a glow, making Freya's eyes water.

She shuddered. Then, against her will, she went inside.

If Freya had hoped for a single moment of alone time, she was mistaken. She was subjected to a tour of the temple first. The priestesses lived in simple rooms with bunk beds behind the main temple, which was open to the public. There was a courtyard, and chilly autumn air swept over Freya as she walked its perimeter. The priestess showing her around was named Esja, and she seemed nice enough, considering Freya's opinion of how poorly Vakker's orc priestesses treated Brenn.

In the middle of the courtyard was an ugly tin bird bath big enough to drown in. Freya began to ask what it was for, but two other priestesses entered the courtyard with soap, brushes, and towels.

Steam rose from the surface of the tub.

"I've already bathed today," Freya protested.

"A cleansing," said Esja. "To purify you for the goddess."

Freya made a conscious effort not to roll her eyes as Esja gestured for her to strip down. She removed her clothes and passed them into Esja's outheld hand. Esja coughed, gesturing to Freya's ankle. Sighing, Freya handed her the last knife hidden on her person.

"I will be wanting that back," she said.

Esja pursed her lips. "You won't need weapons here. Any violence committed in a temple will be retributed by the goddess."

Freya held her tongue. She knew from experience this was untrue.

As she approached the tub, she tried to hold herself tall, but the cold and her dissipating strength made it difficult to keep her head high. After being bedridden for weeks, she would be weaker, she had to remind herself—and she'd been not just bedridden, but nearly murdered. It was perfectly fine not to be at her best.

In contradiction of Freya's grumpy attitude, the bath was quite nice, less of a bath than a brushing. The priestesses fragranced the tub with a eucalyptus oil. The smell soothed her and her aching skin, made her feel more awake. One priestess brushed her hair while the other gently ran bristles over her back.

"The hands," Freya heard one of them whisper. She quickly withdrew her hands under the water. The relaxing feeling left as quickly as it had come.

She was more on guard afterward. She chided herself for not being protective of her privacy in the first place. Vessels of the goddess as they were, Freya had seen how judgmental these priestesses could be.

When she rose from the tub, still covered in suds, they did not demand she go back in. One of them patted her with the towel, and the other helped her into an itchy woolen robe. It was blessedly unfeminine, formless and ugly.

Nowhere to hide knives, though, Freya noted. She would have to get an emergency weapon somewhere, and she imagined she was not allowed to leave, even though no one had explicitly told her so.

Esja informed Freya of a strict schedule of prayers, preparing meals, picking and drying herbs, polishing metal. All very dull, but she'd been made to do worse.

Esja seemed apologetic about the many responsibilities. "We have only delegated work to you that you should be able to do in your condition. I know you are just new and only staying for a while. But there is always more work than we have the time for."

"How long is a while?" Freya asked, and Esja once more pursed her lips. Freya surmised she would be stuck here for months.

"You'll join us for dinner and a meditation session tonight," Esja said. "We'll start you on your duties tomorrow."

"Lovely," Freya drawled.

"Do you have any restrictions with your diet?"

"No," said Freya. She wondered where the food came from—where it had been purchased, caught, or gathered; who had prepared it; what the kitchens were like, as she had not been shown the inside. These were all things to be aware of at Vakker Castle.

For all she knew, the food here could be poisoned. But then, she didn't have her queen to protect from poisoning.

The temple did not have a separate dining hall. They had a small, drafty room with a long table and benches on either side. A small hearth burned at the corner with a simple herring stew from which the orcs ladled portions. Communal, Freya noted with some relief. If the food was poisoned, they would all go down.

She mopped up the stew with a hearty slice of half-stale bread and ate it reluctantly. Her strength would be necessary to get out of here whenever they decided to leave her alone. There was no conversation at dinner, and Freya was grateful. Only the scraping of silverware and the slurping of stew filled the room.

When they were done, two of the priestesses came around and collected everyone's bowls. Freya licked hers clean, not caring what they thought of her. She filed out of the room with the others, noting that amidst the elaborate designs of the robes, hers alone was gray and drab. Perhaps this was the kind of garb intended for novices.

But the different robe seemed another way to set her apart.

At the exit to the courtyard, Freya glimpsed an opening into the scullery, where the two orcs who had gathered the plates were scrubbing them clean. They were chatting. Freya recognized their conversation for what it was. The same kind of gossip that echoed through the castle kitchens.

Freya slid out of line, invisible as ever, and hid against the inside of the open door.

"No, I swear. In her personal bedchamber, not the infirmary," the one on the left said, and Freya's skin flushed hot with anger.

"Are you sure? It sounds made-up," the one on the right said.

"I heard it from someone who was there. She said the queen never left her side, day or night. She was utterly sleepless and distraught."

Stand up for your queen, Freya begged the second orc with all of her heart. In the silence that ensued, someone splashed water, and Freya almost thought her wish would come true.

"She's just an attendant?" the orc on the right asked.

"A handmaiden, I think. They call her the queen's shadow, but it sounds like the queen was hers, if you catch my meaning."

Freya reached for knives that weren't there.

Someone cleared their throat behind Freya. She did not jump; she had heard Esja's authoritative footsteps approach and expected to be reprimanded.

"Are you cleaning or gossiping?" Esja asked the two orcs dryly.

The two priestesses did jump. It only took them a moment to notice Freya, two feet shorter than Esja.

"You would not speak ill of your queen, surely? When you know her trusted handmaiden is here with us, no less?" Esja said.

The two bowed their heads. Sorrier for getting caught, Freya thought.

"No, Esja," they said together.

Esja shuffled Freya away from the door without touching her. The others were in the courtyard, sitting on the cold ground in rows. No one showed signs of feeling the chill.

"I must apologize for their behavior," Esja whispered. "Some of us get bored, and recent events have caused excitement. It's not often we are called to the queen's side. I am sure they did not mean anything by it."

If everyone was talking about the queen like this, Astrid was not respected in this place. Perhaps the priestesses' devotion to the goddess offset the loyalty to their queen.

"It's fine," Freya snapped, and found a place at the back of the courtyard to sulk.

Esja took a spot at the front of the gathered group, facing away from them. The last dregs of sunlight dissipated. Stars poked through the veil of night, and a cool breeze uninhibited by the walls of the temple rushed through them.

"We will start with a prayer," Esja said, and Freya frowned through the chant, though she obediently closed her eyes. They were swirling up some kind of magic between them, but she knew not what it was for. She wished she had paid closer attention to Brenn's explanations of her magic.

"Close your eyes and allow the goddess to flow through you," Esja said when the chant ended. "I shall wake you all in a quarter hour."

Freya tried not to make any noise that would garner unwanted attention, but she wanted to laugh at them all. What exactly was this supposed to accomplish?

Minutes passed, and Freya's mind wandered. With her eyes closed and just the sounds of nature around her, Freya finally found she could focus.

An assassin was on the loose, and Freya needed to figure out who she was. Her gut told her the assassin was still in the area. Varin had not discovered the culprit, despite what Freya was sure were his best efforts. The assassin had to be an expert at what she did—not just at archery, but stealth. Making herself invisible.

Someone like Freya.

No. Not so much like Freya. Someone like the person Freya used to be. She did not slink into tents and cut throats. She did not poison people anymore.

She allowed, just a bit, for her old self to leak into the new.

The assassin, if she was such an expert, would not have missed any of her marks. If that was an assumption Freya could work with, then the assassin had intentionally swiped Freya's ear with her arrow the first time around. Not a true attempt, but a warning, perhaps.

A warning of *what*? To create fear? To keep everyone on edge? Would it not have been better to have killed Astrid from the start? That was what Freya would have done. She would have taken out her target and been long gone, but the assassin's target was still alive.

She wasn't thinking about this in the right light, even now.

Freya brought herself back to the human who snuck around camps, doing the bidding of the latest warlord to defeat a competing warband.

The assassin had also targeted, and killed, King Skarde.

This was not one warband against another. This was one warband against two—one person against everyone. Ulfur would order such an assassination done, or the assassin could work for someone else gaining power in Lynby, a rival warlord to Ulfur's rule. It was hard to get consistent news from Lynby, even with her contacts, due to the disorganization and shifting power structure.

Think, Freya, think.

The king's brother had been murdered by poison. Was it possible whoever had poisoned him was also the person who had killed Skarde and nearly killed Freya? But why the different techniques?

The arrows had been daubed in poison, Freya reasoned. She thought back to when the first arrow had grazed her ear, how irrationally she had acted in the aftermath. Perhaps it was not only because of the possibility of losing Astrid. Poison would also have induced this behavior, but the cut had been smaller, and Brenn had taken care of it before it had gone too far.

Poison and arrows, arrows and poison. Why not a poisoned arrow for the king's brother, too? Why the delay between the assassination of him and the king, when Freya would have taken them out in succession?

She was so, so close to answers. And she was also tired. A bone-deep weariness had settled into her body, no longer fueled by the adrenaline of the new environment. If her body was not at her best, her brain wasn't, either. She clenched her fist to quell the urge to pound it into the cold, hard dirt.

"You may wake," Esja said from the front of the group.

Freya's frustration boiled over. The quiet was the first opportunity she'd had to truly think through everything. She needed to get out of here.

And she needed a drink.

CHAPTER TWENTY-EIGHT

There was little Astrid could do about the assassin on the loose.

Varin had guards investigating the castle, searching rooms, fortifying weak spots. What good was any of it? They were unlikely to find the assassin's journal, wherein she'd laid out all her plans. A creeping frustration overcame Astrid as she was subjected to meeting after meeting to discuss suspicious finds and motives. None were fruitful.

During the fifth meeting of the day, Astrid looked behind her for Freya's presence. Of course, Freya was gone. Astrid had looked back, again and again, and Freya was still not there, and it was Astrid's fault.

The things Freya had said to Astrid had stung in a way only Freya could hurt her. There was a kernel of truth to each one—Astrid had pushed Freya away for as long as they'd known each other. Freya, with her watchful gray eyes, had told Astrid she was interested in a million ways, had showed her love in just as many, and Astrid was the one who'd chosen not to act. Always, she'd been the one holding them back.

An ache started behind Astrid's eyes.

Varin held up a key for which no one knew the lock and sighed. "I believe some unfortunate historian can no longer enter their dwelling. I don't know if this warrants a meeting."

Astrid stood and marched to the exit.

She was aware of the silence that ensued, but she did not care, particularly, how she came off. The guards at the door shuffled after her as she briskly walked out, out, out, into the night air and under the moon.

She stuffed her hands under her armpits. "Help me," she murmured to the sky. Freya did not believe in the goddess, or perhaps not in her power, but Astrid wasn't above begging. She kept doing the wrong thing, and at this rate, she'd never get anything right. Nothing ever went as Astrid Karrsdaughter wished.

She needed all the help she could get.

A warm hand curled over Astrid's shoulder. She avoided looking back—the same gesture she'd repeated all day, undoubtedly noticed by others.

"You must be tired," Ruga said.

"I am quite sick of not going anywhere with this," said Astrid.

"And missing Freya?"

Astrid huffed. "She is always there. I am not coping well."

Ruga stepped in front of Astrid. Her eyebrow quirked, but she said nothing. Astrid was never so straightforward with her emotions. In Ruga's absence, in allowing herself to have Freya... She'd changed.

"She needed to be put somewhere safe where she could heal. Brenn was right, and so were you to follow through," Ruga argued.

"She has served others her whole life," Astrid said. "It is not right of me to force her to do anything."

"You're thinking about the things she said before she left," Ruga said knowingly.

"Have I not pushed her away?" Astrid asked. The ache behind her eyes worsened. The tears would come soon, and she did not want to shed them in front of anyone except Ruga. The guards who'd followed them were not far.

"You have pushed many people away," Ruga said. "Many more than you needed to."

"I know." Astrid had pushed Ruga away, too.

Astrid had thought that, as queen, creating distance commanded respect. Maybe in another time, another world where Ulfur didn't exist, she would have become queen and been allowed to flourish in a peaceful, golden era of Torden.

In this place, where enemies could lurk in the shadows, she'd needed to be unequivocally strong and impenetrable.

Yet everyone had seen her break for Freya.

She cursed herself once, then twice, and then the tears came.

Ruga enveloped Astrid in her arms. Their dynamic had always been like this—Ruga the caring sister, even though she was younger, and Astrid being cared for. Astrid had pushed Ruga away, emotionally and physically. She had not resisted when Freya proposed Ruga's marriage. Ruga was not far in Branwen, but she was free from the burdens Astrid had handed to her every day. Free to choose for herself what she wanted. Free to choose love.

Astrid had given Ruga the fate she wished for herself.

With Ruga's arms around her, Astrid waited until her eyes dried and a deep cold crept past her cloak. She dabbed her face on the furry hem and breathed in painful gulps of night air.

Someone approached quietly, footsteps on the dry ground.

Astrid did look back this time. It was Hedda. The former captain of Astrid's félag was careful to look at her queen and not at Ruga, even though Ruga was the one who said, "Hello, Hedda. How can we help you?"

"Ruga," Hedda said, nodding. "Your Majesty, Guthmar and his retinue will be leaving soon. He wishes to speak with you."

Astrid had asked Guthmar what was going to happen with Sydlig's throne, and in response, he had locked himself in his rooms. She suspected, in the absence of the king and the king's brother, Guthmar himself would serve as king in the interim until Sydlig's council had time to sort out the succession.

The assassination of the king would make this a difficult job to hold, particularly for someone who would rather watch birds than rule a country.

Astrid felt a pang of sympathy for Guthmar. She had not wanted to be queen; she knew what it was like to have such responsibility thrust upon you.

"I will speak with him," Astrid said.

When they got there, Guthmar was packing his bags with the help of Alvor and Tassi. Tassi removed several items from the bags—gifts, Astrid realized, from people around the castle, ranging from silverware in the kitchens to the book with the birds. Alvor muttered to Tassi, but his hunched shoulders gave no room for this indulgence.

Astrid understood why. It did not look good to come home with a series of trinkets from the country where the king had been murdered.

One of the guards from Guthmar's retinue was present, but there was no sign of the other staff.

"The serving staff was sent home," said Tassi, brusquely, when he saw Astrid's unshielded bewilderment. "Our other guard is with your armorer, who was kind enough to offer fresh equipment for the rest of the late king's retinue."

King Skarde's guards still roamed the castle, angrily upturning whatever mattresses or upholstery they felt would contain the assassin's secrets. Astrid had been careful to appease them with as much food and drink as they wished so they would be less inclined to turn around and stab her.

"Only brought the servants because my cousin insisted," Guthmar grumbled from his luggage. His voice was gravelly, like he'd been crying or drinking. When he looked up, his eyes were red, and his horns twitched.

Astrid recognized this brand of exhaustion well. "If you need any assistance, just let us know how we can provide for you."

"Who is this?" Alvor asked.

Ruga stepped forward. Had they really not met? Astrid supposed Ruga had been by her side while Guthmar dealt with his own problems.

"Ruga Karrsdaughter. The queen's younger sister, and Queen Consort of Branwen." Ruga shook hands with Alvor, and her face brightened. "Oh, do you hunt? My wife loves to hunt. Perhaps we can arrange a visit in a more peaceful time. Branwen is such a beautiful island. A change of scenery might be beneficial—"

"I'm sorry, but I don't think now is a good time," Alvor said, taking back her hand. "We should discuss the succession."

"Of course." Ruga backed away politely.

Where would Guthmar be without his spouses? Astrid wondered as Guthmar rubbed a hand down his face.

"The council is not fond of me," said Guthmar. "But then, they were not fond of Skarde either."

"Guthmar," Tassi warned.

"It's all right, dear," said Alvor. "We should be transparent."

"Thanks, Alvie." Guthmar patted her hand. "The council may go with me, or they may go with someone else. We will have a mourning period for the current king, of course."

"Of course," said Astrid.

"I know it has been said, but I want to extend our sincere condolences for your loss," said Ruga.

Guthmar looked up at her with wet eyes. "He was an unkind man, certainly to me."

"You've had other losses," said Alvor.

"The loss of my freedom," said Guthmar.

An awkward silence ensued.

"In any case," Astrid said, "we are grateful we could host you here, Ambassador. I have enjoyed your presence immensely."

She was surprised to find it was true. Whatever the political forces around Guthmar—however they beat him down—he was a ray of sunshine in an otherwise bleak world. Someone who could find the good in little things. A rarity to Astrid, who saw the world so differently. She was swept up with the sudden urge to hug him.

Guthmar threw his arms around Astrid. His enthusiastic squeeze was unlike Ruga's assuring hugs, but it was still the warm embrace of someone who had come to like her, and that was nice, too. Astrid returned the gesture.

"I will let them know you had nothing to do with Skarde's death," said Guthmar. "But they may blame you anyway, you know."

"I know," Astrid said with a sigh.

"I hope your little shadow is healing well," he added in a whisper.

Astrid held her tongue.

"I am sorry that your citizens were hurt by the attacker," said Alvor. "Even with the number of guards present… It's just appalling that everything happened the way it did."

Tassi's lip curled like he wanted to say something.

"May I hug you as well?" Guthmar asked Ruga.

"Why not?" Ruga said. She hugged him too, and then Guthmar sighed with the weight of the world on his shoulders.

"Back to packing. We must go home with haste."

Astrid and Ruga left them. It was kind of Guthmar to consider Freya's health amidst his own turmoil. Astrid did not envy the journey he had ahead of him, no matter how short he might rule.

A strange feeling overcame Astrid, and she stopped at a window and looked out into the night.

Something wasn't right. There were answers in this castle, but the person best at seeking them wasn't here to find them.

A falcon crossed in front of the moon. Even when Freya wasn't physically here, part of her remained.

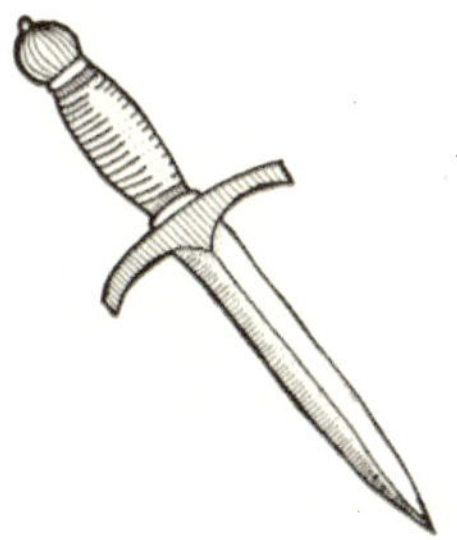

CHAPTER TWENTY-NINE

The Rosebriar Inn was quieter than Freya's last visit.

The smell of ale, stale bodies, and freshly mopped floors brought back the memories of the night Astrid had fled here. An appropriate place to return to, Freya thought. How different things had seemed back then. A night filled with hope. Freya knew she might never feel that way again.

She picked a table at the back corner, warm enough to feel the hearth and keep both exits in view. Two groups huddled close to the hearth: one trio of orcs, one pair of humans. They spoke in low voices. This time of night, it was late enough to be considered early.

Back at the temple, Freya had gone to bed, waited until she couldn't anymore, and then crept out of the shared sleeping quarters to the stable. The horses did not spook—they were unused to crime, their whole lives cared for by priestesses who wore robes like Freya's. Freya had taken one with ease, mounting the horse with the help of a stool, though the ride had been taxing with her recent weakness. She'd slipped into the night like a spirit, stolen alms in her pocket. She would repay the priestesses as soon as she got the chance.

A sleepy barmaid set a tankard of ale before Freya. She had a tentative sip. The ale was lukewarm, hardly worth the stolen money spent to buy it.

Freya could not afford to stay the night. She had to act soon. There wasn't time to sleep.

Returning to the castle was a great way to get herself tied up and dragged to the temple via armed guard. The best thing she could do was bide her time until she could find and confront the assassin on her own. If none of the priestesses had woken when Freya stole the horse, they would certainly report back to Astrid about Freya's absence in the morning.

Unfortunately, Freya couldn't afford to wait. All time left to spare had been used up during her healing period. A distracted Astrid had left everything to Varin. Freya liked the steward, and generally trusted his competence, but he was busy—things slipped past him, as she'd discovered when she first arrived in Torden. He could not put the kind of focus on the assassin that Freya could. And surely Sydlig's council would send investigators to resolve the king's death. That was, if they didn't send an army and blame Torden instead.

Freya drummed her fingers on the table. Ever since the temple, she'd felt an unusual clarity. Suspects filtered through her mind. Many of the visitors were suspicious, but most wouldn't be motivated to kill a king.

The door to the Rosebriar Inn opened, and an orc and a human entered.

Freya shivered against the sudden gust of cold. She made note of the newcomers' garb—cloaks like everyone wore in autumn, no weapons at their hips—and let her eyes fall back to her drink, wary of appearing too interested.

The two approached the hearth. Freya waited for them to settle.

"Freya?" one of them said.

Freya's eyes snapped up. She squinted at the newcomers in the low light of the room. Her knuckles tightened around her ale—she recognized them. Two of the ambassador's servants. Hjotra, the orc, and Ingirun, the human.

She tried to compose herself, gave a little wave. What were Guthmar's servants doing here? Was Varin doing a thorough investigation? If it had been up to Freya, she would have locked down the castle and refused to let anyone leave until she had alibis from every last one of them, and at least two stories to corroborate each. *And* a dead assassin in her hands.

Guthmar's attendants took the seats across from Freya. They smelled of fresh laundry and looked bright, well-rested. Freya felt a prick of envy. She might smell like eucalyptus, and maybe a bit like horse, but she doubted she exuded restfulness.

Once, Freya had winked at Hjotra at the staff table in the dining hall. Guthmar's attendants called her handsome, she remembered. She did not feel handsome now.

"Whatever are you doing here?" Ingirun asked gently. She held up two fingers to the barmaid when the barmaid passed and received a grunt in exchange. "Have you sworn yourself to the goddess since we last saw you?"

Freya tugged at the novice robes. "Something like that."

"We heard you were hurt," said Hjotra.

"Yes," said Freya curtly. "Perhaps not a conversation to have around others."

The two exchanged a half-frightened look. Freya tried to cool her agitation. They'd found her, pallid and half-healed, wearing priestess's robes at an inn in the early hours of the morning. Excuses would be lacking in logic. A change in subject was better.

"What are you two doing here?" Freya asked quietly. "I thought you would be with the ambassador."

"We've been dismissed," said Ingirun.

"He never really wanted us there," confided Hjotra. "I'm sure he was dying to get rid of us."

The ale tasted sour on Freya's tongue. "I suppose he didn't know what to do with you."

"No, I don't suppose so," Ingirun said. "His spouses, on the other hand..."

Hjotra rolled her eyes. "Anyway, we've been sent away to find other employment, but traveling all the way to Sydlig is a lot of work. We thought we would stick around and see if there were any opportunities here."

"What brings you to Rosebriar in particular?" Freya asked.

The barmaid set ale before the two attendants. They thanked her, clinked their tankards against each other, and took generous gulps.

"That's good ale," said Ingirun.

"Better than back home. Just another reason to stay in Torden," said Hjotra.

"What brings you to Rosebriar?" Freya repeated.

Ingirun blinked at her, expression blank. "Oh. Uh. We heard there was good business here."

"From whom?"

"Sorry?"

"Where did you hear that?" Freya said.

"From someone in the kitchens?" said Hjotra. "Stars, Freya, you sound like the steward."

Ingirun snorted.

Freya closed her eyes. She needed answers badly. The staff knew everything—she'd made herself approachable to them for a reason. These two had to have some information. Freya couldn't just interrogate them outright.

"Sorry," said Freya. "Long night. I thought this place was a hidden hole-in-the-wall for Torden, so I am surprised anyone from Sydlig has heard of it."

The two relaxed. "That's all right, Freya," said Ingirun.

"Is Varin being his usual cranky self?" Freya said, cracking a smile she hoped looked remotely genuine.

"Ugh," said Hjotra. "Couldn't piss without him knowing. How many questions did he ask us?"

"At least a thousand," said Ingirun.

So Varin *had* done his job. Maybe he'd cleared the two of them early on and given Guthmar permission to release them. The idea of letting suspects go didn't sit well with Freya, but she was glad to have confirmation something had been done.

"Sounds tedious," Freya said.

"Truly," Ingirun said. "Say, do you want to go in on a room together? We've been making stops all day, and we are awfully tired."

"I won't be staying," said Freya.

"I suppose I've never seen a priestess stay anywhere except the temple," Hjotra said good-naturedly.

"Right," Freya said. There was no way these two wouldn't gossip about seeing her in novice robes here. She could only hope it would take a while to get back to anyone important. "Well, it was nice to see you."

"Won't you stay for just another drink?" Ingirun pleaded. "On me. I'm so curious about Torden traditions. It would be nice to know some things before we get established here."

Freya's first instinct was to say no. The years in Torden had made her soft, though. She had once been a transplant to the country, taken in by its people and welcomed despite her past.

"I suppose just one drink would be fine," Freya said.

The barmaid brought another, and the attendants interrogated Freya about Torden's culture: What was Freya's favorite part of Torden? Where were the best markets for fresh fish? What kind of labor would Freya recommend for someone who wanted to get to know the country? How did the forestry industry compare to Sydlig's?

Freya's eyes started to close as she answered the tedious questions. She downed the ale steadily. The faster she sipped, the faster she could get out of here, but they'd know she wanted to escape them if she drank too quickly.

Freya had to leave while she could still get on her horse. She was already so tired. Maybe she could find a wind-sheltered corner of town to sleep in—she'd slumbered through worse conditions. She would just have a nap, and then be on her way.

The sight of the bottom of the tankard was a surprise to Freya. She set it down a little too roughly, her movements sluggish. This damn injury. She needed more rest than she'd thought.

"Well, ladies," Freya said. "I'll be taking my leave now."

She stood from the bench and black spots filled her vision. With a gasp, she grabbed the edge of the table.

"You don't look well," said Ingirun.

She didn't feel well. This went beyond exhaustion, beyond a wound in the process of magical healing.

"Will you please stay? I'll order a room for you at once," Hjotra said.

Freya gathered her bearings, leaning her hip against the table. In front of Ingirun and Hjotra were two untouched tankards of ale. Had they finished their first round? She couldn't remember. She recalled them sipping, but not gulping.

"What did you do to me?" she asked.

"What do you mean?" asked Hjotra. The orc stood to help Freya, touching her elbow, but Freya nudged her away.

She caught a whiff of them again. Fresh laundry. But hadn't they been traveling all day?

To the horse. Now. Freya shoved herself off the table and began to stumble away, but her feet gave out. Her thoughts were slow, her previous clarity gone. "Help?" she called.

"Oi, what's going on here?" Another voice, from the other side of the room. "Is your friend all right?"

"Yes, I think she's just had too much to drink," Ingirun said. She lifted Freya's face from the floor. "How many did you have, Freya?"

"You poisoned me," Freya choked out. She curled her tongue in on itself. The flesh felt fuzzy; a bitter taste coated her mouth.

Freya's ears rang. The only indication a newcomer had arrived was the cold air washing over her clammy face. The air was stabilizing, and she had enough left of herself to look up.

The silhouette of an orc woman stood in the doorway.

Freya reached for the stool next to her head, meaning to swing it around and knock over Ingirun. Her limbs weren't working like they should. Her gloved fingers glanced off the leg of the stool.

A pair of muddy boots stepped into Freya's line of sight. She tried to look up, but her vision was poor, darkening around the edges, spots in the middle.

"Help," Freya croaked.

"I don't know what's going on here," the voice from earlier said, closer, "but I don't like it. I'm escorting this woman upstairs to recover."

"Where did the barmaid go?" someone else asked.

Freya tried to grab the leg of the stool again. A boot stomped on her hand. She whimpered.

Arguing broke out over her head. She couldn't make sense of it. Drool pooled at the corner of her mouth, and she tried to wipe it away, wincing at the crushed bones in her hand. She thrust herself onto her elbows and began to crawl.

Someone grabbed her hair and yanked her head back. Freya tried to resist, but whatever she'd been drugged with was too potent.

Her head slammed into the floor. Darkness overtook her.

CHAPTER THIRTY

Sleep eluded Astrid. She tossed and turned, but guilt ate at her. Freya was trapped in the temple like a caged animal against her will, and Astrid had put her there. She had used her powers as queen to override her beloved bodyguard's wishes.

Now that Guthmar and his retinue had left, Astrid was sure Freya would be upset that she hadn't done more to keep them around. She couldn't see how she could have kept them longer—it wasn't like she could ask them to stay back from a country whose king had just been murdered.

Other things caused her concern, too. Freya, and how she would react when she was fully healed. The assassin, out there somewhere. Ruga, still in Vakker Castle with an assassin on the loose. Sydlig, politically unstable, ready to make a big change with their king—maybe someone who would ally with Lynby and go to war with Torden.

How hard it would be to make up with Freya. How much she wanted her by her side, warming her bed. How deeply it would hurt when Astrid lost her.

She tossed and turned some more.

Hours later, as sleep just barely began to lay claim to Astrid, a loud yowling brought her to full consciousness. She sat up abruptly in bed, upsetting Fenrir—the source of the noise.

Fenrir stopped yowling, tilted his head, and then yowled again when Astrid did not move.

"Very well," Astrid said. "I will do something about Freya."

She'd made a mistake—one of many. Pushing Freya away was futile. They were bound by their wyrd to be together—this, Astrid did believe with all her might. Keeping her distance only delayed the inevitable, and for what?

Astrid pulled a cloak over her nightgown, slid Freya's dagger into its sheath, and checked the window. Thank the goddess she had a window to look out of again—the moment Freya had gone to the temple, Varin had had Astrid's things moved back to her old rooms, assured by the many guards on patrol and the thorough sweep of the castle that she was now safe.

Through the window, the night sky was yet dark, and a chill crept through the glass to Astrid's fingers. She shuddered.

Apologizing would put Astrid's mind at ease. She needed to let Freya know she didn't mean to rob her of her agency. Perhaps the temple was treating Freya well, and she would want to stay.

At the very least, Freya deserved a choice.

Hrothgar and Sigurd, standing watch at Astrid's door, followed her silently to the stables. Two half-asleep orcs sprang into action to bridle her horse. Astrid pinned her cloak closed and accepted Hrothgar's help onto the horse's back, and then the three of them were off. Blessedly, no one told her leaving the castle was a bad idea, though it occurred to her Freya or Varin would have. Or Hedda.

The night ride to the temple was objectively peaceful—but the peace was misplaced, stifling in its solitude. Lanterns lit the way as they approached the town. The bugs were dead, most birds gone south.

Astrid arrived at the temple with the gut feeling that something was very wrong.

"I'll run ahead," Sigurd offered.

Astrid wished she could approach herself, that it was proper to do so. She watched from horseback as Sigurd rang the bell at the entrance and a priestess came to greet her with a furrow in her brow.

"Something is amiss," Astrid said to Hrothgar. She dismounted the horse and led it by the reins to the entrance.

"We don't know when," said Esja, the head priestess. "One of the others heard her wake, but they thought she needed to relieve herself. Three priestesses heard the horse leave."

Gone, then. Freya was already gone. Like Astrid, when she was caged, she would find her way out, one way or another.

Esja paled when she saw Astrid. "Your Majesty. Can I get you some tea?"

"Do you know where Freya may have gone?" Astrid asked.

"We do not know, Your Majesty. I apologize."

Astrid's heart twisted.

"She will be back soon, I'm sure," said Hrothgar. "She is extremely competent, Your Majesty. She can care for herself."

Despite her worry, Astrid recognized the truth in Hrothgar's words.

"I tried my best to make her feel welcome," said Esja. "I do not think she liked it here."

"She didn't," said Astrid. "We will have to let her come back on her own."

Astrid could give her that—time away, chosen on her own terms. She assured Esja she laid no blame upon the priestesses.

"I am sorry to keep you up and busy," Astrid said to her félag.

"It's what we are here for, Your Majesty," said Hrothgar.

Gratitude swelled in Astrid's chest. No matter how much she isolated herself, she was not alone.

The lanterns around the stable were fully lit when Astrid returned. A stable girl ran toward the main castle, stopped when she saw Astrid, and turned around and ran back.

Astrid allowed the staff to take her horse with her pulse racing. "Why are we so active tonight?"

"We had an unexpected visitor, Your Majesty," the stable girl said.

"And who might that be?" she asked.

Shrouded in shadow, Tassi stepped forth from one of the stalls. "I'm the visitor." He bore deep bags under his eyes, and his clothing was soiled with dirt and sweat.

"I thought you left," Astrid said. "Did something happen?"

The assassin, she thought. Oh, stars, the assassin.

"Is Guthmar well?" she asked, voice rising.

"For now, he is, yes," said Tassi. "He has Skarde's old guard. They do not like him, but they will defend him." He cleared his throat. "He is kinder to them than Skarde was."

Astrid touched Freya's dagger under her cloak. "What's happened, Tassi?"

"I have kept something from you," Tassi said. "I wasn't sure it was worth sharing, but now I think it is important. It's about—"

Everyone looked up as another horse approached. The animal moved unnaturally fast, as if enchanted. As the horse and rider entered the ring of light from the stables, Brenn came into view. The stable staff rushed forward to help her from her horse.

"Why are you gathered here?" Brenn asked, breathless.

"Finish what you were saying," Astrid ordered. "Brenn, you will have to wait."

"I met Guthmar years ago. He is a good man, and I knew I wanted to marry him," Tassi started.

Astrid tried to hold her composure.

"He has his quirks, as you know. I love him deeply, and I always will. His heart is so big—he loves everything, everyone, and so I accept where his heart goes, and I am happy to share his light with others."

"There is no need to defend your love," Astrid said. "I understand the things you appreciate about him."

Tassi nodded in acknowledgment. "A month before we left for Torden, he met a woman. She was a visitor to the Sydlig court, a well-respected adviser with connections to nobility. She was witty, kind, and a good listener. When Guthmar talked to her, she genuinely cared about everything he said, no matter how odd or mundane."

Astrid's blood chilled. "Tassi," she said, "are you meaning to tell me you barely know…?"

"I have gotten to know Alvor over the past few months. She…is quite different than I am. But I believe she hides much."

Alvor, only married to Guthmar briefly before coming to Torden. Impossible. Why would King Skarde have let Guthmar take someone so new to court with him to serve as Sydlig's ambassador?

"She's our assassin?" Astrid demanded. She turned to Brenn. "Did you know this?"

"Of course I did not know," said Brenn. "I think Freya would have."

"Freya would have been more cautious of someone new," Astrid said, knowing she was coming off as snippy, beyond the point of caring.

"Perhaps she missed this one thing," Brenn said gently.

"Freya doesn't miss anything," said Astrid.

"I don't know if she is an assassin," Tassi interjected. "She fell ill shortly after we left for Sydlig. She stayed behind in Vakker—in the city. Her stomach is not good. Guthmar wanted to hold everyone up and wait, but she insisted we go on without her. I had a feeling...and I tried to follow her to the city, but I couldn't find her."

"Was she poisoned?" Astrid asked.

"I don't know. She didn't have the king's brother's pustules, if that's what you're asking. But that was a late symptom," he threw in quickly.

Astrid grabbed Tassi by the shoulders. There was fear in his eyes, and also defeat. She wanted to shake answers out of him. "What are you hiding from me?"

"Only my hunch, Your Majesty," he said.

"And what," Astrid said, "is your hunch?"

Tassi swallowed. "I hesitate to say. I do not like to throw around accusations. And it would hurt Guthmar."

"Unless Guthmar has been the assassin all along, and he poisoned Alvor?" But that didn't make sense. Even if Guthmar was adept with poison and arrows, he'd been there for the second assassination attempt, just as frightened as everyone else. Astrid had seen him string a bow, and his form was poor. He would not have been able to make the shot that killed King Skarde.

"He wouldn't," Tassi said. "He would never."

Brenn nudged her staff between the two of them. "Queen Astrid, I hope I do not speak out of turn, but I must insist on your attention immediately."

Astrid released Tassi. He slumped back, closed his eyes.

"Go," said Astrid. "King Guthmar needs you."

"Yes, Your Majesty," said Tassi. "Thank you for hearing me."

As Tassi mounted his horse, Astrid turned her acid glare to Brenn.

"Your Majesty." Brenn curtsied.

"You know where Freya is," Astrid guessed.

Brenn's knuckles were white against her staff. "She's not safe, Queen Astrid."

Astrid's mind went blank. "She's not safe?"

"She's in danger," said Brenn. "I don't know where she is. I saw a poor image of a woman playing the lyre, lined in red and fraying at the edges."

"The Rosebriar Inn," Astrid whispered. It made sense that Freya would go there, and the connection to Astrid touched her. But... "What kind of danger is she in, Brenn?"

"I would go immediately," Brenn said.

"We're hours away. Will we make it in time?"

"We have to try," said Brenn.

Astrid lifted her head at the stable girl. The staff rushed forward, helping everyone onto their horses. Astrid, Brenn, Hrothgar, Sigurd.

And Hedda, running from the castle. She wore no armor, unlike Hrothgar and Sigurd. Astrid caught sight of the scar on her face, the flash of short blue hair pulled back, the angry glare in her eyes.

"I'm coming," Hedda choked, hands on her knees for support. "Please get me a horse."

"We need to go," said Brenn.

"You'll have to catch up," Astrid said. She was calm—a leader sending her soldiers into battle. This, she knew how to do. This, she would do for Freya.

She had no choice.

CHAPTER THIRTY-ONE

Head throbbing, hand aching, Freya came to on the floor of a candle-lit room. Dimly, she recognized the layout from her last stay at the Rosebriar Inn. Her first thought was that she needed to warn Astrid the owners could be bought off not to intervene when crime happened before their eyes.

Her second thought was that she was going to die.

She tried to lift her head and swore. No concussion, she didn't think, at least. Just sore, and whatever poison had been in her drink was clouding her thoughts. Not fatal—not yet.

Her hands were bound behind her back. She shifted her whole body to get a better view of her surroundings.

A figure sat in a chair before the fireplace, her silhouette limned in warm light. The woman's horns curled around her pink-haired head, unmistakably orcish.

With effort, Freya adjusted herself until she was sitting up. She would not die without looking her killer in the eye.

The figure before the fire rose. She stepped in front of Freya with the same muddy boots as earlier. Defiant, Freya lifted her head and looked into her murderer's face.

"I should have known," Freya said.

Alvor smiled. "I quite like you, Freya," she said. "It's really not personal."

"Taking someone's life is always personal," Freya countered.

Alvor bent to Freya's eye level. "I don't plan to kill you."

"No?" said Freya. "Could have fooled me."

Alvor tilted her head. "Walk me through it. Why would I want to?"

"I won't play games with you. If you're going to kill me, just do it."

Alvor stared until Freya couldn't stand to stare back. Freya shifted her shoulder. The rope around her hands was tight, constricting. She was losing feeling, her fingertips—*bare* fingertips—tingling.

"I used to do this, too, you know," Freya said. "When you want to usurp someone, you kill their leader. When you want to destabilize someone's rule, you take out their second-in-command."

"Funny to think a human considers herself the second-in-command to the orc country of Torden," said Alvor. Her inflection was playful, almost mocking, and Freya tamped down her anger.

"You have always watched us," said Freya. "You let Guthmar wander free and observed on your own. You know how important I am to Astrid."

Alvor whistled. "Not even a title. You *are* close."

"I wish you would kill me already and spare me your monologue."

At this, Alvor laughed. "It's a wonder you've made it this far in life, goading people as you do. Fortunately for you, I am entirely unbothered by your taunts. I've heard worse."

Freya twisted her wrist. It was going to pop, but she thought she could get it out of the rope if she slid it at an angle. Something in there was already broken.

"You don't work for King Skarde," said Freya, "or else you would not have killed him."

"On the contrary, I think plenty of people who worked for King Skarde wanted to kill him. None of them are as brave as I am, though," Alvor said, good-humored. "Guthmar will be king now, and things will be better. You'll see."

What exactly was she playing at? Did she really think the council would want Guthmar to be king? For that matter, did she actually love Guthmar, or was she just a plant to gain access to the leadership of two major orc countries? And *you'll see...* Did she really mean to let Freya live?

Freya could not ask any of her questions. Alvor was a cat, toying with the mouse she'd caught, and Freya did not intend to be a compliant mouse.

"I think I'm drawn to you," Alvor said, "because I see much of myself in you. Every time you enter a room, the first thing you do is check the exits. Your back is always straight. You are alert at all times, vigilant over anything that could hurt your liege. From stairs to assassins."

"So you did push her?" Freya said, despite herself.

Alvor laughed again. "That would be rather childish, wouldn't it?"

"I would not put it past you."

"I did not push her." Alvor stood straight and stretched her legs. "Stars, you are rather short to the ground for a spymaster."

Freya licked her lips. No weapons, nothing to fight back with. Unless she could use the furniture. And the fire.

The poker, then. Thrust it into the fire, then into Alvor's eye.

The rope chafed at her wrists as she continued to twist.

"The staff in Vakker Castle love you," Alvor said. "Even Guthmar's servants became fond of you. They almost didn't accept my bribe."

"A shame they did."

"You can be charming when you need to be," Alvor continued. "I would say you've been a good spymaster to your queen."

"Not good enough, apparently," Freya said dryly. "You still convinced Guthmar's attendants to drug me."

"Try not to be offended. I'm very good myself."

Was it possible Alvor was a free agent? Or perhaps she really did love Guthmar, and she'd done this for him—eliminated a source of terror in his life, taken a shot at some sort of personal vendetta with Astrid.

Or she could be hired by someone powerful. Someone from Lynby.

"I can guess who you work for," Freya said.

"It won't matter by the time this is over," said Alvor.

"And when will it be over, exactly?"

Alvor smiled, and realization washed over Freya.

The plan was to lure Astrid here. Freya lashed at her bindings, abandoning the attempt to hide her efforts.

Alvor watched but didn't stop her. "You'll need your energy for later," she said. "Might want to rest."

Freya had nearly gotten her wrist out of the ropes, but she hit a sore spot—where it had been trampled on before—and curled in on herself in pain.

They weren't alike, Freya thought. If she had to kill someone, she would have done it by now. If she meant to lure someone, they would already be here. And she wouldn't be talking to the bait.

Alvor brought a pitcher of water to Freya and poured her a cup. Freya licked her lips, suddenly aware of how thirsty she was. Alvor held the cup to Freya's mouth and gently tipped it back.

Despite herself, Freya drank. She would need her strength to get out of these bindings and kill her captor. The water was crisp, cool, and clear.

Alvor took the edge of her cloak and dabbed at Freya's sweaty forehead. "There, there," she said. "I'm sorry for this, Freya. Really."

Freya said nothing. *We are not alike*, she thought.

Part of her knew this wasn't true.

CHAPTER THIRTY-TWO

When they reached the Rosebriar Inn, Astrid breached the door so fast, it splintered under her boot.

The innkeeper looked up, jaw agape.

"Where are they?" Astrid demanded.

Astrid did not wear her crown, but the authority in her voice was commanding enough. The barmaid stepped back, unblocking the stairs to the second story.

Astrid thundered up the steps. The others were still dismounting their horses outside, but she couldn't wait. She pounded on the first door until it opened, then the second, and the third. She'd made it to the fourth when an arrow half-penetrated the wood of the door, sharp and true, its point sticking at the level of Astrid's chest. A strong bolt from a crossbow, as Freya had guessed.

Hrothgar touched Astrid's shoulder, and she jumped.

"Allow me to go in first," they whispered.

"She's armed," said Astrid.

Brenn scuttled down the hall, Sigurd on her heels. "I can help."

Brenn's eyes closed, and a high-pitched, inhuman hum emitted from her throat. At the tip of her staff, a large half sphere emerged, shimmering and translucent. A shield large enough to cover them all. Astrid touched it with her finger. Though it appeared intangible, it was solid as oak.

"Together, then," Astrid said. Everyone bundled in behind Brenn, and Astrid kicked the door in.

An arrow bounced off Brenn's shield, then another. The room was smoky, dark, unlit, like the fire had recently been put out. A sound, a fiddling—another arrow being loaded and shot. It, too, bounced off the shield.

A muffled shout came from somewhere to the right. Astrid's shoulders tensed. She drew Freya's bone-handled dagger.

"Reveal yourself," she ordered.

Hrothgar's sharp intake of breath was the only warning Astrid had. She scruffed Hrothgar and Sigurd by the back of their necks and ducked.

The arrow landed in the wall behind them. The angle was just to the side, just barely through the shield's defense.

Brenn's rhythmic chanting filled the room. The tip of her staff began to glow and became brighter and brighter until the center of the room was washed in light. Only edges and corners remained in shadow.

Astrid bent to Freya. She was curled on the ground, eyes wide. Someone had tied a rag around her head, stuffed into her mouth, and her hands were tied and bruised.

She was alive, though. Astrid could not help the smile that came to her face. *Freya was alive.*

Astrid ducked again as another arrow whizzed past her—she was almost too slow to react. No time to celebrate. She looked up, around, eyes wild, dagger ready.

There. In the corner.

Every day since Freya arrived in Torden, she had protected Astrid. It was Astrid's turn to return the favor.

Astrid dove toward the source of the arrows. Back in the center of the room, Hrothgar cursed and Sigurd pushed past the barrier.

The crossbow came down over Astrid's head. She swore, slashing at it with her dagger until she heard a yelp and a clatter. The crossbow, on the ground, smashed beyond use. Astrid stood over the orc who had nearly stolen Freya's life. In the low light, Astrid saw Alvor's eyes—feral and panicked. A rush of power flooded Astrid as she knocked Alvor to the ground.

Her fist made contact with Alvor's face. Alvor drew a sword with one hand, a wicked-looking knife in the other, and leapt at Astrid. Astrid only parried in time to miss losing her head.

Astrid gripped the dagger clumsily as she parried the attacks, out of practice with wielding a weapon. The heavy weight of the dagger barely repelled Alvor's wild blows. Exhaustion ran up her arms each time the weapons made contact.

Astrid was losing. Her opponent was too capable.

Hrothgar approached, but Alvor swung at them, too. Astrid took the opening to get closer to the knife and slammed her hand into Alvor's fist. The knife clattered to the ground.

Alvor stepped back, sword drawn.

Astrid looked to Hrothgar. They nodded. Her muscles were warm, ready, and suddenly they felt sure. Her grip on the dagger became more natural, an extension of herself. But of course. Astrid had wielded dozens of daggers in her day. She'd used swords for most of her life. She fell into her old self, letting her overthinking drop away.

The muscle memory came back to her.

Hrothgar moved in on Alvor's left, and as she parried, Astrid swung in, twirled the sword around her dagger, and disarmed Alvor once and for all.

"Search her," Astrid said.

Hrothgar and Sigurd rushed forward. Sigurd held Alvor's hands over her head as Hrothgar shook through her pockets. They extracted another small knife, the kind used as a last resort when all other options were exhausted. There were no other weapons.

Alvor squirmed out of Sigurd's grip and lurched for Astrid. Astrid thrust her palm into Alvor's shoulder and Alvor twisted, falling to her knees. Sigurd knelt to pin Alvor's hands behind her back.

Astrid pointed the dagger at Alvor's throat.

"Lucky you brought your priestess," said Alvor, chest heaving. "You all would have been dead."

Astrid pressed the tip of the dagger into Alvor's neck. A bead of blood welled against the blade.

"You're not wrong," Astrid said. "It seems the goddess chose our side."

To Astrid's left, Hrothgar stood, holding their sword out. But Astrid had already won. Together, they'd disarmed her, neutralized the threat.

Astrid had protected Freya.

Her hand shook. She was not scared, not buzzing with adrenaline.

She was angry.

She had welcomed this orc into her castle, allowed her to integrate with Torden's citizens, given her room and board and her husband a warm welcome despite the forced circumstances. She had been a good host, and Alvor had violated her home. Ruined the sanctity of the place that housed Astrid and the people she loved.

"I should kill you," Astrid said.

There was a cracking sound, as if someone's bones had broken. Astrid's head whipped around.

Brenn had Freya standing, holding one of her hands. The skin of the hand looked fresh, bearing only its old scars but none of the new dark bruising. An on-the-spot bone healing, done so suddenly that Brenn swayed with exhaustion. In the doorway, Hedda had arrived and was trying to make sense of the scene.

"Don't kill her," Freya said hoarsely.

Astrid looked to her félag, to Brenn. Only Freya could have defied her. Only Freya could stop her from going through with this act of vengeance.

"She hurt you," Astrid said, voice cracking. "She wanted you dead."

Freya touched each of her own wrists, the side of her head, her shoulder. Astrid's eyes followed every movement, counting the places she had been injured. Unbidden, the dagger pressed deeper against Alvor's neck.

"Get it over with," Alvor snapped.

"Why shouldn't I?" asked Astrid.

"She's working for someone," Freya said, flexing her recently healed fingers. "We need to know their agenda. Maybe we can use her as leverage."

"We can't keep her alive," Hedda said. She stepped into the room. "She tried to kill the queen. She *did* kill King Skarde."

"Hedda has a point," Astrid said. "We can't harbor a king-killer, even for answers. Sydlig won't stand for it."

"So kill me," said Alvor.

"She wants to die," Freya said. "The person who gave her the orders—or who hired her—wants her to die, too. That way, we'll never know."

"I don't have any answers worth giving," Alvor said from her knees.

"Let me look at her." Freya put a hand on Astrid's arm. Her skin was cold. Bare skin to bare skin.

Astrid backed away.

Freya stooped to Alvor's level and, without warning, grabbed her chin and made her look up. "I know your kind," she said.

"I bet you do," Alvor said.

Freya threw down her chin. Alvor let her head hang and didn't pick it back up, but through her strands of magenta hair, Astrid saw an expression that would haunt her later: a wicked smile.

"My Queen," said Freya.

"Yes?" Astrid asked, startled.

"Permission to give an order?"

Astrid squinted at Freya. She did not ask permission to do anything, least of all giving orders. In present company, though... Someone who was a killer and an informant in their midst, the félag here...

"Granted," Astrid said.

"You have been wanting something important to do for a while now. To try to prove yourself here, prove your necessity. Your loyalty." Freya turned to Hedda. "Here is your chance."

Hedda looked lost. "Freya..."

"This prisoner is *your* responsibility. Watch her, feed her, and interrogate her. Get some damn answers about what's going on in the rest of the world."

Uncomfortable, Astrid shifted. She would not have thought to do this. Hedda might find it even more demeaning than cleaning the floors.

Astrid met Freya's gaze, and an understanding passed between them—the kind of understanding one could only cultivate through years of trust. To Hedda, Astrid nodded her assent.

Hedda's eyes fell to Alvor. "What will we do with her? After we have our answers?"

"You already have them," Alvor said.

"We'll have to give her over to the Sydlig council," Astrid said. "Until then, as Freya said, she is yours."

Hedda looked down at Alvor, hands twitching at her sides. Of all of them, she looked the least like a warrior. She bore the scar over her nose, her hair pulled back out of her face and ready for action, but she wore common clothes where the others wore armor, her blade in its scabbard, undrawn and unused.

"Very well," said Hedda. "The captive will stay in my charge."

CHAPTER THIRTY-THREE

Three days later, Freya resumed her usual place behind the queen as Astrid wrote to Sydlig's council about the assassin who had killed their king. In the letter, Astrid explained that she welcomed them to come take the assassin as soon as they had their succession in order. Freya hoped that was enough time to get what she wanted out of Alvor.

The decision to keep Alvor around rather than let Astrid kill her had been made in the heat of the moment. Freya could pretend like there were more answers she wanted out of her, like she really did want Hedda to have a task to prove her worthiness, but she knew that wasn't the full truth.

When she'd looked into Alvor's eyes, Freya had seen herself reflected back.

Was Alvor's job not hers, once upon a time? Granted, Freya had never been asked to kill a king, and she did not think she would have aimed for such a large target on someone else's behalf. Too dangerous, too much risk to herself.

But she had killed warlords and those who served them at the behest of others. Was it so different that she'd had no choice, that she'd done what she did to survive, when Alvor was not forced to do the same? If Alvor had come to the queen for mercy from the start, explained who she'd been working for and why, Astrid would have protected her.

As for Freya, she'd only had herself. No one else had been willing or able to protect her. Not until she got to Torden.

She had not yet decided if keeping Alvor alive was another form of protection.

Astrid finished writing and set down her quill. Her back was tense, and, in understanding of their new boundaries, Freya took hold of Astrid's shoulders and massaged them in a kneading motion. Her hands were healed fully, but the recovery from the poison still overwhelmed her sometimes. She had taken to sleeping long hours, but otherwise, she felt not so different from her usual self.

"You always know how to help," Astrid said with a sigh.

"That's what I'm here for," Freya said.

The sound of the crackling fire filled the room. Freya looked down at her queen. If not for Astrid, Freya could've been in Alvor's position somewhere, or dead. It was only a matter of time before her bad luck caught up.

Believing in bad luck was dangerously close to believing in the existence of her wyrd. Freya leaned back, releasing Astrid's shoulders.

"I pray Sydlig doesn't plan to send anyone to Torden any time soon," Astrid said. "I only just got rid of them."

"Or Alvor did," Freya said darkly. "I'm sure they will be busy handling their own affairs for a bit yet."

"I hope you're right."

Freya built up the courage to speak. "Astrid, I want to get something off my chest."

Astrid faced her. "Anything, Freya."

Freya's chest warmed. "We haven't established where we go from here. What we plan to do with ourselves. Each other, I mean."

Astrid tilted her head. "Follow me," she said.

Easy as anything, she took Freya's hand and led her to the bedroom. Maybe that was evidence enough of how far they had come since the beginning. Not long ago, Freya had touched Astrid's hand by accident and faced days of mortification afterward.

Astrid sat on her bed and patted the spot next to her. In the corner of the chamber, Fenrir dozed away. The hearth in this room was unlit, but Freya was sure the luxurious rug kept the floors warmer than they used to be.

Her influence was everywhere.

She took Astrid's hands in her own, but her mind was blank, emptier than it had ever been. She was always thinking, scheming, solving, but when it mattered most, her thoughts failed her.

"I love you," Astrid said, saving Freya from whatever she'd been about to say. "I will always love you. I am worried it will have significant impact on my rule, but I do."

"I'll steer you back to logic if it ever does."

In the dark room, Astrid's eyes were shiny. "I'm afraid that won't be possible someday."

"When I die, you mean," said Freya.

"Yes," said Astrid. "It's not fair. Your life is so much shorter than mine. It feels like a sign. That you're...not meant for me."

Freya squeezed Astrid's hands—skin to skin, pulse to pulse. "I don't feel that way at all," she said.

"Oh, Freya... Stars, I can't make it through this."

Freya broke from Astrid's grip to brush a tear from her cheek.

"Of course I want to be with you," Astrid continued. "I want to be yours in every sense. But I don't know if I can survive the heartbreak of your natural lifespan. I don't know if I can live on five centuries without you. How can anyone compare after I've had you?"

Her voice broke on the last syllable.

In the midst of Astrid's tears, Freya's own formed. She blinked them back and swallowed. No, it wasn't fair. She would always have Astrid, assuming they could keep off the assassins. But Astrid...

There had been a moment, back at the temple, surrounded by priestesses, when Freya had come to the specific kind of clarity some people worked decades to find.

Articulating it would be difficult.

"You're never going to lose me," Freya said firmly. She pressed her palms into Astrid's. "I'm yours forever. When I die, and the goddess takes me to her field and reincarnates my soul, I will come back to you."

The statement did not have its intended effect, heavy though it was said. It did stop Astrid's tears, however. "Now isn't a good time for a joke," she said lightly.

"I'm not making a joke," Freya said. She brought Astrid's hands to her lips. "I'll be reincarnated, I'll age, and something in my bones will remember you, and I will return to your side."

"I don't know..."

"I *do* know. The next time I die, I will be reincarnated again, and I'll come back to you—and the same for the next life, and the next. One day, your body will give out too, and you'll be the one to come back to me. That is our wyrd." Freya kissed Astrid's knuckles. "I know it to be true like I know the sun will rise tomorrow."

Astrid sobbed. "You really believe that, Freya?"

"I do," Freya said. "I absolutely do, with everything I have."

Astrid threw her arms around Freya and crushed her. "Then I believe it, too," she said.

Freya broke free of the hug and planted a gentle kiss on Astrid's lips—a promise of their many years to come.

She pressed her forehead to Astrid's and felt her breath against her skin. The smell of her, the warmth of her—all so intoxicating. All *hers*.

Freya reached for the bronze hair cuff at the end of Astrid's plait and twisted it off. She twined her fingers through Astrid's hair. Astrid moved back as Freya loosened the braid, unraveling the three sections slowly and with care.

An inexplicable melancholy overcame Freya when she was done. She wanted to touch Astrid's hair forever. Astrid sat watching, hair long and wavy and surrounding her face.

"You can braid it again if you like," Astrid said.

Freya smiled at the easy way Astrid read her mind. "Maybe later. I am in the mood for undoing tonight."

She tapped the lace on Astrid's boot. Astrid held it up for her. Freya shifted to the rug, kneeling, and untied the laces from top to bottom.

"What else will you undo?" Astrid asked, eyes playful.

Just like she had been the first time they went to the Rosebriar Inn, when Freya saw she could be happy. Only, this time, Freya had done it.

"I'll work my way up," Freya said.

Astrid parted her legs so Freya could access the lace of her trousers. Freya looked not at the laces, but up at Astrid, who kissed her forehead as she worked. She unrolled Astrid's trousers past the ankle, maintaining eye contact, and tossed them aside.

"Come down here with me," Freya said. "I'll undo the top."

Astrid joined Freya on the rug, facing her so Freya could access the laces of her doublet. Freya's fingers slid through the gaps in the laces, just the layer of Astrid's tunic between them, and Astrid gasped.

Freya took her time. She pulled the laces apart row by row and set the doublet, still warm from Astrid's body, aside.

"Nothing to untie on the tunic," Astrid said.

"It's a little long for my liking anyhow," said Freya.

Astrid lightly punched her shoulder. The tunic reached just to mid-thigh.

Freya tilted forward to kiss her, planting one hand on her thigh. Her skin was so warm to the touch, inviting. Astrid shifted against Freya's touch. She cupped the back of Freya's head in her hand, leaning her head back to kiss her deeper.

Freya tumbled into Astrid's lap. Astrid pulled her up and held her close. Their mouths moved faster, more desperate. The sting of Astrid's tusks grazing Freya's skin was a welcome kind of pain. One Freya could get used to.

Freya clenched Astrid's tunic in her fist.

"This really has to come off," she mumbled against Astrid's mouth.

Breathing heavily, Astrid allowed some space between them. Freya grabbed the tunic from behind Astrid's neck and whipped it onto the ground.

She couldn't help but place a palm against Astrid's midsection. Her soft skin was occasionally marred by a nick from an old wound, from back when she'd been a fighter. Freya allowed herself to circle the underside of one of Astrid's breasts. She looked up into Astrid's eyes and saw softness there, saw love.

Astrid was still a fighter, even if her fighting looked a little different now.

Freya's greedy eyes drank in every detail of Astrid—her collarbones, her elegant neck, her horns—so elaborate, so detailed up close—and her tusks, the redness around her mouth.

"You're gorgeous," Freya said. She took hold of the end of Astrid's long hair and twined it through her fingers.

"You certainly make me feel that way," Astrid said.

Freya released Astrid's hair and shoved at her shoulders until she was flat against the carpet with Freya on top. Freya adjusted her stance, her thighs squeezing Astrid's midsection to either side. Astrid tugged at Freya's tunic, and Freya, laughing, removed her own layers so Astrid could touch her skin.

Astrid put one tentative finger to the fresh scar between Freya's breasts. Alvor's arrow had pierced her there, nearly taking her life. The wound no longer hurt, but the scar would remain. Just one of many, Freya thought.

"We have been through much to get here, haven't we?" Astrid asked gently.

"It only makes me appreciate what we have more," said Freya.

Freya leaned down so their skin pressed together, torsos touching. Astrid's hungry hands roved over Freya's naked back as they kissed. Freya touched her lips to Astrid's jaw, the soft spot under her neck that made her whole body clench, her collarbone. She moved down, taking Astrid's nipple in her mouth. Astrid squeezed Freya's arms as Freya's tongue worked. She licked the underside of Astrid's breast and trailed wet kisses that tensed Astrid's muscles all the way to her navel.

Freya nudged Astrid's legs up as she took her place between them. She looked up at the hills and valleys of her favorite person, the orc who made her feel at home, and a rush of gratitude overcame her.

With a sleepy smile, Astrid stroked Freya's hair with one hand.

"What do you want?" Freya asked.

"You," Astrid said. "All of you."

Freya kissed Astrid's soft belly as her searching fingers found Astrid's clit to a sharp intake of breath. Freya wove patterns into Astrid, learning which movements made her squirm, what she reacted to best. She swirled and flicked and rubbed until Astrid's hips jerked.

"Inside," Astrid choked out. "I want you inside."

Freya's fingers swept down and inside her. Stars, was she soft. She pressed two fingers in, tilted up at the tips, and Astrid gasped.

"More," Astrid said.

Freya slipped in another finger, pumping, watching Astrid's expressions as she rested her head against Astrid's thigh. Her own insides squirmed, heat rising to her face. This was a privilege, one she would be happy to exert for the rest of her life.

"M-more," Astrid said.

Freya pressed a fourth finger into Astrid, and Astrid clenched around her. *Sweet goddess.* Freya bit back her own moan, seeing Astrid's head thrown back, lips trembling.

"More, Freya," Astrid said.

The tips of her fingers and thumb tented together, Freya pushed back into Astrid's cunt. Astrid grabbed a fistful of Freya's hair in her hand and thrust. Freya felt Astrid open for her, past the resistance, and watched as her fist disappeared to the wrist.

Astrid writhed against her. Freya used her other hand to hold her down on the rug.

"More," Astrid said. "Please."

"I told you, 'please' is my favorite word," Freya panted. "But I'm all out of fingers."

Astrid opened her eyes. She was sweaty, tousled, hair everywhere. Absolutely perfect in every way.

"Freya Wedd," she said, "I said I wanted *all* of you. I want every inch of you that I can take."

Goosebumps rose on the back of Freya's neck. She lowered her mouth to Astrid's clit, damp curls of hair pressed to her lips. She tasted her—goddess, did she ever—as she deepened her arm. One inch, two. Astrid was a puddle under her as Freya lapped her up. She pressed in some more, and Astrid shuddered. Her grip tightened in Freya's hair. A moan left her throat, filling Freya's ears and heart.

With a scream and another tightening of her grip, Astrid gushed over Freya's hand.

Freya shuddered, too. She had not removed her trousers, and she knew very well they were wet beyond wearing.

Very slowly, Freya extracted her drenched hand. She wiped it on the rug—it would need cleaning, in any case—and moved up to curl into Astrid's arms.

"You are something else, Freya," Astrid said, massaging Freya's shoulder. She was breathless. Freya was, too.

The room was warmer than it should've been, full of the smell of them, and Freya still tasted Astrid on her tongue. She looked at her hand in wonder, looked at Astrid in wonder that she'd been able to take so much of it.

"What would you say to a private commitment ceremony?" Astrid asked quietly.

"I would say yes," said Freya.

Astrid smiled brighter than the sun.

FREYA & ASTRID

And so it came to be, one crisp autumn morning, that Freya Wedd and Astrid Karrsdaughter were dressed in their finest clothes. The ancient seamstress Dag came to the castle themself to fix the two up in matching white embroidered in gold.

Visitors arrived quietly, known only to Varin, the félag, and the castle guard, the last of whom were kept out of the plans for the ceremony.

First, Ruga Karrsdaughter and her wife Elketh Ceridwen arrived from just over the channel at Branwen. Ruga sat at Astrid's side as Elketh braided her hair. Astrid much preferred when Freya did it, but Freya was occupied with her own preparations.

Astrid thought she must be emanating happiness like rays of the sun. Finally, some time with her sister she could truly enjoy. She was planning on inviting Ruga back soon—or maybe she would have a chance to visit in Branwen some time.

"I am happy for you," Ruga said. "Freya loves you very much."

"She's a weaselly little thing, isn't she?" Elketh said. Ruga elbowed her in the side and Elketh laughed. "Hey! Just an observation. I think it's a good match. Everyone deserves love."

"If she is a weasel, she is my weasel," Astrid said with pride. Any chance she could take to claim Freya, she would, no matter how ridiculous the circumstance.

Elketh and Ruga exchanged a knowing smile.

Next, Brenn arrived alone. She went to Freya's old room adjacent to Astrid's bedchamber, helped her don accessories, and pressed oil into her hair, shaping the curls.

"I have never seen you so dashing," Brenn said.

"I am not dashing," said Freya. "It's all your handiwork and good tailoring."

"Perhaps I should take up grooming on the side."

"You did a good job, Brenn," Freya said. She squeezed Brenn's hand. The gloves were back on, but she would take them off tonight in Astrid's bed. "And I want to thank you for being a good friend, even when I have not been."

Brenn hugged Freya, careful not to muss her hair or wrinkle her clothes. "You are my very best friend, Freya. You always will be."

Freya clutched Brenn's robes with tears in her eyes. Once, she would never have dreamed this could happen to her. She was safe, or as safe as one could be in this world. She had love in her life, in her friends and her allies and her partner.

She had hopes for a future stretching across lifetimes.

They gathered in the assembly room with its tall windows. Sunlight bled onto every wall, bright and warm, and outside, golden trees shed the last of their leaves.

With Huginn and Muninn on her shoulders, Brenn stood at the makeshift altar next to Varin, who had orchestrated the arrangements. The two talked in low voices as the guests entered. The félag filtered into the back, on alert to protect their queen, but also there to celebrate her.

Elketh and Ruga sat toward the front with Vera, the elf librarian, who stared daggers into Elketh at something she might have said—or perhaps she was still holding a grudge about a certain incident involving a ceremonial crown.

"I almost wish Guthmar was here," Astrid said as she looked out over the small crowd. "I bet he loves weddings."

"I would wager you're right," said Freya.

"And my parents," Astrid said sadly.

"Mine, too," said Freya.

"Your siblings?"

Freya smiled sadly. "They never had the chance to grow old. I don't know what they would be like now."

"Stars, Freya. I'm so sorry."

Freya shook her head. "It's all in the past. Besides, this"—she gestured to the room—"is our family. These are the people we love. How lucky are we to have them with us?"

Astrid quite liked this evolving Freya who could now find light in the darkness.

Everyone took turns coming up to the couple to give them their well wishes. Hrothgar hugged Astrid—perhaps remembering their night of joyful dancing together at the Rosebriar Inn—and

Sigurd shook her hand. Elketh and Ruga embraced them both. Vera nodded to each, with respect for at least Freya, if not Astrid. The félag lined up, one by one, and bestowed their wishes upon the lovers.

Hedda came last.

She stood before Astrid and Freya, uncertainty clouding her features. "I cannot say I am fond of you, Freya," she said bluntly. "But you are fortunate to have found love in each other."

Astrid's stomach tumbled with guilt.

"How is the captive?" Freya asked.

"Varin suggested leaving her alone for a month or so. Food and water only, no talking." Hedda shuffled her feet. "But fine, I suppose. We have made her comfortable."

"Good," said Freya. "Thank you, Hedda."

"Thank you, Hedda," Astrid echoed with more warmth. "It means a lot to me that you're here."

Stoically, Hedda bowed and went to her seat.

"She'll forgive you," Freya said.

"I hope so," said Astrid. She did not like that she had distanced so many of her friends. There would be time to repair those relationships. She *had* to make time for it. Only when it came to Hedda was she totally at a loss.

Astrid noted that, when Hedda took her seat, Ruga came over to speak with her. Hedda was guarded and stiff in Ruga's presence. Whatever Ruga said was drowned out by the other chatter in the room, but Ruga shook Hedda's hand—cordial, at the very least, through Hedda's clear discomfort.

"I think Alvor will be good for her," Freya added thoughtfully.

"The responsibility of watching over her, you mean?" Astrid asked.

Freya hummed. "Something like that."

When the sun reached the highest point in the sky, Astrid and Freya clasped each other's hands as Brenn presided over the ceremony. She spoke of their love, their commitment to each other's souls, their dedication that would last through their reincarnations. The ceremony was less formal than a wedding, but that was all right. For better or worse, Astrid and Freya had always done things their own way. They were not going to stop any time soon.

As Brenn finished, the small crowd clapped. Astrid smiled, buoyed by the support of those she loved most. Freya smiled, buoyed by Astrid's contentment.

The kiss they shared at the altar was, perhaps, not very appropriate for a queen to share with her trusted bodyguard and spymaster. A hoot from the crowd (distinctly Elketh's) egged them on. Astrid dipped Freya, and Freya couldn't help the happiness that washed over her, the most happiness she had ever felt in her life.

When they pulled away, their shadows pooled around them, encircling them together, combining their bodies and souls into one. Astrid noticed, and Freya followed her gaze and squeezed her fingers.

The queen's shadow, the shadow and her queen. Inseparable, together as one, always and forever.

THANK YOU

Thank you for taking the time to read *The Orc and Her Spy*, the second in a series of sapphic fantasy romances. If you have the time, please consider leaving an honest review on your favorite platform(s).

If you'd like to receive updates about future releases, deals, and freebies, including prequel story *Freya the Infiltrator*, you can sign up for my newsletter at this link: lilagwynn.com/newsletter

COMING SOON...

THE ORC —AND— HER CAPTIVE

In which Alvor uses her bargaining power against her captors and Hedda's quest to earn her spot at the queen's side forces her to reckon with her anger

ACKNOWLEDGEMENTS

No book is written entirely alone. Once again, I have to start by thanking Sarah Waites, who created the cover that inspired this series and also illustrated its beautiful map. My champions of the first book, Nat Paga, Ceril N. Domace, and Victoria Flickinger, gave incredibly useful feedback that shaped the course of these books. Nat, who messages me with her enthusiasm (and creates fan art!), is a driving force behind why I keep writing. I lucked out with beta readers for this book—Nat, as always, deserves thanks for her detailed lists of things she liked and things I was missing, but I also had the pleasure of Victoria's push for clarity, consistency, and eliminating overused phrases; MD's praise and sense for the cohesion of events and themes; Tusani's astute interrogations when things didn't add up; Rowen's keen observations about grammar and relationship dynamics; Liv's assertion for more grounding detail; Mindi's grammatical corrections and analysis; and Audrey's kind comments about her favorite lines and overarching, big-picture feedback (and for telling me you can't fold parchment). Every one of these readers improved this story, and I'm so grateful. Adie Hart, an extraordinary author in her own right, provided the copyedit for this book, twisting my tangled phrases into something that flowed and calling out elements that didn't quite fit, and I owe her so much. Rae Terwilliger, you rock for supporting me with your art and your kind words. My sisters and my best friend support me by reading my books and falling in love with my characters, and my friends Fel and Matt cheer me on and recommend my books to other people. Most importantly, my partner is the one who helps me bounce around ideas, who cultivated my writing space, and who reads all of my books as soon as they're finished. Lastly, thanks to you, reader, for picking up this book—and a huge apology for how long it took to get it into your hands. I appreciate your patience and your continued interest in my stories.

ABOUT THE AUTHOR

Lila Gwynn is a lesbian author (and avid reader) of sapphic fantasy fiction. In her free time, she can be found binge-reading indie books, casually playing video games, or occasionally writing. She lives with her wonderful butch girlfriend and their many cats.

Bluesky: @lilagwynn.bsky.social
Instagram: @lilagwynn
Website: https://lilagwynn.com

www.ingramcontent.com/pod-product-compliance
Lightning Source LLC
LaVergne TN
LVHW100518110826
845146LV00002B/689

* 9 7 9 8 9 9 4 0 0 2 4 1 4 *